SMILE OF THE STOWAWAY

Smile of the Stowaway

Published by The Conrad Press in the United Kingdom 2018

Tel: +44(0)1227 472 874
www.theconradpress.com
info@theconradpress.com

ISBN 978-1-911546-45-0

Typesetting and Cover Design by:
Charlotte Mouncey, www.bookstyle.co.uk

The Conrad Press logo was designed by Maria Priestley.

Printed and bound in Great Britain
by Clays Ltd, Elcograf S.p.A

SMILE OF THE STOWAWAY

TONY BASSETT

1

'Who the hell are you?' I asked.

He was a brown-skinned man in his early twenties. He had short, black, curly hair. His clothes were tattered and coated in dust. But he was smiling. I shall never forget that. He was smiling.

My wife Anne ran round the back of our motor-home after hearing my shouts. She just stared at this strange apparition of a man crawling out from beneath the vehicle. The man clambered to his feet.

'He must be a stowaway,' I thought.

It was just after seven in the evening on July the thirty-first. Three hours before, we had been queuing at the port of Calais to board a Dover-bound ferry. Crowds of asylum seekers had been scurrying around the lorries and cars, seeking any opportunity of a free passage to England.

Somehow this man must have attached himself to the underside of our vehicle and travelled with us on the boat. Then he must have been our secret passenger for the final twenty-mile stage of our journey from Dover back to our village.

No wonder he was smiling. He was alive.

He may have sustained cuts and bruises. He may have been vigorously shaken about and left bathed in sweat. But he had arrived safely at his cherished destination of England.

Anne looked at him with a kind of awe, then turned to me.

'He's an asylum seeker!' she whispered. I thought she was probably right. The man was wearing a red check shirt and black trousers tied round the waist with a piece of white string. On his feet were a pair of cheap brown sandals.

Underneath my shirt, I felt myself tensing my arms. I felt confident that, if he had been aggressive towards us, I could have coped. He was a couple of inches shorter than me and quite lightly built.

'Please, I'm good man,' he said in a halting voice. Then he added: 'Me... Yusuf.'

Anne, who, at thirty-two, is two years younger than me, turned to Yusuf and, speaking slowly, said: 'Hello, Yusuf. I'm Anne and this is Bob.'

Yusuf nodded. 'Anne, Bob,' he said. 'Hello.' Anne glanced at me and I glanced at her. Then she took me by the arm and led me a few yards away towards the front door of the house.

'Bob,' she said in a hushed whisper. 'We've got to call the police.'

'I know,' I said. 'But let's at least give him a glass of water. He must have had a dreadful journey.' She glanced back at me and gave me a couple of quick nods.

I unlocked the front door and pushed it open. It brushed against a small mound of mail that had collected during our three-week cycling holiday. A faint musty smell could be detected since all the windows had been closed during our absence.

I rushed into the kitchen and found a straight pint glass. I ran the cold tap for a while so that the water would be fresh and not stale. Then I walked quickly back into the garden and handed it to Yusuf. Anne gave me a sudden reproachful look as if she had resented me leaving her alone with him - even though it had only been for a minute or so.

As Yusuf gulped down the water with enthusiasm, Anne went inside to put the kettle on. I quickly scooped up the letters lying on the hall carpet and dropped them on the hall table, next to the telephone.

Anne came out of the kitchen. 'What are we going to do?' she asked in the same hushed whisper.

'I don't know,' I said. 'But we can't leave him out there in the garden, can we? He looks harmless enough. We'll make him some food and then find out more about him.'

'Bob, I don't really want him in our house, but I suppose you're right.'

I gave her a nod. I loved Anne completely and I shared her unease but on the other hand I felt a genuine concern for Yusuf already. I went outside into the garden.

I noticed Yusuf was standing in the doorway, watching me.

'It's all right,' I said. 'You can come in. We'll make you a sandwich.'

But he seemed nervous, anxious about the situation and reluctant to cross the threshold of our home. I found it reassuring he had concern for our feelings. 'Come in,' I said. 'Just come in, please.'

Gingerly, he followed me down the passageway and into our medium-sized kitchen. Anne quickly made him a cheese and tomato sandwich which he ate very quickly while we all sat round the small table. I did not know what to say, so I just said the first - hardly very original - thing I could think of saying: 'Where are you from?'

He looked puzzled.

'I mean, what country are you from?'

'Eritrea,' he said.

I knew almost nothing about his homeland except it was in East Africa and I had a vague recollection it had been occupied by the Italians at some point in the past. I teach English History at a Canterbury academy, but my historical knowledge is not entirely insular.

'Anne, darling,' I said. 'Could we give him another sandwich? The poor man's ravenous.'

Anne gave a nod, smiled at me rather awkwardly then furnished Yusuf with a second cheese-and-tomato sandwich. He gobbled it down with as much enthusiasm as the first. All the while he smiled, often saying: 'Thank you, thank you.'

I did not know what to make of him, but I found myself beginning to warm to him. I knew next to nothing about his journey except that, somehow, he had managed to squeeze under our motor-home and stay there for several hours.

I did not know for certain but assumed he had climbed underneath when we were still in France. He must have been there while our vehicle was in the ferry's car park, during the crossing and during the thirty-minute journey back to our home from Dover. I couldn't help but admire his courage. Or was it courage? Perhaps it was simple desperation to get to Britain, where he presumably hoped his dreams of a new life would be fulfilled.

I knew I could not just keep thinking and looking at him. I had to say something.

'Why have you come to England?' I asked.

He frowned and replied: 'Sorry, your English. You speak too

fast. I'm not understanding.'

'Yusuf, why have you risked your life to come to England?' I asked, speaking slowly but clearly, hoping I was not talking too loudly.

He still looked puzzled. I even wondered whether he understood the word 'England.' So, rather foolishly I suppose, I opened my arms wide as if to indicate a large space - hoping that he would understand I was referring to the country in which he had arrived. It seemed to have the desired effect because suddenly he smiled.

'Work,' he said. 'Work, money, new life, Bob. Better than back home.'

I could not help but admire his courage in following his dream and coming to England.

Anne said: 'I don't know much about Eritrea but I'm sure there must be lots of poverty there. I imagine the children begging in the streets almost from the moment they can stand up.'

Yusuf made no response to this. I doubted he'd fully understood what my love had said. Then, for no apparent reason, he reached into his trouser pocket with his right hand and pulled out a photograph. It showed the face of an attractive mixed-race woman who could have been aged between eighteen and twenty-five.

'Mother,' he said proudly. 'In England. I look for her.'

'Your mother's in England?' I asked, astonished. 'Which part? Which area?'

Little by little, we coaxed out of him that his mother, whose name, Asmarina, was based on the name of the country's capital and was now aged forty-six, was believed to be living somewhere in England after her relationship with Yusuf's father broke down. However, Yusuf had no idea of her exact whereabouts. His father remained in Eritrea, caring for his remaining family.

'You want to find your mother,' Anne asked. 'Is that right?'

'Yes. I look. I look,' he said. We noticed tears were forming in his eyes.

'What's the matter, Yusuf?' I asked. 'Are you in trouble?'

'I'm from poor family,' he said as if he were about to start crying. 'We're eight children. Me, number five. My father work on the farm. My older brother and five sisters work on the farm. It's hard. Sometimes we've no food and go to bed hungry. Two of my sisters need the medicine, but we've no money for the doctor. My younger brother Hamid and I knew what we had to do. We had to leave. Two less bellies to feed, and we've the hope of getting the money. We'll send to my father.'

'Where did you learn English?' I asked him.

'I go to school in my village and I watch films sometimes.'

I was relieved his English was better than I imagined.

Yusuf explained haltingly how his family lived in a village just outside Asmara. They evidently had a small-holding and kept several animals - mainly chicken, donkeys and goats. He, Hamid and Yusuf's friend Yonas had decided in January to leave their homeland and seek their fortune in England.

'We not telling our father we're going,' he revealed. 'We don't want to make him cry. We pay the people...'

'People smugglers?' suggested Anne.

'Yes, the people smuggler. We save for them. We pay five hundred dollars.'

'How did you get that?' I asked.

'I work long hours in factory in Asmara,' he replied. 'All

three, we go on the camel through Sudan. No one's to know or my family will be suffering. We go by night.'

I interrupted to ask: 'Where did you want to go to?'

'Europe,' he said. 'But it's hard journey. Bad people run my country and they have spy. If we're catched...'

'You mean caught,' said Anne.

'Sorry. If we're caught, our family will be punished.'

'That's right,' Anne agreed. 'I think they've got a dictatorship in Eritrea. Is that right?'

'Yes,' said Yusuf. 'But the world do nothing. Then we go by bus to Khartoum. We meet smuggler man from my country. We pay him five hundred dollars so we can journey to Libya. This takes many days - sometimes over desert. My friend Yonas is sick but we've no doctor. We're with strangers who cannot help. We now have no money. We hide in a truck of food going to the seaport.'

He fell silent for a moment before going on: 'Then luck comes. We find a fishing man and he gives us the work. We fish in the light and sleep on the beach by night. This happens for weeks. Then we have money. We must go to the Tripoli. It's four hundred miles, but we take bus and sometimes we walk.

'When we arrive, thousands of people are at the seaport. We sleep inside lorry, but policeman finds us. We must pay him money or he takes us to police station. We all have to pay him one hundred dollars. It's too much, but we're not having the choice.'

This immediately reminded me of my own brush with the law a year earlier. I was one of ten thousand teachers who marched through Central London calling for better pay and pensions. A friend of mine was struck by a police baton and knocked to the ground. When I tried to help him, I was struck too.

I made an official complaint about the policeman concerned and a belligerent sergeant threatened to charge me with criminal damage. I could completely sympathise with our friend.

Continuing his story, Yusuf said: 'We must take a boat to a place called Lampedusa and go to Italy. We find the smuggler man from our country. We pay him a thousand dollars.'

I exclaimed: 'What? Each?'

'Yes. Yonas pay, Hamid pay and I pay. But the fishing boat's no good. We have coat to protect but we're forty and we have children also.'

'Life jackets,' Anne whispered to me.

Yusuf put his elbows on the table and buried his face in his hands. He sat like this for nearly a minute. When he removed his hands and looked up at us, he was red-faced and we could see tears streaming down his cheeks. I put my arm round his shoulder to reassure him.

'We're in the boat,' he went on. 'We're nearly arriving. We see the land, but the pump's stopping. The engine's stopping. The water's coming. We try to call for people on other boats to help. No one's coming. The boat's sinking. Hamid and I find the mast to hold, but Yonas is nowhere. I call for him. I call for him.' Our guest's sobbing became louder.

'He's gone. Twenty are lost to the sea. Hamid and me, we're saved. We swim. We find the land and go to the seaport. Then we got on the back of a lorry and travelled to Calais. I think Hamid is still there. We're crying a lot for Yonas.'

As Yusuf paused again to reflect upon the loss of his friend,

I remarked: 'I know a little more now about what you've been through. You've obviously had a terrible time.'

I wanted to ask Yusuf how he managed to remain beneath our motor-home for so long without falling onto the road, but I felt certain he would be grateful to have an opportunity to lie down after such a gruelling journey. Also Anne was concerned about a cut on his left forehand. She placed a flannel under a warm tap, washed the wound, applied some ointment and covered it with a plaster.

'There,' she said. 'That should heal fairly quickly. D'you want to come into the living room and sit down?'

'Thank you, Anne. You kind,' he replied, as he slowly followed her into the next room. 'Some people they find a man hiding under car. They get angry. You don't get angry. You give me food. You give me medicine. You and Bob, you kind.'

'Thank you, Yusuf,' Anne replied.

She made him comfortable in one of our living-room armchairs. Within seconds, our guest was asleep.

As we returned to our seats at the kitchen table, Anne suddenly laughed.

'What is it, darling?' I said.

'I wish I'd taken a photograph of the moment Yusuf's head emerged from under the van,' said Anne, who was still wearing the red T-shirt and white denim shorts she had travelled home in.

'How on earth did he manage to cling on for so long?' I said. 'He must've tied himself to the chassis in some way. It must've happened while we were stuck in the traffic queue in Calais or waiting in the car park before we boarded the ferry.'

'You'll probably find some rope on the ground when you move the van,' she agreed. 'Anyway it's time to call the police. He's an illegal immigrant. We're likely to get into serious trouble if we don't report him. We don't want to risk getting into any trouble. Yes, I think we should call the police. Who's going to make the call - you or me?'

2

In six years of marriage, my wife and I had barely exchanged a cross word. But I sensed that an argument was about to erupt between us over the fate of the stowaway.

'I don't think we should call the police,' I said. 'At least, not for the moment. Think what he's been through. He's travelled more than five thousand miles. He's been cooped up in Calais with thousands of other migrants. Then somehow - don't ask me how - he's attached himself to our vehicle. What he did was incredibly dangerous. What if he'd fallen onto the road when we were in fast-moving traffic? He'd more than likely have been killed or seriously injured. Can't you see how desperate he must be to settle in England? So let's have a think about it. Let's... well, let's at least wait until tomorrow. You see, I think we should give him a chance. We shouldn't just shop him to the authorities.'

'What?' said Anne. 'We let him stay here?'

'Why not? It's only for a short while. He's had a terrible time. He doesn't want us to call the police. He wants to work and earn money for his family. He's obviously come over here to better himself and to look for his mother. His sisters are sick. We should let him stay for a while until he finds work.'

'I suppose he doesn't want to claim asylum right now because many of his fellow-countrymen have been turned down,' said

Anne, glumly staring down at the table. 'Or he's not telling us the full story.'

'I feel sorry for the guy. He seems so genuine,' I said. 'He wants to help his family. He's had a nightmare journey. He was nearly drowned and then could've so easily been killed on the A2 coming up from Dover. Let's give him a chance. I know there are a lot of people who don't have any sympathy for asylum seekers and yes, we have to have some kind of control over immigration. But he's a human being.'

'Yes, but he could be a criminal,' Anne suggested. 'Don't you remember the case of the family from the Midlands who invited a homeless man into their home? It was on television. He went mad with a knife. He murdered the woman, who was fifty, and her thirteen-year-old son. Her husband only survived because of life-saving surgery.'

My darling Anne looked distraught and was breathless.

'They'd fed him,' she said quickly. 'They'd given him a job and let him stay with them. Then I can remember, about six years ago, a nurse in the North of England was stabbed to death by an asylum seeker from Iran. Police failed to warn her he'd killed a previous girlfriend.'

'All right, but I think I'm a fair judge of character. He doesn't seem to have any of the characteristics of a criminal. I think we should put him up for a few days. But look -- I won't let him stay unless you agree one hundred per cent. And if he puts a foot out of place, we immediately call the police.'

'All right. We'll let him stay for a short time - until he sorts himself out,' Anne replied with a reluctant nod of agreement.

'I promise you, if he puts a foot wrong, we dial 999,' I assured her, convinced we had nothing to fear from his presence in the cottage. 'I quite like the man. He doesn't appear to have any of the characteristics of a criminal. I think we should put him up for a few days.'

Anne smiled. 'You know, you're a kind man, Bob. All my family keep telling me that, and I do love you, you know?'

'I love you too, darling,' I said, kissing her on the cheek.

We spent the next two hours unloading our belongings from the white motor-home, which I had bought for £19,000 two years earlier. I had decided it was money well spent. We had had three holidays abroad with it already.

We had gone on the trip to France partly because our beloved Labrador, Alfie, had died of cancer in May at the age of twelve. We thought a break would help us to deal with our grief.

However, we were glad to have arrived home and memories of our much-missed faithful friend now was a little more distant. We were fortunate to live in such an idyllic part of England. Our sleepy village, Chasehurst, is located just a few miles from the ancient cathedral city of Canterbury.

Hop gardens and fruit farms abound in the area and the quiet lane outside our home, 'Fairview,' is adorned during the summer with a host of wild flowers. These include an array of white daisies and pink foxgloves.

The red, pale yellow and white roses had flourished during our absence, although the shrubs and bushes that stood proudly at the front of our land badly needed pruning.

By now it was, I suppose, about ten in the evening. We were both racked with fatigue. After a light meal, we glanced into the living room. Yusuf was still sleeping soundly.

'Shall we let him stay here overnight?' I asked Anne. She

looked at me for a few moments, then gave a quick nod.

'All right,' she replied. In silence, we went upstairs to our bedroom.

I spent a few minutes unpacking my suitcase and, as a result, Anne, whom I had married six years earlier, was in bed before me. Wisps of her blonde hair, her lily-white forehead, her slender nose and small mouth were just visible above the bedsheet. I slipped beneath the duvet, reached across and cuddled her warm, naked body.

'It's all quite exciting, isn't it, darling?' I said.

'What d'you mean, darling?'

'I mean having a stranger around - having a stowaway in our own home! We've never really had an adventure of our own, but we're certainly having one now.' She smiled at me in the semi-darkness.

'Yes, darling. I see what you mean. It's like we're partners in crime.'

We made love passionately.

I felt the joy of our love was heightened by the thought we could be in contempt of the law. It felt as if we were sealing a covenant with each other.

'I hope we've made the right decision,' Anne said later as we both settled down to sleep.

At about four in the morning, I needed to visit the bathroom and rose from our bed. I thought I would also check on Yusuf.

But as I drew close to the bedroom door, I realised Anne had locked it from the inside. I must admit I was shocked. I felt suddenly guilty. Should I have allowed my personal suspicion of the authorities to influence my attitude towards Yusuf? Should

I have used my powers of persuasion to try to convince Anne to let him stay with us? What if her misgivings were well-founded and he was some form of criminal?

My heart went out to her. It grieved me to think she might be worried about his presence with us. I felt I had to do my utmost to help Yusuf, but I certainly did not want the act of helping him to damage the relationship between Anne and me. All I could think was, if he betrayed our trust or breached our hospitality, that would mark the end of our involvement with him.

I crept down the stairs. The living-room door creaked open. Yusuf's black curly hair was just discernible over the top of the armchair. Assured he was still slumbering, I returned to our bedroom.

After considering for a few moments whether to tackle Anne in the morning about her decision to lock the door, I resolved I would not mention it. I got back into the bed and, within a few moments, I was asleep again.

3

In the morning I at first wondered if our stowaway might have left us. Our cottage was eerily silent. I rose as the sun streamed past the beige curtains into our bedroom at the front of the cottage. Its rays flickered and danced across the varnished wooden floor.

I looked at the clock. It was just after nine. My forehead was moist with sweat. It had been a sweltering night.

Anne was still asleep. Her breathing, which sounded a little like a cat purring, was to be the only sound. I sat upright for a few minutes, watching over her and listening out for any sound from downstairs. There was none.

I pulled on a grey T-shirt and an old pair of blue jeans before descending the wide oak stairs to the hallway, half-expecting to be greeted by Yusuf. But he appeared nowhere to be found. As I opened the door to each room downstairs, I thought I might suddenly find his smiling face. But he was not there. I tried the upstairs rooms as well to no avail.

He must have upped sticks and gone.

I was disappointed. I had championed his cause. Yet it appeared he had chosen to seek his fortune elsewhere. We'd fed him, given him somewhere safe to spend the night, tended to his wounded forehead and listened to the heart-breaking tale of his flight from the harsh regime in his homeland. Yet he'd turned his back on us and gone without a word of thanks.

For a moment, I felt hurt. Despite the risks, we'd done our best to help him. So this was how he repaid us? But amid my feelings of disappointment there was also some sense of relief. I would have had to explain his presence to friends and neighbours and possibly relatives, too. If he were living with us, we might be courting trouble with the authorities. Above all, his presence risked upsetting Anne.

The pillow, sheet and duvet Anne had given him were piled neatly on the armchair where he had slept. He could have simply discarded them loosely on the settee, I thought. At least, he had had the consideration to leave them folded up.

Anne had meanwhile been disturbed by the sound of my footsteps going about the cottage. She was lying quietly in our bed, considering the prospect of getting up. Her first thoughts, she told me later, were about Yusuf. She remembered she had locked the bedroom door. She realised now I must have unlocked it at some point. It was a sign to me she was still uneasy about Yusuf remaining in our home.

She cried out to me: 'Darling!' I looked in on her.

'Yusuf seems to have gone,' I said. 'I can't see him anywhere in the cottage. But there's no note - nothing. His bedding's piled up neatly in the living-room.'

'That's very strange,' she said. 'Perhaps it's for the best.' Then she added: 'I don't like saying this, but is anything missing at all?'

'I never thought of that,' I replied. 'But I've been in every room now except the bathroom. Everything seems in order.'

'Darling, how d'you feel about him leaving without a word?' she asked.

'Well, it seems rather ungrateful,' I admitted. 'I mean, after all we've done. I suppose I feel sad, but part of me's a little relieved as well, I suppose. How d'you feel about it?'

"I think it might be for the best, although he seems a pleasant enough guy,' she confessed. 'Anyway, I'm going to get dressed now and I'll be down in a moment.'

'OK,' I said. 'I'll go downstairs and make some tea.'

I had just gone down the stairs and was about to enter the kitchen when I thought I could hear a faint clicking noise coming from somewhere outside.

I unlocked the back door and stepped into the rear garden. It was a bright morning without a cloud in the sky. To my surprise, I then noticed the two loose wooden boards on the side of our shed had been nailed back. Whoever had carried out the repair work had possibly entered the shed and used some nails and one of my hammers, I told myself. Had one of the neighbours carried out the job as a favour while we had been away?

But I was more perplexed by the clicking noise that had first lured me outdoors. It was coming from the front garden.

I edged past our old Ford Mondeo and the motorhome to reach the front drive. It was then I realised Yusuf had not left us after all.

As I walked past our flower beds and unkempt front lawn, I could see his right arm moving about energetically. I reached the bottom of the gravel drive and could see he was standing in the lane, clipping the overgrown shrubs. I was surprised to find him there. But I was also delighted.

I realised he must have risen before me, fixed the shed and then found my garden shears at the back of the house and set himself to work in the lane. He was toiling away, unaware of my presence, still wearing the grubby red check shirt and torn black trousers he had arrived in.

'Hello!' I said. 'You're working hard.'

He turned in surprise. 'Hello, Bob!' he said. Then, evidently unsure of what else to say, he returned to his task. He had found some black refuse sacks and was filling them with the cuttings.

Later that morning, after Anne had got up, we provided Yusuf with a towel and suggested he was free to have a bath if he wanted.

He readily agreed to the idea. I had an old white shirt I had worn at school some years before. Luckily it fitted him. I also found a pair of blue jeans he could wear. Anne shortened each trouser leg by two inches with pins while he was in the bathroom.

She also put his old clothes in the washing machine. As she was doing this, she found a passport and birth certificate in his pockets, which she handed to him when he came downstairs into the kitchen.

Afterwards we made Yusuf tea and buttered toast before sitting down round the table to discuss his future.

He appeared frightened when I mentioned we could drive him to the police station if he wanted us to.

'No police. I'm good man,' he said. 'I want work.' He picked up his passport from the window sill where he had placed it before breakfast.

'Look - passport,' he said excitedly, handing it to me.

The blue passport, issued by Eritrea's Department of Immigration and Nationality, gave his name as Yusuf Osman. His place of birth was stated to be Asmara and his date of birth given as August the sixth 1993.

'I'm not illegal,' he insisted. I smiled faintly.

'Yusuf, Yusuf, your passport doesn't give you the right to be in Britain, but don't worry,' I told him. 'You can stay with us for a few days - until you've fully recovered from your journey.' Turning to Anne, I added: 'I agree with you the best thing would be for us to let Yusuf stay in the motor-home. We can give it a good clean and make it very comfortable for him. It's fortunate we have it. It means he can stay there and be self-contained while we work out what to do in the long term.'

'All right. If that's what you want,' she said.

'Is that all right with you, Yusuf?' I asked.

'Thank you, Bob. You good man,' he said. 'Thank you, Anne. You good man.'

She quickly corrected him with a terse: 'Woman.'

'Woman,' he repeated.

Over the next few hours, the pair of us cleaned out the Swift diesel motor-home and found some spare bedding for Yusuf.

My blue Ford Mondeo was parked behind the Swift Lifestyle vehicle, which was inconvenient. We needed it for a trip to the shops the next day, so I drove both vehicles out into the lane and re-parked them so the Mondeo was at the front.

While swapping the two vehicles round, I had expected to find some rope. I was thinking he must have secured himself to the chassis in some way. All the doors of our motor-home had been kept locked throughout the time we had been in Calais on the advice - or rather really instructions -- of police, so he could not have gained entry to the van and travelled inside at any time during the journey.

It would seem he had secured himself to the underside of

the vehicle. My first thought was he might have used rope or cord to tie himself on. He would then have had to untie it in order to free himself at the end of his perilous ride.

However, there was no sign of any rope. Out of curiosity, I got the most powerful torch I owned from the garden shed, walked to the side of our motor-home and manoeuvred my way beneath it.

By doing so, I finally solved the mystery of how Yusuf had gained his passage to England. He had not tied himself to the chassis after all. There were two steel crossmembers beneath the vehicle, a short distance apart from each other. They held the lower part of the vehicle together. Each one was five or six feet in length.

Although there was a space of only about sixteen inches (forty centimetres) between the top of each joist and the van's floor, Yusuf had managed to wedge himself into that gap and used the two struts to support his body. Just one slip could have been fatal.

I was sure he must have been endowed with the luck of the devil during his flight from France. He could have burnt himself on the exhaust system, but that would have been the least of his worries.

Whenever the van lurched or braked suddenly, he could have been hurled onto the road - and then perhaps mown down by a vehicle behind. When the road became bumpy, again his life would have been on the line. It was miraculous he had survived.

I later passed on details of my discovery to Anne, but for some reason we decided not to discuss the issue with Yusuf.

4

Yusuf soon made himself a comfortable retreat inside the motor-home. He quickly learned how the bed should be lowered at night and how the cooker and toilet worked. I wondered about giving him a front door key but decided I would need to talk to Anne about this first.

Anne was still not totally convinced we were acting for the best. While Yusuf was eating some food in the kitchen, she drew me into the living-room.

'He's an illegal immigrant. I keep thinking he should be applying for asylum,' she said.

'But he's such a nice guy,' I said. 'He's been toiling away in the garden since daybreak. You saw yourself he was terrified when we mentioned taking him to the police. As far as we're concerned, he's gone through the right channels. He's got some sort of right to be here.'

Anne held her hands up to her face. 'If it's a genuine passport, yes. But why travel here, clinging onto a motor-home, if he's got the right to be here?'

I had to admit the rights and wrongs of the situation were unclear.

'Look,' I said. 'He's been working so hard. You saw yourself he seemed terrified when we mentioned taking him to the police.'

I had to admit the rights and wrongs of the situation were unclear, but Anne had, until being made redundant a year earlier, been working as a librarian - and this gave me an idea.

'Why don't you go to the library and look into the facts about claiming asylum?' I suggested. 'They must have loads of books on the subject and you can also do some online research.'

'Yes,' she said. 'That sounds sensible. I'll go over there early next week.'

Later that day, as Anne was working on the till at the Village Stores, Yusuf knocked on the back door.

'Mister Bob,' he said. 'I work.'

Our visitor's work ethic was impressive. He now stood there, bristling with energy and eager to impress us further. Our back garden had become overgrown over the previous two months. We had lost interest in tending it since the death of Alfie. I at once handed him the shears and let him prune the trees and bushes. At the same time, I made a mental note I would later give him a small sum of money for his trouble.

After leaving him to his own devices, I happened to notice our amiable next-door neighbour, seventy-two-year-old Stephen Rigden, was putting his refuse bins out.

'How was France?' he asked.

'Great. Weather was terrific, the scenery in Burgundy was wonderful and we sampled some fantastic wines. Only drawback was it was a bit expensive. Dijon with its ancient houses and palace was magnificent. We worked it out that we must've covered two hundred and fifty miles on the bikes.'

'Aren't you whacked after all that cycling?'

'We did sleep rather well last night!'

'I expect I shall be holidaying in the Med.'

'What part?' I said. 'France, Italy, Greece?'

'No, Gillingham,' he replied. 'I'll be stopping with my son in the Medway towns.'

I smiled and then he became more serious.

'Bob,' said the tall, grey-haired former builder. 'I noticed a guy in a red shirt cutting your bushes this morning. Have you got yourselves a gardener?'

There was a pause as I wondered what to say. I could have pretended Yusuf was being employed as a gardener - but then Stephen might notice our guest coming and going from the motor-home.

'He's our new lodger,' I explained. 'You know Anne lost her job with the library? Well, to be honest we've been having a bit of a struggle financially - even though she's got a part-time job at the shop. Don't spread it around, of course.'

'Of course not,' said Ridgen.

'We just need that little bit of extra money coming in. It helps with the bills,' I said.

'Don't blame you,' he said.

Before it became dark, I glanced through the kitchen window. Yusuf's work-rate was phenomenal. He had virtually transformed the rear garden in a single afternoon, filling more than a dozen black refuse sacks with cuttings from trees, shrubs and bushes. Each bag was neatly tied and they were stacked tidily at the side of the house.

Now he was kneeling on the ground and proceeding to weed the flower beds. He only stopped when I told him Anne had prepared a meal for us all and he needed to come in.

Once he had stepped into the kitchen, I took him aside. I explained, in the simplest words I could find, that, for the moment, he should try to avoid contact with our elderly neighbours - Stephen and Marion Rigden on one side and eighty-five-year-old widow Linda Morrison in the adjoining house. Yusuf looked blank.

'Bob means you stay with us, lodge with us,' Anne explained gently.

'If anyone asks, you're the lodger,' I told him.

Yusuf gave a quick nod.

'Oh, I see. Lodger,' he repeated. It was clearly a new word for him.

After the meal, we all sat in the living-room. This was a twenty-seven feet long room with an oak-beamed ceiling and inglenook fireplace.

As I watched television, Anne took it upon herself to try to improve Yusuf's English. She wrote down some basic English sentences in an exercise book and then showed it to him. She read each phrase to him, explained in turn what each one meant and then invited him to repeat them to her.

Finally, he went off to the motor-home and later told us he spent an hour learning the phrases Anne had taught him before he went to sleep.

After Yusuf had been with us for more than a week, the three of us settled into a steady way of life.

Our day would begin with breakfast on the terrace outside our living-room patio doors. We enjoyed extensive views across farmland.

Sometimes I would go on a cycling trip to the town and back while Anne would teach Yusuf some English. On other occasions, Anne and I would go shopping or visit some of my teaching friends. We would often return to find our visitor had carried out some tasks in the garden. We realised he was doing this work to impress us and to convince us to let him stay at Fairview.

Around this time we gave him a front door key so that he could go into the kitchen to make himself a sandwich if we were out.

When I returned from visiting the school on Tuesday, August the eleventh, Anne greeted me with a kiss and said she had something to tell me.

'Bob, dear, we can't go on like we are - providing Yusuf with meals and accommodation,' she said as we stood together in the middle of the living-room. 'He needs a job. I've just the idea. Why don't we contact one of the fruit farms? There are lots round here and they're crying out for labourers. I've been phoning round and there is one just up the road in Sissenden. They were very interested when I told them about Yusuf. He could work part-time if he wants.'

'Great idea!' I said. 'We'll have a chat with him later in the week after you've done your research.'

On Wednesday August the twelfth, Anne finally found time to return to the library where she had once worked. There she spent more than three hours huddled over books and peering at a computer screen, trying to discover how an immigrant like Yusuf should set about claiming asylum.

On her return, she found me in the living room and explained it was a lengthy process.

'You contact an office in Croydon and they call you in for a biometrics check a week later in which they note all your physical features,' she said. 'They also carry out medical tests - including checking your blood pressure, blood cholesterol and blood glucose.

A week or two later you get your first interview. You must bring your passport, birth certificate and proof of address. They then take up to six months to make their minds up.'

'I imagine there is some kind of fee involved,' I suggested.

'Yes, it's not cheap. It costs nearly a thousand pounds and at your first interview they decide whether to detain you or release you while they ponder their decision. But right now you're extremely unlikely to be detained. They just haven't got the staff.'

'Don't asylum seekers usually have a lawyer to fight their corner? I think Yusuf might need one,' I said. 'After all, Britain might not want him. He's penniless and single. If he was in touch with his mother and living with her, he would probably be in a stronger position, wouldn't he?'

'Yes, but actually he has got one really strong card - he's Eritrean. Of course, he'd have to convince them he'd face persecution if he returned. He's meant to apply as soon as he can and he's not really meant to work till it's all sorted.'

'The authorities will never know the exact date when he came here - because of the way he arrived,' I observed. 'I think we should let him take this farm job and have a couple of months working in the sun. He's had an exhausting journey and he needs to raise a bit of money so he can apply.'

'That all sounds sensible,' Anne replied.

'If the police or anyone comes knocking, we'll say he came as a lodger. We won't mention how we accidentally brought him on our chassis! Would they necessarily believe that anyway? I think we need to have a heart-to-heart chat with him. We need to find out what he wants to do with his life - where he sees himself going. I was wondering if he wants to improve his education, for instance.'

I was due to return to my post at school at the beginning of September and my life would then become extremely hectic. I did not want to burden Anne about this, but the September term was stressful and I knew I would have less time over the coming weeks to concern myself with Yusuf.

Just at that moment, I noticed through the front window our guest was sitting in a green wicker chair, sunning himself in the front porch.

'Yusuf!' I called. 'Could we have a chat?'

He walked hesitantly into the room with a quizzical look on his face.

'Yes, Bob?' he asked.

Anne and I sat down on the settee and we invited him to make himself comfortable in the armchair.

'We've been talking about you and your situation,' I began. 'Anne's heard that a farm near here might be able to give you a job picking fruit.'

At first Yusuf was cautious when we mentioned the prospect of him picking and packing fruit. He told us he had heard most workers on Kent fruit farms were from either Romania or Bulgaria and he wondered how he would be accepted by them.

'I don't want to do that,' he insisted, making a gesture simulating a man breaking a stick with his two fists.

'No get on,' he said. 'They greedy and fight.'

'We can't offer you work here. We can't afford to,' I said.

'I work for you,' he said.

'No,' I said. 'You work for money - at the farm.'

Eventually, he realised Anne and I were adamant and, when he realised he would have the chance to earn good money, he quickly warmed to the idea of farm work.

'I am so thankful to you, Bob, and to you, Anne,' he said.

'That's good. We have enjoyed having your company,' I told him. 'Look, we're willing to let you stay on in the motor home for a few weeks. But eventually you'll have to claim asylum and sort your situation out.'

He was about to rise from the armchair and return to the porch, but I stopped him.

'Yusuf,' I said quietly. 'How d'you see your future? D'you want to study at all?'

'Yes, I like to study. But I also need to find mother,' he declared. 'Now we're having summer. Maybe I work on the farm and then maybe go to find mother.'

Anne interrupted.

'We know you've had a rough time,' she admitted. 'But we feel that, in around two months' time, you should apply for asylum. I can explain what you've got to do. I will help you. We will phone the immigration people in Croydon and get an appointment.'

'Thank you, Anne. Thank you, Bob. You have been a great help to me. Where is this Croydon?'

'It's a town about sixty miles away where the asylum centre is based. I can drive you there.'

'I will go. Bob, Anne, I am so grateful to you. Even now, in the middle of the night, I am crying for my friend Yonas. But I stop crying when I am thinking how good it is to be in England after everything I have been through. It wouldn't have been possible without you and your kindness.'

Anne added: 'Your asylum claim may be turned down in any case, but at least this way you get a nice summer holiday in England.'

I said: 'If the authorities make a fuss about your case, you can always plead ignorance.'

We had gradually become used to his ways and, in my heart, I suppose I was afraid of losing him to some detention centre - although I think we both realised that, strictly speaking, there should be no delay in his applying and what we were doing was essentially wrong.

That night, after Yusuf had gone to bed, Anne and I continued talking about our new friend.

'The situation in England's crazy,' I told her. 'Asylum seekers are turning up in the backs of lorries all the time. I even read about two found in the engine compartment of a school coach when it returned from France.

'Often, when the police catch them, they've no way of taking them to a detention centre. Sometimes they're simply given the address and told to make their own way there. Of course, many of them disappear en route.'

On Thursday of that week, we decided to buy Yusuf some clothes. Until then, he had been sharing my rather limited wardrobe. This was becoming increasingly challenging for me and, when I returned to the academy, I would have to focus fully on my work. I did not want to begin a school day without being able to find a suitable shirt or pair of trousers to wear.

On August the twelfth, the three of us set out in the Mondeo for the shops of Canterbury. We bought him underwear in Marks & Spencer. Then we trawled round the charity shops. We found him two smart white shirts, four casual shirts, two pairs of trousers and a dark-blue winter coat. The total cost was around fifty pounds.

5

Early in the morning, two days later, the sun rose in a cloudless sky. I glanced from our bedroom window. The pink foxgloves and white daisies in the lane tossed and nodded their heads in the gentle breeze.

Anne had made an appointment for her and Yusuf to visit a farm two miles away in the next village of Sissenden.

Finch & Davies, first established in 1953, was one of the largest farms in Kent. They grew apples, pears and plums for supermarkets and the wholesale trade.

Yusuf's appointment was at ten am, but two hours beforehand he was nowhere to be seen.

'I've an idea where he might be,' I told Anne. 'You wait here in case I'm wrong.'

There is an idyllic spot a few hundred yards from our cottage. You walk a short distance towards Chasehurst village and then take a turning on the right through the woods. After a brief woodland walk along a public footpath which crosses a stream, you come to a clearing overlooking open fields. A smart brown wooden bench had been installed there in honour of a former chairman of the parish council, now deceased. If you sit there, surrounded by wild flowers, you can see for miles across East Kent.

It was a place where Yusuf liked to come and think. Sure

enough, on this occasion, I found him rapt in thought, sitting on the bench.

'Don't you want some breakfast?' I called out as I approached him.

'I'm no hungry,' he said. 'I think I stay in village today.'

I knew Anne would be annoyed with him. She had spent some time the previous day, phoning the various farms located in our part of East Kent. They were all desperately in need of fruit pickers. She knew, if Yusuf borrowed my spare bicycle, he could make the daily journey to Finch & Davies in just ten or fifteen minutes. She did not want him to lose the opportunity.

Eventually, with some reluctance, he walked back to the cottage with me.

After Anne spent a short time discussing the matter with him, he finally agreed to accompany us to the farm. He put on a white shirt and black trousers Anne had pressed the evening before. I gave him one of my old ties - a dark-blue tie I had hardly worn but no longer cared for.

At a quarter to ten, we all jumped into the Mondeo and, with Anne at the wheel, we set off for the farm.

Finch & Davies has more than five hundred acres of land, most of which have been turned into orchards. They also have several huge barns which are used as pack-houses and storage areas.

We noticed apple trees as far as the eye could see. The green fruit of late summer were gradually ripening before us, bringing, here and there, the dash of a reddish hue to the maze of green-coloured branches and leaves and the brown trunks of the trees.

The main office was in the original farmhouse built in the

middle of the nineteenth century. We parked in the large car park behind and then pointed out the reception area to Yusuf.

As we approached the main door, I cracked a joke at Yusuf's expense - referring back to his journey into Britain riding beneath the motor-home. I told him: 'When the tractor hauls a full load of fruit back to the farm, be sure you travel ON TOP of the cart.' My joke, once explained, failed to impress Yusuf, although it made Anne smile.

Anne introduced herself to a well-dressed lady who was standing by the door, the managing director's secretary, Sue Wickens.

'This is Yusuf Osman,' Anne told her. 'And this is my husband, Bob.'

'We were so glad to receive your call, Mrs Shaw,' she said. 'We're so desperate for pickers. So this is Mr Osman? Yes, he'll do fine, provided he's got all the necessary paperwork. And this is your husband?'

'Yes, that's right. We've brought his passport,' said Anne, indicating to Yusuf he should display it. He began to slip it from his pocket.

'That's fine,' said the well-spoken secretary. 'What I want you to do is see our Mr Edwin Moreton, the site manager. He can tell you about the pay, the hours, the accommodation and things like that. Mr Osman's your lodger, you told me?'

'Yes, he's staying with us for the moment. He's a very willing worker.'

'That's good to hear. Now you just go out of this office and into the next building. I'm afraid it's a bit cold in there! Ask for Mr Moreton. Anyone'll tell you. Good luck!'

We left the main office, crossed the car park and entered

the huge pack-house through a half-glazed metal door. A Romanian worker in a blue protective coat and transparent plastic cap went to fetch Mr Moreton. As we waited, Anne mentioned that she had an inkling she knew the manager.

'If it's the man I'm thinking of, he's a regular library user. He reads a lot of technology books,' she informed me.

After ten minutes, a stern-faced Englishman wearing similar blue overalls and carrying a file of documents approached us.

'Hello, Anne!' he said. 'I'm not in trouble, am I? I phoned and they said I could have the book for another week.'

'Hello, Mr Moreton,' she replied with a smile. 'I'm not working at the library any more, I'm afraid. '

'Oh, I see. I'd heard about the cutbacks, of course. I'm sorry about that.'

'Not to worry. Look, this is Yusuf Osman. Mrs Wickens asked us to introduce him to you.'

'Oh, that's right. So you're Yusuf, are you? I'm guessing you're not Romanian, are you?'

'He's from Eritrea. Show him your passport, Yusuf,' said Anne.

'We've got to be careful. We had the immigration people down here last year.'

'We've found him honest and very hard-working,' Anne assured him. 'We can both vouch for him.'

'OK,' said Mr Moreton. 'He'll have to go in the office to sort out the paperwork. If you're prepared to work hard, son, we pay the minimum wage of six pounds seventy pence an hour. Obviously, you don't get paid during any breaks such as lunchtime. But last year some of our top workers took away nine pounds an hour on piece rates.'

'That's cool, isn't it?' said Anne, looking to see Yusuf's reaction. He remained stone-faced.

'We'll need him six days a week - maybe seven,' said Mr Moreton. 'The work'll be picking to start with. If we choose, we might give him a turn in the pack-house. If you work hard, you can earn good money, son. You'll make lots of friends. The accommodation's quite good. We've got a fleet of fairly modern caravans.'

He added: 'Are you into football, son? There's a soccer pitch and we've got some table tennis tables. It's like a holiday camp here.'

'He'll be staying with us for the moment,' Anne explained. 'We're only in Chasehurst.'

'Oh OK,' said Mr Moreton, nodding his head. 'Look, we'll take him. We're desperately short of people. We'll do this, Anne, because we know you, but I must be frank with you. If he steps out of line, he's out of here.'

'You won't have any problems,' I said. 'I'd bet my life on it.'

Mr Moreton turned to Yusuf.

'My parents called me Edwin, but everybody knows me as Ted,' he explained. 'Now I have to ask you this. How d'you feel about going to bed early and getting up early? The best time to pick fruit's when it's cool, very early in the morning. We'll need you at four-thirty am. Will that suit you?'

'That's all right. There's a bicycle he can use,' said Anne, who was surprised at hearing the early starting time. 'Is that all right, Yusuf?'

'Yes,' he said.

'I take it you've no allergies to fruit, bees or wasps, son? And you're not colour blind?'

Anne turned to Yusuf. 'He's asking whether you become ill -- become sick -- if you touch fruit? He's also asking if you become ill because of a bee or wasp attack and if you've got any problem with your eyes?'

Yusuf nodded. 'No problem,' he said.

'I'm helping him with his English,' Anne explained.

'That's OK. We've got all nationalities,' he said. 'All right, young man. We'll see you at the crack of dawn on Monday.'

'Goodbye, Mr Moreton,' she said. 'Don't worry. We'll make sure he's here at four-thirty.'

As we walked slowly back to the car, Yusuf had a question for Anne.

'What's this word "son"? Does he think he'll be my father when I pick the apples?' he asked.

'No, no,' said Anne. 'It's a term of endearment. Oh God! How can I explain that to man from Africa? It means he's being friendly. He doesn't want to be your father. He's probably going to treat you like a son.'

As Yusuf got into the passenger seat of the car, he said: 'The English language can be very strange.'

6

Anne offered to drive Yusuf to the farm on his first day. Secretly, because of his earlier reservations, she had been concerned he might fail to report for work. She set her alarm for a quarter to four in the morning, roused him from his bed in the motor-home and travelled with him to the farm for his four-thirty am start.

But when he returned on foot from his first full day at work, he surprised her by proudly handing Anne the thirty pounds he had earned.

'This for you. This for food,' he declared.

From that time onwards, he regularly cycled to and from work. I had given him two cycle locks and told him to make sure he locked his bike to a post or railings - or his new mode of transport might quickly disappear.

I explained: 'There are lots of people there on low wages who cannot afford to buy a bicycle and would relish the chance of having yours.'

So much physical effort was required in his job that, during his first week, spent picking plums, he came back exhausted. He would wolf down a meal cooked by either Anne or myself, spend an hour learning English and then go straight to bed.

But as his second week progressed, he was to become more accustomed to the physical strain. He would arrive back at three pm or four pm feeling less exhausted.

Anne continued with her part-time job helping out at the village shop for two afternoons a week, while I had begun travelling to Canterbury. I was visiting the academy so I could prepare lessons for the forthcoming term.

However, an unexpected incident occurred on Thursday, August the twenty-seventh that upset both Anne and myself. It concerned our neighbour, Stephen.

Both Anne and I returned home that day at about the same time - around half past five. We noticed an ambulance, a police car and a small white van parked outside the Rigdens' house. Yusuf had a worried expression on his face as we entered the hall.

'Oh, Bob, Anne,' he said. 'Something bad is happening next door. Medical people are coming. Police are coming.'

'Are you talking about the house where Mr Rigden lives -- the tall man who saw you gardening?' I asked.

'Yes. He is sick They are taking him from the house and driving him away.'

'I think I'd better pop next door and see if Marion is all right,' Anne muttered.

'I'll come too, in case there's anything I can do,' I said.

Stephen's wife, Marion, is aged seventy-four. She moves around her semi-detached red-brick cottage with the aid of walking sticks and suffers from mild dementia.

Anne pressed the doorbell. A young paramedic in a smart, dark-green uniform came to the door.

'We're from next door,' Anne explained. The paramedic immediately beckoned us in and I followed my wife through the dimly-lit hallway. We could see Marion was sitting in an armchair in front of the fireplace in the beige-coloured living room. She was surrounded by dark, 1950s furniture. A faint smell of stale cigarette smoke hung in the air.

'Before we go in,' I whispered. 'What has actually happened?'

The paramedic looked us both sternly in the face.

'Mrs Rigden found her husband slumped on the floor of the conservatory an hour and a half ago,' he whispered. 'His head was badly bruised and covered in blood. He was lying motionless, barely breathing.'

We spotted two men in white overalls and facemasks moving around at the far end of the house.

The paramedic went on: 'One of the panes was smashed in the conservatory door. Fragments of glass lay on the floor beside Mr Rigden. More slithers of glass lay on the patio outside.' He paused for breath.

'To add to the mystery, £20,000 in savings, which they'd kept in a cardboard box, has gone missing,' he added. 'A forensic team are checking the conservatory.'

Anne and I looked at each other in astonishment. We had known Stephen and Marion since we first bought the cottage and moved in six years earlier. They had been friendly, helpful neighbours.

Without waiting any further, Anne rushed forward to see Marion, who was wearing a long, pink floral dress with a white cardigan, and asked if she was all right.

'Yes, thank you, dear. It's Stephen,' the old lady replied.

After ensuring Marion was comfortable, Anne made some tea and asked the paramedic to make sure the social services department at Kent County Council had been alerted.

'They've taken him to the Ashford hospital,' Marion

announced loudly. 'I can't get there. It's twelve miles.'

'Would you like me to drive you there?' Anne asked.

'Would you do that, dear? Our son's away.'

'It would be the least we could do,' said Anne.

Fifteen minutes later, Anne helped Marion into the front passenger seat of the Mondeo and the pair set off to the hospital.

But when they arrived, sadly, they learned Stephen had died during the journey in the ambulance. After Marion had had a long conversation with one of the nurses, Anne drove her back to Chasehurst. She stayed with the old lady at her home for another hour until some distant relatives arrived and began attending to her needs.

By the time she left the Rigdens' house, the police had posted a constable at the front door to monitor any callers.

Later in the evening, after our meal of beef Wellington, I noticed for the first time Yusuf had a small bandage on his left middle finger and there were traces of blood on the left sleeve of his shirt.

'Have you cut yourself, Yusuf?' I asked. He pulled the sleeve towards him and examined it.

'I prune the bush. I cut my hand,' he explained. 'Yusuf will be on the repair soon.'

'On the mend,' said Anne between mouthfuls of beef. After the meal, Anne examined the dressing. Yusuf had tied it himself in a haphazard fashion after finding our first aid box in the bathroom. Anne applied ointment and then secured the bandage properly.

The following day, she was teaching Yusuf some English phrases in the living room and I was preparing a lesson on Tudor kings when there came a loud knock on the front door.

A tall, stout man in a brown suit and yellow tie whom I had never seen before was standing in the porch as the door creaked open.

'Mr Shaw?' he asked. I nodded. 'I'm Detective Sergeant Kirwan from Kent Police. Just wanted to ask you a few questions.'

'Would you like to come in?' I said.

I led him a few yards into the cream-walled hallway and then stopped. I was reluctant to let him meet Yusuf in order to avoid any awkward questions about our guest. I stopped by the oak stairs. 'What can we do for you then?' I asked.

Perhaps he sensed my hesitancy and found it strange.

Speaking with a slight Irish accent, he said: 'We're investigating a suspicious death - your neighbour, Mr Rigden.'

Anne, who had been listening intently from within the living-room, bade Yusuf remain where he was. She placed her finger upon her lips, indicating to him to remain silent. She then came to join us in the hall.

'Hello, officer,' she said. 'I spent a few hours with Marion last night. It's been a terrible shock.'

'She's bearing up well in the circumstances,' said the twenty-five-year-old sergeant. 'Can I ask where you both were between three pm and four pm yesterday?'

'I was at the New East Kent Academy, preparing for the school term for the whole afternoon,' I explained. 'I got home at five thirty.'

'And I was at the Village Stores, working at the checkout all afternoon. I got back at the same time.'

'Would there have been anyone else in the house?' he asked, as he made a note of the details in a small notebook.

'Only our lodger,' I said.

'And where's he now, sir?' he asked.

'Well, actually, I believe he's in the living-room,' I said.

'Could you call him, sir?' I called out his name. Yusuf walked timidly and uncomfortably into the hallway.

'What's your name now?' the sergeant asked.

'Yusuf Osman,' he replied.

'Where were you yesterday afternoon, sir?'

'I work,' he said.

The sergeant continued: 'What time did you arrive back here?'

Yusuf looked at Anne for help in understanding the question.

'He means: 'What time did you get home?'' she explained.

'I home at seventeen hundred,' he said.

Anne looked towards the detective. 'Five o'clock,' she said.

'I'm quite familiar with the way the twenty-four-hour clock operates,' he said somewhat curtly.

'Where d'you work, sir?'

'He works ten minutes away at Finch & Davies, picking fruit,' said Anne.

'And they'll be able to verify you were there until - what? - four-thirty pm or five pm, will they?' he asked Yusuf.

Our lodger glanced towards Anne for possible guidance. Then he said: 'What does this mean: "Verify"?'

'They'll confirm you were at work, will they?' the sergeant demanded.

'Yes, I work,' Yusuf insisted.

Turning to me, the sergeant asked: 'How long's he been lodging here, sir?'

I informed him Yusuf had only been with us for a month

and he was one of hundreds of immigrants who were working at the farm.

'Yes. They're mainly Romanians and Bulgarians. He doesn't look like one of them,' the sergeant declared.

'No,' I replied. 'He's actually from Eritrea.'

'Oh, OK. Well, I don't think I need take up any more of your time at this stage. This is an ongoing investigation.'

I recalled seeing how heartbroken Marion Rigden had been at the hospital and on her return home alone to her house the evening before. I turned to the sergeant.

'Have the police got any idea what happened?' I asked.

'Well, at the moment, it's being treated as a suspicious death,' he said. 'But there seems to be some money missing. We're awaiting the results of a post mortem. It could turn into a murder inquiry, but it's too early to say that, so please keep that under your hat. Bye for now.'

He then opened the front door and walked off down the drive.

All three of us returned slowly to the living-room. I slumped down into our brown leather settee. I sat there for a few minutes, staring at the beige carpet. I had been amazed to hear our neighbour Stephen might have been the victim of a murderer and the motive might have involved the couple's life savings.

Naturally, it had been surprising to hear they kept such a large sum of money in their home. This, to my mind, had been foolish. I was entirely aware elderly people mistrusted banks - even more so since the financial crisis of 2008 - but I felt it had been unwise to stash so much money away at home.

Nonetheless, I had every sympathy for Marion Rigden,

who had lost her husband in such appalling circumstances and presumably would now face additional hardship in paying for his funeral.

Who could have carried out such a crime in our idyllic country village? The most likely explanation was an opportunistic thief had been prowling round and noticed easy rear access to the Rigdens' house. Believing the house to be empty, they had smashed the pane in the conservatory door and quickly found the money - presumably hidden somewhere in the garden room.

Then, to their astonishment, old man Rigden had confronted them. There had been a fight. Our neighbour had been struck on the head and, being elderly and frail, had succumbed to his fate.

In the past, I had taken a keen interest in the subject of rural crime. A policeman had once informed me that, despite a popular misconception burglars were older folk, in reality they were often young - perhaps teenagers or young men in their early twenties. They often acted on a whim after a long lunchtime drinking session had provided them with 'Dutch courage.'

The young criminals preferred to target premises where they could arrive unnoticed, make an easy entry and make an easy departure. Acres of farmland lay behind our homes, which provided a simple escape route if one were needed.

Burglaries rose in the summer as windows were often left open - another attraction for opportunistic thieves.

'Yes, that's how it must've been,' I told myself.

7

The autumn term began on Monday, September the seventh. I was rushing around the whole week like a deranged city trader after a stock market crash, trying to organise activities for the one hundred and eighty new Year Seven pupils starting their secondary education.

It was also a critical week at the farm. Members of the workforce, including Yusuf, were being transferred to picking apples for the first time.

Within a few days, I was as exhausted as our lodger had been during his very first week filling boxes.

But, on the Thursday of that week, he was waiting eagerly outside the front door for me as the Mondeo trundled up the drive after work. He was sitting on his favourite wicker chair and was sunning himself next to the bay window.

'I'm wanting a car,' he informed me. 'I have licence - look.'

He produced a shabby driving licence issued in East Africa which I doubted was legal for use when driving in England.

By this time, he was regularly paying us thirty pounds a week towards his food and electricity, but he informed me he had been saving all the rest of his earnings of more than £250 a week, after deductions.

Someone had informed him there was a blue Ford Fiesta on sale for £525. It was fifteen miles away. Would I accompany him and give him advice?

Not only was I weary after having to deal all day with dozens of fresh-faced, excitable Year Seven pupils. I seriously doubted whether he would be able to afford the huge amount of money required to insure a car.

But Yusuf was almost like a man bewitched by a black magic spell. For ten minutes, he begged me to drive him to see this vehicle, which had a 'mere' seventy thousand miles on the milometer and upon which he had set his heart.

In the end, I had to promise to take him to see the vehicle the following day. It was the only way I could calm him down and see my way to getting past him and into the house.

Once inside, I quickly phoned my car insurance company and went onto comparison websites. As I had suspected, the companies would only provide insurance cover for a hefty fee.

As I tried to explain to Yusuf, he was an Eritrean. He was only twenty-three. His employment record amounted to three weeks as a fruit picker. He didn't have a full UK driving licence. The details did not make impressive reading for the underwriters.

Most of the companies would have wanted him to pay his whole annual premium in advance - and the cheapest I could find was £840 just for third party, fire and theft cover. If he insisted on paying his premiums monthly, each instalment would cost him something like £170.

It took a while, but I managed to convince him the cost of the insurance made it impractical for him to get behind the wheel. When he finally realised the full implications, he gesticulated wildly with both his hands.

'Too much!' he declared. 'Too much!'

It was a shame. For the moment at least, he would have to

get around on just two wheels.

However, this brief episode in our lives sent us an important message. It showed our guest had gained in confidence and was finding the urge to become more independent.

Over the past few days, I had become increasingly puzzled about how poor Stephen could have met his death. One aspect of the whole conundrum stood out in my mind: Was it just coincidence he was found severely injured among broken glass at around the same time Yusuf was discovered with a cut finger?

I am afraid to say, I was now beginning to wonder whether Yusuf could have been involved. Perhaps Anne had been right to express misgivings, I told myself. We did not really know about our stowaway's past. Was it possible the Eritrean was lying to us? Was it possible that his finger had not been cut while pruning, that he had intruded into our neighbour's back garden and that he had injured himself while smashing the conservatory door?

I tried to dismiss the whole idea from my mind. But, as time passed, I had to admit it was one possible explanation - one of many - as to how our neighbour had been injured and, ultimately, died. To support the theory, Yusuf had accumulated some savings. He was keen to buy a car. Had he also stolen Stephen's money? Surely not.

That evening, after Yusuf had left the house and had retired to the motor-home, I discussed my thoughts with Anne. She shook her head, saying: 'Don't say I didn't warn you. I said it was possible he might be a criminal.'

'Perhaps we've been foolish after all,' I said. 'Perhaps we should've called the police the moment we found him.' I began to realise that, if Yusuf had had anything to do with Stephen's death, he could strike again. Surely our lives could not be at risk from him, could they?

Anne was lost in thought. Suddenly she declared: 'I wonder if he regarded Stephen as a threat? Remember Stephen spotted Yusuf in the garden, suspected he was foreign and started asking questions. You don't think...'

'I think we should tackle Yusuf straight away about it,' I said. 'We should just ask him directly if he went next-door on Thursday.'

'What if he doesn't like being asked about it and turns nasty?'

'Come on,' I said. 'This is the guy who's repeatedly thanked you for the dinners you've been serving up -- the guy who was so grateful when you fixed his bandage. He won't turn nasty. Trust me.'

'You're probably right,' she conceded.

I went to the back door and was surprised to find it locked - just as I had found our bedroom door locked the first night Yusuf stayed with us. Anne had obviously turned the key, I thought. Perhaps she had been regularly locking it once Yusuf had gone to sleep in the motor-home. Or perhaps she had begun doing so since Stephen's death.

I turned the key and, moments later, tapped on the door of the motor-home. 'Yusuf,' I whispered. 'Can I speak to you?'

'Yes, Bob,' he replied, easing the door open. 'I was just writing about foxgloves in the lane.'

'Yusuf, I'm sorry about this, but I've got to ask you a hard question.'

'Ask and Yusuf will answer,' he said.

'Yusuf, when you came home from work on Thursday, did you go into Mr Rigden's garden for any reason?'

'No, first I come here to motor-home. Then I go into house and write English words.'

'It's just there was broken glass at the back of Mr Rigden's house. Perhaps that's how you cut your finger?'

'No, Bob, that's wrong.,' he insisted, appearing upset at me doubting him. 'I cut while pruning. Look!' Although barefoot and dressed in only trousers and a flimsy shirt, he led me to the garden shed by torchlight and showed me the shears. There were traces of blood on the blade.

'Yusuf no lying. Blade cut finger,' he said. I was so relieved.

'All right, my friend. I just had to ask. Go to bed now, Yusuf. You've got an early start.'

As I returned to the back door, I found Anne was standing in the doorway, watching me with a gentle smile on her face.

'I'm guessing you found blood on the shears,' she whispered. I nodded.

'We had to ask,' she said. 'I'm a lot happier now.' She squeezed my hand and we went upstairs to bed.

8

'Hi Anne. Over here!' The shrill female voice rang out around Cosimo's Café where Anne and I were queueing for a table. It was a few days after the start of term. Anne had met me at the school gates and we had decided to stop for a coffee at one of the myriad of coffee shops in Canterbury.

'Come and join me!' the smartly-dressed woman in her mid-thirties implored us. Since most of the space in the room had been taken up by a group of Dutch tourists, it was an enticing offer.

'Bob, this is Prunella Ball,' Anne announced.

'Nice to meet you!' I asserted, grasping her hand.

'I haven't seen you in months,' gushed Prunella, kissing Anne on the cheek.

'I lost my job at the library,' Anne explained, as we both took seats at her table in the window.

Prunella, a tall, slim woman with long, brown hair tied neatly behind her head, said: 'I'm so sorry to hear that. You were there for so many years, weren't you? Hey, Anne. Did you see the story you gave me about the farmer who wants to power his house with rotten apples? There was a huge row with his neighbours. It made a big piece in the Daily Mail.'

'It gives a new meaning to the phrase "apple juice!"' I remarked.

'I never saw the story,' said Anne, ignoring my attempt at humour. 'You must show me a copy some time.' Then, turning to me, she whispered: 'Anne's a freelance journalist - so watch what you say.'

Prunella went on: 'Thank you so much for telling me about that farmer, Anne. What d'you want - tea? Coffee? Let me get them for you.'

'Are you sure? That's very kind. We'd both like a white coffee. Thank you,' said Anne.

'It's the least I can do,' said the journalist, rising from her chrome café chair and heading to the counter. Anne informed me she had got to know Prunella at the library. She was a former Kent Police press officer who had gone onto serve as a staff reporter on two national newspapers. She now worked as a stringer for the national press and was based in Faversham.

When she returned to the table with our drinks, we found Prunella had also bought us all some fruit cake. She said: 'So you're a lady of leisure now, Anne?'

'I've got a part-time job on the checkout at the Village Stores in Chasehurst,' Anne replied.

'Look, I'm glad I bumped into you both. You live in Hopgarden Lane, don't you?'

'Yes, that's right,' replied Anne. 'That cake looks lovely. It's very kind of you.'

'Don't mention it. Listen, I've been making inquiries about a mysterious death in your road. I've had a tip-off it could be murder,' she said.

'You're talking about Stephen, our next-door neighbour.' I told her, sipping my coffee.

'Yes, Stephen Rigden, isn't it?'

'Yes. We're devastated, to be honest,' I admitted.

'D'you know anything about what happened?' asked Anne.

'Only that the post-mortem was inconclusive and they're carrying out more tests -- including toxicology and tissue tests,' said Prunella.

'So they're still treating it as a possible murder?'

'Yes. I know a little about it because I've a good friend who works in CID, Graham Kirwan. He's one of the officers in the case..'

I interrupted to say: 'He's a detective sergeant, isn't he? I believe that's the chap who called on us a few evenings ago.'

She nodded and then I noticed she was glancing at a notebook she must have just retrieved from her handbag. She quietly began reading out some of her shorthand notes: 'The head wound suggests blunt force trauma - possibly caused by a hammer used with substantial force. He lost a lot of blood. That's what Graham told me this morning.'

Sipping her tea, Prunella went on: 'He seems to think someone found out the Rigdens had a hoard of money and took a chance to break in. As there was no vehicle outside the house, perhaps they wrongly assumed the couple were out. They broke the glass in the door and then attacked old Mr Rigden before stealing the money. I'd like to take down a few words from you, Anne, if that's all right, so I've got a neighbour's viewpoint. I'll probably be writing a piece later in the week for one of the Sundays.'

'I'd be happy to help. He was a nice old boy,' said Anne. 'We feel sorry for Marion. Social services have been involved. There are four carers going in every day and her son's been visiting.'

'It looks like an opportunist to me,' I remarked, determined not to be left out of the conversation.

'Looks that way,' Prunella agreed. 'There've been no other reports of break-ins in the area for some time - not since Larry Pearson got put away.'

'I remember reading about him in the local paper,' I said. 'The press called him Light-fingered Larry. But he never turned his hand to violence - he'd run a mile at the first sign of trouble.'

'He was sent down about three years ago. He might be out now,' Prunella suggested. 'Oh, there's something else I discovered. The landlord of the Merry Friar in Chasehurst let slip that Rigden had fallen out with someone - a roofer by the name of Knight. Rigden claimed he failed to repair his roof properly and withheld some of the money. I gather it was a long-running dispute.'

'Small world,' I said. 'I know Miles very well. The Friar's one of my drinking haunts.'

'He's given me lots of stories in the past. People tend to open up after having a few drinks and so publicans are a great source of news. Look, if you could just spend a moment telling me about Mr Rigden...'

'Of course,' said Anne. 'What would you like to know? And, by the way, you must call round for tea if you're ever in the area.'

That night I slept fitfully. There was a lot on my mind. Two of my GCSE History pupils had been disrupting my lessons. At four am, I woke with a start and sat bolt upright in bed, suddenly recalling the conversation in the café with Prunella Ball.

As Anne slept on beside me, I asked myself: 'A house powered by rotten apples? How does THAT work?'

During the second week of term, I returned home from Canterbury to find we had another stranger in our midst - a friendly black cat with an injured paw.

Yusuf had come upon the wounded animal near the farm entrance as he removed the padlocks from the bicycle and was about to travel to the cottage. He heard faint mewing, whimpering noises. The poor creature was lying in a gutter at the side of the main road.

I would have rushed him to the vet, but, Yusuf, who was clearly not fully aware of our way of life, had decided to cycle home with him, clutching the stricken animal in his right hand as he steered with his left.

I was about to suggest we both travelled to the vet's in Canterbury when Anne returned from her job at the village shop. A great animal lover - more so than myself -- she insisted she would immediately drive Yusuf to the surgery. This, she thoughtfully suggested, would allow me much-needed time to mark some history essays.

'This poor animal's bleeding and needs immediate attention,' she insisted. 'I'll make sure he gets it.'

Thereupon, she, Yusuf and the cat got into the Mondeo and set off for the city. We discovered later the cat had been struck by a car, but luckily no major bones were broken. The cost of treatment, which included an overnight stay for the cat at the surgery and pain killers, came to more than two hundred pounds.

As the poor creature - who had not been microchipped -- began his slow recovery at home the following day, Yusuf revealed he had made inquiries at the farm and with its neighbours. No one knew who owned it.

He therefore begged Anne and me if we could keep the animal. I was reluctant and thought more efforts should be made to find its rightful owner.

'Some little boy or girl might be pining for their pet, Yusuf,' I told him. I think he grasped what I was saying, but there were occasions when it suited him to pretend the English I used was 'too hard.' This was one of those occasions.

'I don't understand,' he said. 'That's too hard.'

Anne totally supported Yusuf's desire for us to keep the cat.

'It'll do us good to have a new animal around,' she insisted. 'It'll help us get over the loss of Alfie.'

I sensed it would be pointless to try and argue. I was outvoted, two to one.

'Has the cat got a name?' I asked him that evening.

'Yes,' said Yusuf, as he sat in the armchair with the purring cat on his lap. 'I wasn't allowed to have Ford Fiesta, so I've called the cat Fiesta.'

It appeared to make some kind of sense to Yusuf, although I must confess it did not make much sense to me.

It was at about this time it was first suggested Yusuf might move into a caravan at the farm.

Finch & Davies had fifteen caravans on their land to accommodate their staff, and Yusuf had been shown inside two of them by his workmates. Beds were comfortable and guests enjoyed the use of sinks, showers and basic cooking equipment.

If he stayed in a caravan, he would have to pay forty pounds a week - ten pounds more than he was paying us, but he would be able to avoid the exhausting morning and afternoon cycle rides.

Anne and I also felt it would not be an ideal arrangement

if he stayed in the motor-home for a long period. The vehicle was really designed for short stays. There was no proper heating system.

Anne was reluctant to speak of him leaving us. She had got used to his company and his amusing idiosyncrasies and peccadilloes.

She had become accustomed to teaching him English nearly every night. He had become fascinated by several phrases and would repeat them unexpectedly days later.

Among his favourite sayings were: 'Are there still foxgloves growing in the lane?' 'The apples must be twisted and turned' and 'Mind where you put that bike.'

There was also one he had gleaned from me: 'The damn car won't start.' It was entertaining to hear him recite these words and attempt to copy the near-perfect English accent Anne was teaching him.

Yusuf was unsure when we first suggested he might move into a caravan.

'I like so much to be here with you,' he began. But after a brief discussion he realised that it was time for him to move on.

'You must still visit us whenever you want to,' Anne insisted. 'You will always be welcome here.'

'Yes, you must come over for tea on Sundays,' I told him.

'I know it's time to move,' he said. 'I have new friends at the farm now. But I will miss you both and I will miss Fiesta.'

The following evening, Anne and I visited the farm just before six pm and had a long conversation with Sue Wickens.

'Yusuf would like to move into one of the caravans, if there is a place available,' Anne explained.

The secretary confirmed that there were a number of spare

bunks. She would arrange for Yusuf to move into a caravan with three Romanians at the end of the month, if that suited him, she said.

Mrs Wickens also mentioned she had been very impressed by the improvement in Yusuf's English.

'His English has come on rapidly,' she told Anne. 'Look, Mr Finch has been talking about employing a part-time English tutor - would you be interested in the post? You'd be needed for three hours on a Monday evening and three hours on a Thursday evening to begin with. We'd pay you a hundred and twenty pounds a week.'

A broad smile crept across Anne's face.

'I'd be delighted,' she said.

'We've been fitting out a spare room to hold classes,' Mrs Wickens went on. 'Mr Finch believes it'll improve workforce efficiency if there's better understanding of the language and it'll also bolster team cohesion and esprit de corps.'

'I'd love to do it,' said Anne, who had been complaining recently about the mere twenty-eight pounds a week she earned at the shop.

'Fine. I've got your address and phone number. I'll make all the arrangements and I'll be in touch,' Mrs Wickens added.

As we neared the end of September, we heard Yusuf had turned down an opportunity to be transferred to the farm's pack-house. He said it would be too cold for him. But, as he was such a willing worker, his employers said they would find him a position indoors in their main office as the fruit picking work would come to an end with the approach of winter. It was news he was glad to receive.

9

Summer was slowly vanishing from the apple orchards of Kent, although the branches of the trees were yet laden with the reddening crop. The rich, sweet scent of fruit wafted over the gentle breeze while, here and there, a wild bird scavenged for her final meal of the day.

It was the height of the September fruit-picking season, but Yusuf, Anne and I had a vital task to perform. Yusuf was finally moving from our motor-home to a caravan at the farm - and Anne and I were set to help him.

Until five pm on Thursday, September the twenty-fourth, the fields had been teeming with apple pickers. Any able-bodied man or woman with any free time who came to the farm managers' attention was quickly engaged in plucking fruit from the bountiful trees - provided they could stand and had a ready pair of hands.

Now the day was drawing to an end. Their services and Yusuf's were no longer required until the following dawn.

As soon as he arrived back at the cottage, Yusuf began collecting his few belongings together - his personal documents, his clothes, English books Anne had given him, and a few old gardening tools I no longer required. I had also agreed he could keep the bicycle I had lent him.

One issue had been troubling us for several days - what to

do about Fiesta the cat. Yusuf was keen to take him with him. He argued the cat would be welcomed at the farm because he could keep the mice and rat population down. But Anne had become attached to the pet. Possibly he had begun to replace Alfie in our lives.

In the end, it was decided our cottage would prove a better, safer home for Fiesta. The farm was located on the busy road where he had been injured and the buildings contained hazardous equipment. Here, at our home, there were fewer risks and we kept reassuring Yusuf he could visit Fiesta whenever he wanted to.

So Yusuf spent a few minutes kissing and cuddling poor Fiesta and said a tearful farewell to him.

Then the three of us drove to the farm and helped our lodger move into the caravan that was to serve as his new home.

I was glad in a way he was leaving us. There had been so much discussion about giving shelter to a stowaway and there had been a degree of friction between Anne and me. I can't explain why, but there had been occasions when minor arguments had developed. This had never happened in the past.

I also sensed she had begun to lose her temper with me more readily than before. Perhaps I was just imagining it.

Of course, she had been reluctant to provide Yusuf with a home in the first place and I had adopted a more welcoming approach. Her attitude had then changed. Perhaps this had affected our relationship somehow.

It had proved a little unsettling having him as a guest. We had never shared our home with anyone else before - apart from Alfie the Labrador. So I suppose it had put a strain on our everyday lives.

But, at the same time, I had grown used to Yusuf's company, his readiness to work hard and assist us in anything we asked and his constant cheerfulness.

We had made it clear we would remain friends and he could call round any time he wanted. Yet I would miss him.

One clear advantage in letting him move concerned our legal position with him. I had put to the back of my mind the prospect the police would be unhappy if they probed his immigration status and found he had stayed with us.

It had been nerve-wracking when the detective sergeant called round. But with Yusuf gone, we could no longer be accused of acting wrongly - could we?

That evening, I was able to drive the Mondeo right into the caravan park, which was located behind the main pack-houses. Although it had been specified as being a caravan, it was probably better described as a park home, which Yusuf was to share with three others. Besides the beds, there was a kitchen with a cooker and fridge, a bathroom with a shower and toilet and a communal area with a television.

He introduced us to his three fellow-tenants - all men - who were aged twenty-one, twenty-six and twenty-eight. They were a jovial group of friends who appeared to like Yusuf, patting him on the back and trying to make him feel welcome. Looking back, it is possible one or two of them might have held reservations about him. He was, after all, from a different country from them. However, in front of us, they did not show it.

Anne had bought milk, eggs, bread and some tinned food from a supermarket for Yusuf while he was at work. She had also decided to donate to him some of our saucepans and a small frying pan which we rarely used.

Before leaving him, she cleaned out a cupboard in the caravan's kitchen and placed his food in it.

When it was time for us to depart, I hugged him and assured him once again he could visit us at any time. In return, he invited us to call round on him at his new home whenever we wanted.

Anne kissed him on the cheek and hugged him before we both walked away in quiet contemplation.

I thought I noticed a tear in Anne's eye as we got into the Mondeo for our journey back to the cottage. She was certainly in a rather emotional state. However, she insisted a speck of dust had been blown into her eye by the breeze.

Whichever was the case, I can say categorically we were both a little upset at the departure of our stowaway.

Later that evening, Miles Benton was in fine form when I went for a drink on my own in the Merry Friar. The publican reminded me of a Victorian industrialist with his curly white hair, neatly-twirled white moustache and straggly white beard. He was a stout man of medium build who projected a commanding presence.

'Bob, did you hear about the man who spent all his life driving limousines,' he said, as I sipped my second pint. 'When he retired he had nothing to chauffeur it. That's unlike the man from up our road who was run over by a steamroller. He was chuffed to bits. He was in wards three, four and five at the Kent and Canterbury.'

Over the years, he had developed a simple philosophy. He felt, if he could make his customers laugh, it would produce a happy atmosphere and, as a result, his profits would rise.

'Here's another one,' said Miles. 'I was chatting to a friend about holidays. He said: "Where'd you go this year?" I said: "Greece." He said: "Did you have the shashlik kebabs?" I said: "Yes, I suffered from that for a whole week!"'

I have been a friend of his since we moved to the village. Miles is a sincere, straight-forward man. You always know where you stand with him. If there is a crisis, he will always offer to help. If a small injustice is done, he will shake the walls of Jericho to put things right. In that way, he exhibits the same moral probity as Anne.

After drinking two pints of bitter and ordering a third, I took the fifty-one-year-old landlord aside.

'Miles, one of your regulars is called Knight, isn't he?'

'Gordon Knight. He lives just a few hundred yards away along the main road. It's the house with the antique lamp in the window. Why d'you ask?'

'I've heard he had a big row with my next-door neighbour, Stephen Rigden, the guy who was found dead last month.'

'Oh, I know what you're on about. Yes, Gordon was whinging to me about that fellow Rigden. Your neighbour claimed he hadn't done a proper job. Said there was a problem with the guttering and a load of water was gushing down an outside wall. Your neighbour wasn't very happy about it. He got another firm into finish the job and only paid Gordon half the money. He still owed six hundred pounds, according to Gordon.'

I discovered the police had visited the fifty-nine-year-old roofer's oak-beamed Victorian cottage. Knight left the detective in his front room for a few minutes while he went to fetch the original invoice from another room, along with a letter from Rigden declining to pay. When he returned, his visitor was flicking through the pages of the roofer's accounts book.

'I've heard that Gordon had red pen markings against three names - Stephen Rigden, Lucas Sharp and someone called Couchman,' Miles explained. 'He was forced to admit these were three men that owed him large sums of money. He was considering whether to call in debt collectors.'

'You don't think...' I began.

'No, of course not. Don't get me wrong. He's a big bloke and he can look after himself. I'd a problem getting him to leave the bar one evening and it took three of us to point him in the direction of home. But, as he told me the other day: "I needed that bloke Rigden alive so I could get me money. He's no good to me dead."'

'How did it end with the police?' I asked.

'They just left it at that. Said they'd copy the documents and send them back to him. Said they might drop in on him again.'

I finished my third pint and walked out into the cold evening air. The street lights along the narrow road sent a faint orange glow into the night sky.

I was deep in thought as I wandered back to our cottage. What was the significance of the three names found in the roofer's address book? Had Knight told the truth? Or had he lost his temper and gone round to Rigden's house to try to extract his money? Had he attacked the client in his own home?

I decided it was unlikely the man had been killed in a row over six hundred pounds. Yet curious things sometimes happen.

10

The fading sun was beginning to dip over the horizon as Anne and I drove towards the farm on the last Monday in September. It coloured the darkening sky with a reddish hue.

As we parked behind the main offices, the air was filled with the rich scent of fruit and the aromatic smell of hops which drifted over from farmland across the road.

Anne was taking her first evening class and she was nervous.

Sue Wickens had supplied her with some text books and exercise books as well as a good supply of pencils. She had been allocated a room previously used for storing crates. The walls had been redecorated in magnolia and the floor was covered with a new, light-brown carpet. A large blackboard and easel had been set up beside an office desk for her, while four rows of desks and seats had been installed for the pupils.

It looked as if one of the farm managers had bought a job-lot of second-hand school desks and chairs from a shop.

One by one, members of her first class of pickers and packers began to venture in for the three-hour lesson. I sat discreetly at the back, keen to see how her teaching style would compare with mine.

By the time the session began at half-past six, we counted twenty-six students - fifteen women and eleven men. Yusuf had been one of the first to arrive. He handed an exercise book and text book to every student as they entered. Then he sat down at the front, close to his teacher.

As an initial exercise, she got each student, in turn, to say their name and give details of their age and town of origin.

She wrote down the information and then checked the names against a company list.

As the evening continued, she taught them English words relating to their work - such as names of fruit, types of fruit, parts of trees and words used for factory equipment. She had obtained most of these terms in an email from Sue Wickens. She wrote the words on the blackboard and then got the class to say each one out loud in unison.

Yusuf emerged as the keenest student. It was clear he had benefitted greatly from the assistance Anne had given him and he appeared more proficient in English than the other scholars.

'Right, class. What are "nutrients"? Anyone?' Anne asked at one stage. Yusuf's hand shot up.

'Things that give the trees food so the fruit can grow,' he said.

'That's right,' she said. 'Nutrients provide nourishment in order to provide life and growth. What is "canker"?'

'A fungal disease of the apple,' said Yusuf, before she had even finished the question.

'That's right, Yusuf,' she replied. 'And what is "controlled-atmosphere storage" - normally simplified to "CA storage"?'

Yusuf's hand was raised again.

'Yes, Yusuf?'

'It's managing oxygen, carbon dioxide, nitrogen and temperature to make the apple store best for the apples.'

'That's correct. It's a means of providing an atmosphere best suited to the particular variety of apple and ensuring the fruit do not ripen too quickly. Well done, Yusuf.'

I mumbled at the back: 'Anyone else know anything about apples?' Three of the students turned round and smiled, but none of Yusuf's classmates appeared to share his enthusiasm and the session continued in the same fashion.

When it was finally over, I could see the experience had had a major impact on Anne. She looked drained after standing up for more than three hours and trying to explain the intricacies of the English language to the group - some of whom appeared reluctant to learn.

'It was tougher than I thought,' she told me, as I lay next to her in bed that night. 'It's not just two sessions a week. There's all the lesson preparation and I'm also expected to set homework. I don't know if I'm going to be able to carry on with it.'

'Don't worry,' I told her, trying to sound encouraging. 'Teachers often feel like that at the start. As things progress and you notice improvements in their language skills, you'll find it rewarding and you'll realise taking this job was the right move for you. I thought you did very well.'

Life can be strange. I have decided, after thirty-four years on this planet, that although I have more knowledge than I did as a child, I have no greater level of comprehension. My philosophy breaks down into a simple phrase: The more I know, the less I understand.

I will give you an example. Two months ago Yusuf was camping out in Calais with other destitute young men desperate to start a new life in Britain. He took a life-or-death decision to travel across the Channel as a stowaway.

Now his world had been transformed. He had just moved

into his own home - albeit, one he shared with three other people - and he had been head-hunted for the position of farm messenger, a post he had launched into with his customary energy.

We invited Yusuf round to the cottage for tea on Sunday, the fourth of October. It was ten days since he had moved out. We felt sorry for him. We wondered if he might be lonely.

But as he tucked into egg and cress sandwiches and cupcakes in our front room, we discovered he was enjoying life. He had been accepted as a trusted and reliable member of staff at the farm and all his workmates enjoyed a laugh and a joke with him, except for one - Lucas Sharp.

Sharp was an accounts supervisor who had inexplicably taken an instant disliking to our friend. The more the staff lauded Yusuf, the more Sharp's loathing intensified.

I knew little about thirty-five-year-old Sharp at this time, but over the coming weeks I learned a lot more. He was the beloved nephew of Jane Taylor, a wealthy widow with three sisters - one of whom was farm secretary Sue Wickens.

Jane, whose late husband had been a successful builder, was a long-stay hospital patient who, inexplicably, doted on her nephew. She allowed him to use her thatched cottage as a leisure retreat while she was away.

But instead of taking his wife and sons there for relaxing weekends, the wretched man was in the habit of taking his married lover there, we soon discovered.

The cottage next to farmland at the end of a country lane was an ideal place for a lovers' tryst.

The two-bedroomed property, in the remote hamlet of Chivingden, was surrounded by trees and a high hedge which cocooned it from the prying eyes of neighbours and dog walkers.

After a brisk walk up the lane - which rejoiced in the rather unimaginative name of The Street - a pedestrian would arrive at this picturesque dwelling. Often the only sound you would hear would be birdsong, drifting through the air from nearby trees, and the toll of the bell from the nearby church. Visitors would detect a faint aroma of Kentish wild flowers - particularly honeysuckle and phlox.

After Yusuf began his new job, Sharp was to annoy him in the same way a scavenging wasp irritates a party of picnickers. Every time Yusuf had cause to enter the accounts office, Sharp would make an insulting remark. He would joke: 'Watch out! Here's the camel herder' or 'Hold onto your money, it's peasant boy.'

Somehow Yusuf managed to rise above it. He declined to respond, but I knew he was deeply hurt by these remarks. No one at the farm supported Sharp's bullying ways and some of the staff resented his behaviour.

A few days after our conversation with Yusuf over tea, we discovered another new development in our friend's life - he appeared to have found a girlfriend.

Anne had spotted him walking around the farm hand-in-hand with a twenty-one-year-old Romanian girl, who went by the name of Kristina Petrescu.

I was glad to see his life had changed so dramatically in such a short space of time. He had faced years of struggle in his homeland, he often told me. Now he had the promise of a stable and happy future.

We found out about Yusuf's romance after Anne's second

English class. As usual, he had been the star pupil, asking dozens of questions and providing dozens of answers.

Anne noticed a slight change in his personality. He was more self-assured, more confident. As the students filed out of the classroom at the end of the session, she began to understand why.

Kristina, a girl with a sallow complexion and long, dark, curly hair, took his hand and was momentarily seen staring into Yusuf's eyes.

When Anne returned home, she was more solemn than normal. When I asked how the class had gone, she at first said simply it had been 'the usual.'

It took a few minutes of questioning before she admitted Yusuf had a girlfriend. Eventually, Anne opened up and described the young lady who had caught our friend's eye. Anne did not seem happy for him and I could not conceive why this was.

'I'm concerned about the girl. That's all,' said Anne. 'Perhaps she's too young for him.'

'Come on!' I said. 'He's twenty-three and she's twenty-one. The ages are just right.'

'But he's an old twenty-three-year-old, while she seems very immature. She's always interrupting the class by giggling. He wants to get on and his career's looking up. He's now the farm messenger, and he's doing very well, by all accounts. I'm just concerned she may hold him back. She may turn out to be a bad influence.'

Then I thought I detected a tear beneath her right eye. She bent down to stroke the cat.

'He didn't even ask after Fiesta,' she murmured.

It appeared to me while I had, in many ways, been glad to see Yusuf move on with his life, Anne was taking his departure rather badly.

I decided this was just a sign she had still not moved on since the death of our beloved Alfie. Perhaps Fiesta was not filling that void. Maybe we would have to consider getting another dog, I thought.

Around this time, I heard from friends of friends there was a furious row at Lucas Sharp's home in Broad Oak, Canterbury between him and his thirty-two-year-old wife Gemma - who attended school in the 1990s at the same time as Anne.

Sadly, it took place in front of their children at about ten o'clock at night - a time when the two boys should have been asleep.

I know some of the details because one of the boys, twelve-year-old William --who was Lucas's step-son -- was in one of my History classes. Gossip travels through a school faster than a toupee flying off in a hurricane. I blame paper-thin walls in the social housing.

'You've been with that floozie again,' Gemma was reported as saying. 'I can smell her on your clothes.'

'I don't know what you're talking about,' was his quick riposte.

'I know you've been with that Bennett woman. Don't she know we're married or don't she care?'

'I was working late,' he apparently claimed.

'Then why wasn't you answering your phone?' she demanded.

It is claimed that Gemma then made several allegations about her husband's conduct with the Bennett woman - all of which he denied. But she then went on to say: 'I'm not putting up with this any more. Either you end your grubby little affair or you can kiss goodbye to your marriage because I've had enough!' Evidently, she added: 'If you hang around with that blonde bitch any more, I'm going to do for you,' or words to that effect.

A few days later, Anne was nearly involved in a car accident when she arrived to hold an English class. She was driving the Mondeo through the farm entrance when she had to brake hard to avoid colliding with a gold-coloured Toyota Land Cruiser. Harsh words were immediately exchanged.

The driver of the other car was an attractive blonde woman in her late twenties that Anne learned later was Rosie Bennett. She was accompanied in the passenger seat by a man she recognised as Lucas Sharp. He had interrupted one of her lessons for some matter of minor significance and Yusuf had later identified him as Sharp.

It was around this time we heard from Stephen Rigden's family our neighbour's death was no longer being treated as a possible murder case. A second post mortem examination of the body had given the cause of death as 'acute myocardial infarction' - a heart attack.

Stephen's son, Michael, told us his father had been rushing from his lounge into the conservatory when he suffered this massive attack. There would still need to be an inquest, but the pathologist believed, while in the throes of his heart attack, he had crashed headlong into the double doors, smashing his head against the glass.

A family member had found the money that had been thought to be missing. It was inside Stephen's desk drawer in his study. Stephen's widow, Marion, had been confused at the time of her husband's death because of her dementia.

Michael also told us a detective constable from Kent Police, who had been responsible for a team of officers carrying out a search of the home, had been disciplined. His superiors believed he should have included the desk in their searches.

If the money had been discovered earlier, Kent CID might not have wasted so much time and human resources on investigating the death.

The names of several people had been mentioned as possible suspects in the case. Obviously, they were all now free from suspicion. Poor Marion was also free to organise a funeral and lay her husband to rest.

11

While September is the harbinger of autumn, it is not until October we see the last vestiges of summer being shaken off and a new world developing - a world of darker evenings, soup-sharing round the fire, chilly nights, early morning frosts and mists. It is also a time we recall omens from the past and ancient traditions.

Anne and I knew it was now time for Yusuf to apply for asylum. But just as we were about to arrange this, our lives were shaken by an event no omens had predicted. Yusuf was accused of a betrayal of trust. His job at the farm was placed in jeopardy.

On the afternoon of Friday, October the ninth, Yusuf somehow managed to cycle from the farm to our cottage. But I'm not sure how he did it. He was shaking and in tears when he arrived.

Anne put her arm round him and comforted him, while I made all three of us tea. It took us a long time to work out what had happened - and I am not sure even now, nearly a year later, I fully understand the circumstances.

But, little by little, as we sat round our kitchen table, his account unravelled.

'Lucas ask me two days ago to take money to bank,' he began breathlessly.

'Slow down, Yusuf,' said Anne.

'I cycle to bank. I hand money to woman behind glass and she gives paper receipt,' he continued, close to tears. 'I cycle back and take receipt to Lucas. But today the security man says no money given to bank. They keep asking and asking: "Did you take money?" I say: "No. I give money to bank." But they are not believing. They say: "Don't come into work, Yusuf."'

'You've lost your job?' I asked.

'Yes. They say work finished.'

We questioned Yusuf for some time. Eventually, we began to understand more about what had transpired. Our friend had, for the first time in his role as the farm's messenger, been asked on the Wednesday of that week to take a large envelope of money to the firm's bank.

He had been given strict instructions by Sharp to take the envelope containing £950 to a branch in Canterbury, four miles away. Yusuf claimed he did exactly as he was asked.

He set off on my old bicycle with the package in his jacket pocket at around two pm and arrived at the bank at just after ten minutes to three. After queuing for twenty minutes, he was invited to the counter by a middle-aged blonde lady, one of the cashiers. He handed over the envelope, which she opened. She then found the company's account on her computer screen and credited the money. Finally, she gave Yusuf a receipt. He then cycled back to the farm, arriving at about three forty-five pm and handed the receipt to Sharp.

Yusuf thought no more about it. However, earlier that Friday afternoon, he was called into the main office to speak to the farm's head of security, Peter Cheeseman. An inspection of the firm's bank account had led them to believe the money had not been paid in.

At this point, Anne went to the living-room, picked up the phone and called Sue Wickens. The farm secretary was reluctant to talk about the situation since an investigation had been launched. But she informed us that Yusuf had not been dismissed. Rather he had been suspended from work until the investigation was completed. When Anne returned to the kitchen, she relayed Mrs Wickens' remarks to the two of us.

'Don't worry, Yusuf,' she insisted. 'You have not lost your job for good. You have been suspended.'

'What does this mean?' he asked.

'It means you stop work for a short time,' I said.

'So I have not lost my job?' he asked.

Anne explained: 'Mrs Wickens says everything depends on the investigation. If the investigation finds you innocent, you will return to work.'

'But if they decide I took the money...'

'Then, sadly, they will probably say goodbye to you for good, Yusuf.'

'So no guarantees,' he said, surprising us with a newly-learned word.

'No guarantees,' Anne confirmed.

Yusuf appeared reassured a little on hearing this. He tried to resume his story.

'Mr Cheeseman ask me about journey to bank,' he said. 'They ask me if anyone sees me on bicycle. They ask me who I speak to at bank. They ask if I take the money. I deny. I say: "You know I was given the money to pay in. Of course, I pay in. You think I want to lose job?"'

I was unsure how Anne felt, but I believed he was telling the truth. We had been suspicious of him after Stephen was fatally injured and wondered about our friend's cut finger. Yusuf had told us the truth about that. Hadn't he? This chain of events involving the missing money created some fresh doubts. But we both believed it was unlikely Yusuf would have taken the money.

Yusuf resumed his story. He said: 'This Mr Cheeseman - he like secret police. I think he fail to get a police job. It was like a - how you say? - interrogate.'

'Interrogation,' said Anne, helpfully.

'Yes, interrogation,' Yusuf agreed.

He described how Mr Cheeseman paced from side to side as he questioned Yusuf. Eventually, dissatisfied with Yusuf's account, he entered the private office of the managing director, David Finch, which was a few yards away. The two men held a private discussion, which Yusuf was unable to overhear. A few minutes later, Mr Cheeseman reappeared to say he was being sent home without pay until they had discovered the fate of the missing money.

Yusuf added that, when he returned to the accounts office, Lucas Sharp scowled at him as if to say: 'What've you done with the money?' Yusuf said nothing to him. Then, as he was collecting his jacket from a clothes peg, Sue Wickens entered the room and took Yusuf aside. She then fired more questions at him about the missing funds.

'Did you or did you not take the money?' she demanded. Again, Yusuf insisted he was an honest man. How could he have taken the money? He insisted to her that he loved his job and wanted to keep it.

'She frown at me and ordered me to leave, so I come here,' he sobbed.

Anne was concerned about our friend's mental state. We had never seen him look so depressed.

'Would you like a sandwich?' she asked. Yusuf nodded. She made him a ham and tomato sandwich and we all had some more tea.

'You're in Britain, a country founded on principles of fair play and justice,' I told him. 'If you didn't take the money, they'll eventually realise you weren't responsible. Would you like us to visit the farm and speak to Sue Wickens in person?'

'Thank you both for your support,' he replied. 'But I think it's best to leave things as they are. They investigate. This takes many days. Then Yusuf will be found innocent.'

Anne beckoned me to follow her into the living-room again. 'Back in a minute!' she told him, closing the kitchen door.

Once we were alone, she asked in a low voice: 'D'you think there's any chance he took the money? They are such fools. How could they trust someone they don't know with banking nearly £1,000?'

'I can't see how he would have taken the money,' I retorted. 'Look what he stands to lose -- his job and his accommodation. He wouldn't put all that at risk. And you can see how upset he is. That speaks a million words. I bet it's all a mix-up at the bank.'

Anne said: 'I tend to agree. My only concern is that there might be some evidence we haven't been told about.'

'It looks bad for Yusuf, I grant you,' I said. 'But they've got a duty to treat these things seriously. There are rules about how an employer deals with an issue like this and they're obviously just following guidelines. I'm sure this whole incident will turn out to be some kind of misunderstanding,'

At that moment, there was a knock on the living-room door. It opened and Yusuf's head peered round.

'Is everything OK?' he asked. 'I hope my problem at the farm hasn't caused trouble.'

I immediately glanced towards him.

'Yusuf, excuse me, but I have to ask you this. You didn't take that money, did you?'

He looked at me plaintively. 'Bob, on my father's life, I tell you there's been a mistake. I'd never take the farm's money. I'm loving my job.'

I walked over to him and put an arm round his shoulder.

'That's the answer I wanted to hear,' I said. 'Look, we believe you.'

Anne came towards us. She said : 'You have been honest with us, Yusuf. I expect you will be cleared as soon as all the facts are known.'

'You'll see that I'm innocent,' he insisted. 'I go now.'

'Yusuf, you can stay a while longer if you want,' I told him.

'No, I go to the caravan. Thank you for the sandwich and the tea.'

Anne quickly said: 'Don't worry, Yusuf. I'm sure everything will turn out all right in the end.'

But I am not sure he heard her final words as our friend had already opened the front door and begun to cycle away.

I am sorry to have to say, perhaps understandably, Yusuf did not take his moment of disgrace in good heart. From the moment he heard the shameful words: 'Don't come into work,' he suspected Sharp had engineered his downfall.

Kristina had overheard some of the staff in the orchards and in the pack-house gossiping. Sharp was spreading rumours

Yusuf was in England illegally; he had no right to be in Britain; he was part of a criminal gang; and he was not to be trusted.

When she informed Yusuf of these alleged comments, it had not helped to improve his impression of Sharp.

Our friend tried to blot the idea from his mind, but the nagging thought kept returning Sharp was to blame for the loss of his job. He knew his accounts supervisor lived in Canterbury, but he was, for some time, unsure exactly where. Moreover, he wanted to believe he still had a small chance of gaining his job back. If he went round to Sharp's house to challenge him, he decided this might upset his wife and children. That would not help the situation.

However, he knew Sharp was a regular customer at the Pilgrim's Rest, the only public house in Sissenden, which was also known as the 'Fruit Pickers' Pub.' After a week spent brooding about his suspension from work, he eventually became determined to confront Sharp and question him.

He mentioned this plan to Kristina. She totally supported him and the pair set out on Saturday, October the seventeenth for the roadside tavern.

Kristina told me later, when they arrived at the eighteenth century former coaching inn, a darts match was in progress in which the loathsome Sharp was taking part.

Yusuf decided to bide his time. He and Kristina sat in a corner, out of the way of the darts players, drinking with a small group of other Romanians from the farm.

Just before eleven pm our friend, who by all accounts had drunk five or six pints of strong lager, spotted his chance, according to Kristina. The darts match had finished with a victory for the home team. Sharp was making his way to the men's toilets.

Emboldened by alcohol, Yusuf followed him to the urinals and, I was told, began by shoving him against the wall.

'I been sent home because of you!' Yusuf shouted. 'You a complete bastard!'

'Hold on, little man! Don't you come making accusations about me. You shouldn't even be in this country. You're an ignorant peasant boy. You shouldn't be picking apples here - you should be back home, sowing crops and looking after your camels.'

Yusuf apparently managed to punch his detractor - who was about the same height -- on the chin with a powerful right hook. Sharp fought back, and for several seconds the pair were trading insults and blows.

Two other men arrived in the toilet - one of whom was believed to be pack-house manager Ted Moreton. They prised the pair apart.

Yusuf was led away, but, as he left, he turned his head. 'Tell more lies and I kill you,' he reputedly screamed at his foe.

Kristina, who had been drinking vodka and orange all evening but somehow remained sober, was furious with Yusuf when he returned to his seat, she told me later.

As they began walking home, she told him: "That's very clever of you - making threats to kill him. Don't you want to get your job back? I thought you just wanted to talk -- to have it out with him.'

'Men like that, you can't talk,' said Yusuf. 'I was wrong to say I'd kill him. I've no intention of that. It was the fire of the moment.'

He looked over his shoulder as they walked in single file down the dimly-lit, tree-lined country road. There appeared to be no sign of his adversary.

Kristina told me: 'Yusuf was full of regrets afterwards. He's saying to me: "Ted Moreton saw me fighting. I hope he is not telling Mr Finch."'

12

Anne and I were shopping in the city a few days later when we heard a voice calling from the other side of the street.

We both looked round. A short woman with long, straight, brown hair was waving at us. Anne realised it was her former school friend, Gemma Sharp, who was crossing the road to speak to us.

Gemma, who was without either of her children, appeared to have let her dress standards slip since Anne had last seen her.

While my wife looked smart in a blue patterned dress and fawn coat, Gemma was wearing a tatty pair of blue jeans, a turquoise top and an old, charcoal-grey jacket.

'How are Bill and Richard?' Anne asked.

'They're good. Bill's doing great at school,' said Gemma.

'You haven't met my husband Bob before, have you?' said Anne. 'Gemma, this is Bob, one of Bill's teachers, I believe. Bob, this is an old school friend of mine, Gemma Sharp.'

I reached across and shook her hand warmly.

'Yes, he's doing fairly well. His essay on the Battle of Bosworth Field showed promise,' I assured her.

'Pleased to meet you. Anne and me lost touch a few years back,' explained Gemma, who attended the same Canterbury secondary school as Anne.

'I've started to see your Lucas from time to time,' Anne stated.

'You're not working for Finch & Davies?'

'Yes, I am,' said Anne, who was careful not to mention the scandal engulfing the accounts department where Gemma's husband worked. 'I'm running English classes for the new staff. They're going very well.'

Then Gemma took my wife by surprise by reaching across and hugging her.

'It's so nice to see you again,' she said. 'We used to hang around a lot together.'

'That's true. We did. We had some good times, didn't we, before boyfriends came along and spoiled things!' laughed Anne.

'Then marriage and kids,' said Gemma.

'We've not been so fortunate -- I mean, we haven't had children yet,' said Anne.

'That's a shame, but there's still time. Anyway, we should try to link up one evening. Maybe we could go for a meal, you and me?'

'Yes, I'd like that, Gem. Are you still in Broad Oak?'

'Yes. Shall we swap numbers?'

Gemma consulted her mobile phone screen. She read out her number and Anne tapped it into her phone's memory. Then she read out her own number for Gemma to record.

'Let's not leave it too long!' said Gemma, as she headed off towards one of the department stores.

A few days passed. The farm managers celebrated Apple Day (October the twenty-first) with a festival at which hundreds of school children were invited for tours. Yusuf had previously been looking forward to the event. But when it came, he spent the day on his own, sulking inside his caravan.

But, on Thursday, October the twenty-ninth, Yusuf returned to the cottage with good news. The company had strongly suspected he had stolen the £950. However, Mr Cheeseman had contacted the bank and discovered, mercifully, the whole of Yusuf's visit had been filmed by the bank's CCTV cameras.

He was clearly seen queuing, handing over the money and being given a receipt.

Yusuf hugged me, kissed Anne and then performed a traditional folk dance in the living-room. He strutted round in a small circle, swinging his hips from side to side and waving his hands about.

'Yusuf say the truth,' he said. 'I innocent.'

It transpired our friend had been framed by Lucas Sharp. Two payments were due to have been made into the bank that week - one on Monday and one on Wednesday.

Sharp had secretly pocketed a payment of £930 due to have been paid in on Monday. When Yusuf handed him the receipt he had received from the bank cashier on Wednesday, the supervisor had destroyed it.

Then, the next day, Sharp had informed Mr Cheeseman only one payment had been made into the bank that week. He pretended the money the cashier credited to the firm's account on Wednesday was the money he, Sharp, had been due to pay in on Monday. He told Mr Cheeseman: 'I had my doubts about Yusuf all along. I've been proved right. He's a thief.'

But the head of security was no fool. Once he had seen the CCTV evidence clearing Yusuf, suspicion immediately fell upon Sharp. He was interviewed and showed all the tell-tale signs of guilt. Mr Finch and Mr Cheeseman, who sat together behind a desk, noticed he was extremely nervous. He was perspiring. He appeared deeply troubled. Eventually, he confessed it was he who had stolen the money.

He gave the two men a verbal admission along the lines of: 'I took the money and destroyed the evidence of Yusuf's transaction. As the chief accounts manager had noticed the takings were down, I had hoped to blame the imbalance on Yusuf. I didn't think there'd be any proof of Yusuf going to the bank.'

Sharp had believed, wrongly, the company would accept his evidence as a trusted employee over that of Yusuf - a relatively new member of the workforce whose character was largely unknown.

The company called in the police. A constable accompanied Mr Cheeseman and the disgraced supervisor to Sharp's house, where the £930 was found hidden in a wardrobe. Sharp was sacked and then given a court date on which he would appear before the city magistrates, charged with theft.

A journalist - possibly Anne's friend Prunella -- found out about the case from making routine calls to the police press office. The local newspaper reported on the affair under the headline: 'Accounts clerk charged with theft.'

David Finch invited Yusuf into his office. He apparently told him: 'I hope there are no hard feelings, old chap. You can get back to your job now, starting tomorrow morning.'

But despite the fact Yusuf had been through a humiliating ordeal and had spent three weeks being distrusted by his friends, there was no official apology over the way he had been treated. Anne and I were dismayed by this. We felt he should have at least received a letter from the managing director and possibly a gift of flowers or wine as a token of their remorse.

After telling us his news and spending a few minutes playing with the cat, Yusuf happily cycled back to the farm. He was planning to celebrate with Kristina.

'It's funny that he never seems to be far away when there's a spot of bother,' I said as we watched him cycle off down the lane. 'That's the second time he's come under suspicion for something. But I'm glad his honesty has shone through.'

'I'm sorry I ever doubted you about him,' she confessed. 'You must be a better judge of character than me.'

'Well, I suppose strangers will always be blamed first. Trust has to be earned,' I declared.

My darling wife cupped my face in her hands and kissed me on the lips for several seconds.

'I love you so much,' she said. 'And I'm so glad he has been cleared.' She went on: 'Yusuf has been through a terrible time.'

Then, taking my right hand, she tugged me towards the stairs. 'And now I am going to show you just how much I love you,' she added.

Meanwhile, the farm's decision to sack Sharp and reinstate Yusuf did nothing to halt the bitter hostility between the two men.

Yusuf told Kristina he regarded the sacked accounts supervisor as a silver-tongued fraudster and xenophobe who would stop at nothing to suit his criminal purposes. Sharp regarded the farm messenger as an arrogant peasant who had no doubt tricked his way into Britain and was now trying to ingratiate himself to gain promotion and money.

The conflict between these two men was to endure for a while longer.

13

Shortly after Yusuf returned to work at the farm, he called round to tell us a Hallowe'en party had been planned for the evening of Saturday, October the thirty-first and we were both invited.

Anne spent an afternoon making costumes - a practice at which she was adept. Her mother had been a fashion designer and had passed on her sewing skills to Anne.

She produced for me a Grim Reaper outfit which consisted of a full-length black cotton robe with matching face-veil and waist sash. We managed to find a novelty item for me to carry -- an old, rusty, long-handled scythe that, years before, had belonged to my great-grandfather.

It had once been used to slice through thick grass on a Kent farm that had long since passed from the family. It had never seen use as a fashion accessory, as far as I knew. We covered the blade with brown tape to avoid any unpleasant mishaps.

For herself, Anne chose a witches' garb consisting of an extremely short, black dress with a zigzag hem and a black pointed hat. I joked a witch could easily catch a chill prancing among the tombstones in such a short dress, but she failed to find my comment amusing.

We attracted a lot of laughter as we stepped from the car in our lavish costumes and made our way to the caravan park, where the party was being held. Luckily, although it had rained during the previous week, the day itself turned out fine and dry.

Kristina and Yusuf had spent hours preparing. A huge banner that stretched between two posts proclaimed 'Happy Hallowe'en.' Caravans had been decorated with bunting and balloons. Pumpkins carved into jack o' lanterns, and with tea lights inside, had been arranged on trestle tables laden with sandwiches, sausage rolls and vol-au-vents. One table - stacked with homemade cider, beer and wine - had been erected beneath a banner declaring: 'Witches' brew.'

Kristina and her Romanian friends had baked a large circular cake which was coated with marzipan and then topped with a witch's face and hat made from black icing. Cleverly-crafted black paper mobiles in the shape of bats hung from ropes.

'You've worked hard, Kristina,' I said, greeting her with a kiss on both cheeks.

'Thank you. We all have,' said Kristina. 'You're both very welcome. I hope you enjoy your evening.'

As Anne kissed her on the left cheek, I added: 'You like Hallowe'en?'

'Of course. We celebrate at home. We have Transylvania.'

'Dracula's castle,' I said.

'Yes. Many tourists come. But this party isn't just Hallowe'en. We also celebrate with Yusuf. He's had bad time. He was tricked and then questioned like the Stasi.'

'We knew he was innocent all along,' I said, noticing Yusuf himself had suddenly emerged from the crowd and was standing next to Kristina, holding her hand.

I patted him on the back. 'We're so glad you're back in work,' I told him.

Two hours later, the party was in full swing. There were more than fifty adult guests and 15 children. I was fully entering into the spirit of the party, half-expecting to win a prize in the best costume contest.

But as I downed my third pint of cider - safe in the knowledge Anne would be driving us both home later - my hopes were dashed. The coveted prize of a box of chocolates was awarded to a Bulgarian fruit picker who had arrived in an elaborate skeleton outfit with authentic-looking bones and a hideous facemask.

During the evening, Romanian music was played incessantly. One of the male pickers had brought a piano accordion. As the strains of his music filled the air, a small group of men and women held hands. Then they skipped, swayed and whirled around together, demonstrating a series of Romanian folk dances.

I discovered Yusuf was a fan of Eritrean-born singer Helen Meles, one of the most successful pop stars to have emerged from modern Africa.

One of the music tracks played at the party was a haunting love song in her native tongue. Yusuf could afterwards be heard humming part of the melody.

At around ten o'clock, I decided to try my luck at the apple-bobbing contest. A tub of water had been set up on one of the trestle tables.

'What d'you win if you manage to prise an apple out of the water?' I asked.

'An apple!' said Kristina. 'I'd have thought you'd have known that since you're a teacher!'

'I was hoping I might've won a tenner!' I said, bending

down over the tub. I chose the reddest, ripest apple I could see, opened my mouth as wide as I could and lowered my head towards the water.

I should have been more wary. As my face approached the surface, Kristina ducked me in the ice-cold water. I had never seen anyone guffaw so much as Kristina. Her gales of laughter rang out across the farmyard. Yusuf, who had been watching from a distance, walked over and joined in the hilarity.

Kristina provided a towel. My hair was quickly dried. However, I noticed Anne did not seem to be joining in the fun.

'Aren't you enjoying the party?' I asked her a few minutes later, when we were on our own.

'Not really,' she said. 'I've just had a huge row with Kristina.'

'What was that about?' I said.

'I mentioned the sandwiches appeared to be running out. I was only trying to be helpful. She blew up. She said she had worked solidly organising it and all I did was complain.'

I brought her a glass of wine and a sausage roll, but I was unable to lighten her mood. We decided to leave the partygoers to enjoy the rest of their celebrations. We returned to the car and Anne drove us home.

Five days later, a dazzling display of bright, fiery colours - red, white and green - lit up the November sky as the residents of Chasehurst celebrated Bonfire Night.

Every few seconds, a rocket or a host of rockets would soar into the air above the village and then captivate their earthly audience with a crackling shower of fire.

We stayed at home as I had a lot of marking to do and Anne wanted to watch a programme about zoo animals on the television, but we spent a few minutes gazing out of an upstairs window at the fireworks as they soared above the fields.

The following day, Friday, November the Sixth, the name of Rosie Bennett by chance cropped up again. I ran into Gordon Carsten—a teacher who, like myself, was a member of the local committee of the National Union of Teachers. Moments after spotting him in the staffroom at school, he began recounting details of an extraordinary incident that had occurred the previous evening.

He told me Mrs Bennett had visited the school at about a quarter past six just as the school football team's coach arrived back following a match in Dartford. She informed Miss Bushby, the school secretary, she had received an urgent phone call from a man with a slight foreign accent.

'What was the call about?' I asked with increasing curiosity.

Carsten replied: 'He said something like: "It's the school here. We need you to come in urgently. It's about your son." But Miss Bushby knew nothing about it and, as you know, the headmaster's away at a conference.'

'How bizarre!' I said. 'Her son would be Mark Bennett, wouldn't he?'

'That's right - Year Seven, Mr Hodson's class. By all accounts, she asked if it was urgent because she was meant to be on her way to some place called something like Chivingden. The caller insisted she come. He said the headmaster needed to see her and she should go to the secretary's office. Evidently, the caller's number was withheld. After tackling her son to see if he'd got himself into any kind of trouble and receiving a negative answer, she set off for the school, leaving her mother to care for the two children.'

'Sounds like a hoax call,' I suggested.

'Yes. That's what Miss Bushby thought. Strange, isn't it? She phoned round the extensions, but all the teachers had gone and poor Mrs Bennett walked off mystified into the night.'

'Very strange,' I said. 'That Mark's big for his age and I had to separate him from the Roberts kid in the playground the other day. They were having a bit of a fight. Maybe he's been bullying him.'

'Perhaps it was a genuine call after all,' said Carsten. 'I'll make a few inquiries. If there's a bit of bullying going on, we need to nip it in the bud.'

On the same day, Friday, we were shocked to discover Lilac Cottage, the isolated retreat where Lucas Sharp had been holding secret rendezvous with Rosie Bennett, was in the news. A fire had broken out - supposedly the result of a rogue firework landing on the roof - and a man's body found amid the ruined kitchen.

Our daily newspaper had a single column story on the twenty-first page. It said :

'MAN'S BODY FOUND AFTER COTTAGE INFERNO

> 'Police and fire chiefs are investigating after a man's body was discovered inside a blazing country cottage.
>
> 'A stray firework is believed to have sparked flames which destroyed part of the thatched roof.
>
> 'The dead man is understood to be in his thirties or forties. Police, who are at present treating the incident as suspicious, are attempting to identify him and trace next of kin.
>
> 'A spokesman for Kent Fire and Rescue Service said

two crews were alerted to the incident in the hamlet of Chivingden, near Canterbury at around seven twenty pm on November 5.

'Moments before they'd been responding to reports of an out-of-control bonfire at a Guy Fawkes party being held a few hundred yards away. The fire fighters raced to the cottage and began tackling the flames.

'Using breathing gear and a hose reel, one crew entered the kitchen at the rear of the secluded property, Lilac Cottage, where the partially-charred body was eventually found. The team spent more than twenty minutes extinguishing the flames.

'Station officer Bill Stephens said: "It's fortunate we were nearby at the time the blaze started. One of our fire fighters spotted smoke pouring from the rear of the cottage just as the neighbour's bonfire was being brought under control.

'"The two crews immediately switched their attention to the cottage fire. Speed's obviously essential in these cases as flames spread quickly on thatched roofs. We managed to control the fire before it could do much damage.

'"Unfortunately, the body of a male person was recovered from the kitchen, where it appears the fire had started."

'A Kent Police spokesman said: "Our officers are investigating the incident. At present, it appears a firework may have set the roof of the kitchen on fire. We're not releasing the deceased man's name until relatives have been informed."

'Neighbour John Craddock, 41, of The Glebe, Chivingden, said: "We heard a really loud bang like a bomb going off, but, because it was Bonfire Night, there were a lot of other bangs and we didn't take much notice. Someone told me it's thought a giant firework crashed through the cottage roof and set it on fire."

'The fire-damaged house is understood to belong to Mrs Jane Taylor, a 45-year-old widow, who lives alone. She was not available for comment.'

Anne was dumb-founded when I showed her the story.

'You don't think that's Lucas Sharp, do you?' was her first reaction.

'Could be anyone,' I replied. 'Could be a passer-by killed while trying to put the fire out. Anyway you've got a class tonight, haven't you - the one postponed because of Guy Fawkes? You'll probably find out then if, by some quirk of fate, it was Sharp.'

I had managed to get that afternoon off because Yusuf had informed me there was a problem with the front tyre of my old bicycle. It had become slightly deflated and he suspected a puncture. In addition, the pump was no longer working. We drove into the city with the bicycle in the back of the car. After finding a space in a car park, we wheeled the bike to the cycle shop and bought a new pump and tyre.

But as we left the premises with our purchases, more ill luck befell Yusuf. He came face-to-face with two fellow-Africans - two men he had known a year earlier and had hoped never to meet again.

Yusuf's first thought was to run away. But, perhaps because I was there, he decided it would be best to see why they wanted to speak to him.

When they beckoned him to follow them into a side road, away from the city's busy ring road, he begrudgingly agreed.

Black-haired Sam Tedros, thirty, was a large, muscular man who was well over six feet tall. With a heavily-tattooed neck and arms, he had the appearance of a nightclub doorman.

His twenty-seven-year-old friend, Jaefer Beraki, was about the same height as Yusuf, -- around five feet eight inches tall -- with short, dark-brown hair parted in the centre. However, he was much slimmer and nimbler than his companion.

'Please wait,' Yusuf implored me, handing over the tyre and pump for me to hold. 'I'm speaking to these men and I come back.'

I idly browsed over the range of bicycles on sale in the shop window while waiting for Yusuf to talk to his fellow-Eritreans.

The conversation, held entirely in Yusuf's mother tongue of Tigrinyan and relayed to me by Yusuf later, began with Tedros welcoming Yusuf to Kent. Tedros then ordered Yusuf to pay them £1,000 for arranging his transport to England.

Yusuf insisted he no longer owed them any money. He had found his own way across the Channel.

Tedros disputed this, claiming: 'We did a lot of work for you, helping you get to France. This work's gone unrewarded. We need compensation for that.'

Yusuf explained he had only a little money, but somehow

Tedros knew he had found work at the farm. He grabbed our friend's arms and thrust Yusuf up against the outside wall of the shop. Beraki sneered and spat in Yusuf's face.

Yusuf told me Beraki made threats and ordered him to pay them the money within four days.

Our friend was warned he would have to sell drugs for them unless he found the money. Tedros allegedly said: 'If you're unable to pay, there's a fantastic opportunity for you to sell drugs for us to all the tens of thousands of young working people and students in the city. Within a short time, you could wipe out that debt of yours.'

Yusuf then made some sarcastic remarks, along the lines of: 'It's wonderful to have options. But I'll have to decide which one of these wonderful opportunities I take.'

Tedros then told him: 'Don't be sarcastic, Yusuf. It doesn't suit you. You've only a short time to decide.'

As they walked away, Beraki called out : 'We keep changing our mobile numbers, but it's easy to get a message to us. Some of our boys work in the car wash in St Peter's Road.' Then he added in English: 'Be seeing you!'

When Yusuf returned to the bike shop, he looked shaken.

'Everything all right, Yusuf?' I asked.

'Yes,' he retorted, rather abruptly. "We go.'

I had overheard the raised voices of his companions and had suspected they were threatening him over money for some reason. Yusuf explained the whole of the conversation to me as we travelled back to Chasehurst.

14

Saturday morning was dull and overcast. I rose at nine o'clock with the intention of going to visit Yusuf and help him fit the new bicycle tyre.

But my mission was interrupted by a loud knock on the door just before ten. Glancing through the front window, I noticed a friendly, smiling woman in a light-brown coat standing by the front door. It was Prunella Ball.

'Is Anne around at all?' she asked. 'I wanted a quick word.'

'Yes, I'll just call her. Come in,' I replied. 'By the way, the house powered by apples. I looked it up online. There's an aerobic digester which creates gas from the apples. Is that right?

'Absolutely,' she said.

'That's amazing!' I said.

The journalist, who was wearing a navy-blue skirt and white blouse beneath her coat, waited at the foot of the stairs as I went to see if Anne was dressed.

Moments later Anne came down to greet her friend in black jeans and a pink T-shirt.

'This is unexpected,' said Anne. 'How are you? Everything OK?'

'Ace,' Prunella replied. 'But I need your help with something. You know you told me on the phone the other day you'd started working for Finch & Davies? I wondered if you knew a guy called Lucas - Lucas Sharp?'

'Yes, I know him vaguely,' she admitted. 'He's my friend's husband. I sometimes see him when I turn up to run classes.'

'I'm afraid he's dead. He's been murdered in Chivingden,' she said.

'Oh my God! You'd better come into the living-room,' said Anne, who had been faced with blank looks at work when asking about the cottage fire.

I took Prunella's coat and hung it from the bannisters before following the women into the room. The journalist made herself comfortable at the end of the settee, while Anne sat in an armchair and I seated myself on a dining chair by the window.

"I'm just on my way back from visiting Chivingden and thought I'd drop in,' said Prunella. 'I was pretty sure you'd know him. God, Anne, what happened is so horrendous.'

I interrupted to say: 'You say Chivingden. Is this anything to do with that fire at the thatched cottage?

'Yes, Bob. It is.'

'So Lucas Sharp was overcome by fumes? That's what usually happens with house-fires.'

'No, it didn't happen like that at all, Bob. I'm not sure how to tell you. It's so hideous, so gruesome. It's hard to find words to describe it. He was killed by a firework wired to his head.'

We chorused: 'Wired to his head?'

'Yes,' said Prunella. 'The police doctor, Theo Harryman, said he'd never come across a murder like it in his thirty-five-year career - and he must've seen some grim sights.'

'So you're obviously writing a story about it?' I asked.

'Yes. There'll be major reports in the Sunday papers tomorrow. I've been playing my part. I'm also writing a piece for

Monday's papers. But I don't think the full gory details will appear. The editors of family papers have to ensure material's acceptable to families. While you're munching your cornflakes with the children at the breakfast table, you probably don't want to read about a man's head being blown off.'

'Oh my God!' cried Anne. 'So there's no way it could've been an accident?'

'The police don't think so. They're working on the theory he was tied to a chair, an industrial firework was fixed to his head and it blew up.'

'You've really got us intrigued now, Prunella,' I said. 'D'you have any more details?'

'All I can tell you is my detective friend Graham was having a fireworks party at his home in Maidstone and his boss, Detective Inspector Russell Woods, asked him to meet him at Lilac Cottage. The place is owned by Sharp's aunt, who's in hospital having tests.

'One of my reporter friends has discovered Sharp hated fireworks. An older boy hurled a banger at him when he was aged four. It exploded by his feet, causing no injury but instilling him with a lifetime aversion.'

Anne butted in. 'He must've been feeling a bit down when he died. He'd just been sacked from his job,' she informed her friend.

'That's right, but there's obviously no suggestion of suicide. He's thought to have spent the day cleaning his car and Graham tells me he'd been due to meet his girlfriend at the cottage, a woman called Rosie Bennett.

'Well, to cut a long story short, he entered the place at around seven pm and was astonished to find someone had fixed a Catherine Wheel to the kitchen wall and lit it.

'When he went to inspect this strange spectacle, police believe he was attacked from behind by an intruder who forced a handkerchief containing some kind of chemical round his nose and mouth.'

'Chloroform?' I suggested.

'Yes, that's what the police think, but they're carrying out tests. Anyway, the pungent vapour spread through his nasal passages and lungs and he must've keeled over. When officers arrived in the fire-damaged kitchen, they found him dead, tied with rope to a chair.'

'God, how terrible. He wouldn't have stood a chance,' said Anne.

'That's right. So if there's anything you can tell me about Mr Sharp, that would be very helpful,' said Prunella.

'I'd say Lucas is about five feet eight inches tall,' said Anne. 'It would require a fairly powerful person to overpower him and hold a rag containing chloroform round his face long enough to take effect.'

'Yes. Graham said it looked as if someone had broken in through the back door. Then they've lain in wait for him. After the explosion, Sharp's body remained seated on the chair in his blue jeans, blue check shirt and brown jacket, which were saturated with blood. It's thought the killer made off through the front door - possibly by bicycle. Apparently one of the scenes of crime team noticed some fresh bicycle tyre tracks on the grass verge at the front of the cottage and some more inside the garden next to the gate. There's also part of a shoeprint by the back door. They know Sharp got there by car and came through the front door.'

I asked: 'Any of the neighbours see or hear anything?'

'Most of the neighbours wouldn't open the door to me, but those that did saw and heard nothing significant.'

I remarked: 'Even if they did hear anything, they might have attributed the noise to Bonfire Night festivities.'

'Absolutely,' said Prunella. 'Police think he was killed between half-past six and half-past seven.'

'What happened to the girlfriend, the Bennett woman?' Anne asked.

'Graham says she turned up as the police and fire crews were at the scene. One of the fire officers took her aside and had to break the devastating news to her.'

'At least she wasn't harmed,' said Anne.

'That's right. She isn't thought to have been around when the murderer struck.'

I immediately remembered Rosie Bennett had been mysteriously summoned to the school by a mystery phone call, delaying her arrival at Lilac Cottage. I mentioned this to Prunella, who was excited to hear the details.

'So she had been due to meet him earlier?' Prunella asked. 'That's really interesting. Someone had her interests at heart by delaying her journey. If she had turned up at the agreed time, maybe we would have been looking at two murders. Thanks for telling me that, Bob. Obviously, I will have to check that with the school and the cops, but that might give me a small exclusive.'

'D'you know much about the Bennett woman?' I asked her.

'Only that her husband Neil works as deputy manager of a supermarket and he's a keen member of Kent and Sussex Caving Club. I've been told they're going through a divorce.'

'What about the firework that's meant to have crashed onto the roof and caused the fire?' I asked. 'We read about it in the paper.'

'There was a fire, of course,' Prunella explained. 'But there was no firework on the roof. The killer piled up some clothes from a laundry basket on the table next to the curtains. He set them alight and the fire then spread to the roof. Graham says the killer probably thought the whole cottage would be destroyed, including the body, but the fire brigade arrived very quickly and it was soon put out. A coil of wire which is thought to have been wound round Sharp's forehead and neck to support the firework was found on the kitchen floor among the debris.'

'Any idea what kind of firework was used?' I asked.

'It was a mortar. Some of the cardboard packaging survived. It had the words: "Artillery shell" on the side.

'Good God!' I exclaimed. 'The words "artillery shell" put you in mind of the First World War.' I paused for a moment and then said: 'If my knowledge of the law's up to date, fireworks like that are only legal in the United Kingdom if they're part of an organised display. They're on restricted sale.'

'One of the lines of inquiry being followed by police is to focus on the origins of the bizarre murder weapon,' Prunella said. 'You might've thought the killer might've used a gun instead, but guns can be hard to get hold of. It's possible he got access to a supply of illegal fireworks and decided to use one of those.'

'Gruesome,' said Anne. 'I'm afraid this has upset me.'

I went over to Anne and put my arm round her, consolingly.

She told Prunella: 'All I can tell you about Lucas Sharp is he was meant to pay nearly £1,000 into the farm's bank account in the second week of October, but he kept the money for himself. Then he tried to frame a friend of ours, Yusuf Osman, our ex-lodger, over the theft. Luckily, our friend was cleared and Sharp got the sack at the end of last month. Police were called in and the case was due to come up in court.'

'I'm not surprised to hear that. Graham says Sharp had enemies. Thinks he owed a man some money for drugs.'

'I'm going to be seeing Gemma, Lucas's wife, over the next few days,' Anne revealed. 'I'll see if I can arrange for you to meet her.'

'That'd be great if you could do that. She's refusing to talk to the press at present.'

'I can understand why,' I commented. 'She must be in a hell of a state, poor girl.'

'Yes, but the more information the police and press can get, the more quickly the killer can be found,' said Anne.

'Absolutely. Couldn't agree more,' said Prunella. 'Oh, there was one other thing. As Graham and DI Woods left the murder scene, Graham began peering at Sharp's red Astra estate, which he had parked outside the cottage two hours earlier. Under the street light, he noticed what appeared to be a series of Chinese letters etched on the side of the vehicle. Well, the inspector took a torch from his pocket and examined the five obscure symbols across the entire length of the nearside car door. Each one was twenty centimetres high.'

'How bizarre!' said Anne.

'Yes. The two detectives thought so as well. By all accounts, Graham said: "It looks freshly done. What the hell does it mean?" To which the inspector replied with words to the effect:

"I don't know but I'm damn well going to find out."'

Over the next few days, Anne received several phone calls from Prunella Ball, inquiring whether Anne had been able to arrange a meeting between her and the dead man's widow. I listened to some of them when Anne switched the call to speaker-phone. On other occasions, she explained the content of the conversations to me afterwards.

Anne had for various reasons been unable to speak to Gemma - mainly because the phone had been constantly engaged or left off the hook. Eventually she managed to leave a voicemail message on Gemma's mobile phone, but she waited in vain to hear back from her childhood friend.

However, during the phone conversations with Prunella, Anne received more details about the progress the police were making.

Prunella had managed to speak briefly to Rosie Bennett shortly after Detective Inspector Woods, a tall, slim detective with greying hair and gold-framed glasses, had interviewed the heartbroken lover.

'The inspector is a stickler for victimology,' Prunella us.

'What does that mean exactly?' asked Anne.

'It means he makes it a priority to study the victims of the crime. He believes the surest way to solve murder cases is by obtaining as much information as possible about the victims' lives. That's why he made a point of personally interviewing the dead man's widow and his girlfriend as a matter of the first importance.'

'Oh I see. That's interesting,' said Anne.

'He spoke to Rosie Bennett first,' Prunella went on.' She

explained she had first got to know Lucas Sharp when they worked for the same Herne Bay supermarket a few years ago.

'He had formerly been scruffily-dressed, Rosie told him. But after his marriage, his image changed dramatically. She came across him again in Canterbury two months ago, by which time he was working at the farm's accounts department, and they started dating. She eventually found out he was married, but by then she was so smitten with him she decided to continue the relationship.'

Eventually, Prunella disclosed, the lovestruck pair began spending time at Lilac Cottage.

Prunella revealed the owner, Jane Taylor, had been widowed in 2005. She was one of four sisters: Andrea, Martina, Jane and Sue. Andrea was Sharp's mother and the youngest sister, Sue, was Mr Finch's secretary at the farm, Sue Wickens. Martina was married to Ted Moreton, the pack-house manager. So Sharp was the third member of the family to obtain a job at the farm.

Prunella informed us that, in Rosie's police statement, she claimed she got off the bus in Chivingden at about twenty-five minutes past seven.

Prunella told Anne: 'I've got part of Rosie's police statement here, which I got from Graham. It says: "You could smell burning wood most of the way up the lane. There was a police cordon around Lilac Cottage. A police sergeant told me a man's body had been found and when they described the clothes, I knew it was Lucas. I called my mother. She begged me to come home -- I was so upset. I haven't stopped crying since. I was really shocked when I learned he might have been murdered."'

Prunella told Anne she had called round at Rosie's home in Sturry to interview her.

'She was fairly happy to talk to me, although she was still upset,' said Prunella. 'She was unaware her boyfriend had been dismissed from his job and was due to appear in court on a theft charge. She said he was a fantastic man - very friendly and considerate. She couldn't believe he had stolen any money as he had been deputy manager at the supermarket and highly trusted.'

Prunella noticed that Rosie had photographs of her husband, Neil, hanging on the wall above her stone fireplace. These included images of her husband at two of Britain's most popular destinations for caving enthusiasts -- Alum Pot in North Yorkshire and Gaping Gill, near Ingleborough.

Amusingly, when she asked if her husband was in a cave right now, Rosie told Prunella: 'No, he's probably shifting boxes in the Canterbury supermarket where he works!'

Rosie said her husband had been unaware of her plans to meet Sharp at the cottage.

'No. I haven't spoken to him for two weeks. He knew nothing about my relationship with Lucas,' she told the journalist. 'We've been separated for months.'

Neither had she informed her son Mark nor seven-year-old daughter Cheryl of her date at the cottage.

But when Prunella asked if anyone else knew of the rendezvous, Rosie's response was: "Only my mother -- and the bus driver.' It appears Dennis, the driver of the 1B bus which travels through Chasehurst, was a former schoolfriend of Rosie's. For some reason, she had mentioned to him she would be in Chivingden at seven o'clock on Bonfire Night.

15

The morning of Stephen Rigden's funeral was frosty and bright. As we walked down the lane towards the church, the long grass was adorned with flecks of ice. Our shoes crunched onto the dark-brown leaves, many the size of a man's hand, and I pulled my scarf more snugly round my neck.

Over the tops of the hedgerows, the fields were decked in a carpet of glistening white crystals.

Within just over fifteen minutes, Anne and I reached the fourteenth century St Mary's Church, which overlooks open country at the edge of the village. We passed through the graveyard with its straggly grass and, in a slow, dignified manner, entered through the side door we always used.

There were fewer than twenty people in the congregation. Many of Stephen's friends and relatives lived some distance away or were too old and frail to attend the early morning service.

Stephen's widow Marion was sitting in one of the front pews along with her son Michael and his wife Yvonne. Our other neighbour, Linda Morrison, had been assisted into the second row by a daughter, who had travelled from Essex. We also recognised the landlord of the Merry Friar, Miles Benton, and Ted Moreton from Finch & Davies.

Most surprising for us was to see Sergeant Kirwan, the tall, slightly-overweight detective who had made inquiries into Stephen's death. We were impressed he had made an effort to attend.

Minutes after we sat in a pew a few rows back, Stephen's coffin was brought inside by four burly undertakers. Then the vicar, the Rev Tim Maxwell-Stephens, welcomed us and we all sang Abide With Me.

Although we were few in number, the sound of our singing filled the church - thanks mainly to the loud voice of the vicar and the rousing support from the seven undertakers standing at the back.

The minister gave a comprehensive eulogy, describing the struggle Stephen's family had faced raising their son in post-war Britain, his early working career as a crewman on cross-Channel ferries and his final years running his own building company.

Stephen had been an enthusiastic golfer and bridge player who had doted upon his son and three grandchildren, he said.

'What his friends also remember is Stephen's great sense of humour,' the vicar said. 'He was at a concert once when a fellow guest loudly criticised one of the performers, saying: 'Whatever happened to melody?' In a flash, Stephen called out: "She's working on the checkout at Tesco's!"'

The vicar said another favourite joke of Stephen's concerned a man who appeared before a judge on a burglary charge.

'The defendant claimed he could not have committed the crime because, at the time, he was driving a coach of shoe repairers from Timpson on their annual outing to Margate. The judge said: "I don't believe your story for a minute. It sounds like a load of cobblers."'

The vicar added: 'Stephen was often the life and soul of the party. He'll never be forgotten. Now let us raise our voices in his memory as we sing together Amazing Grace : How sweet the sound.'

After Stephen's burial in a churchyard plot close to open fields, Sergeant Kirwan walked over to us.

'I don't know whether you remember me,' he said. 'Graham Kirwan, Kent Police.'

'Yes, of course we remember you,' I said at once. 'You were investigating Stephen's death.'

'I wonder if I could just jot down your phone numbers,' he said rather enigmatically. 'I'm not sure I kept them.'

'Here you are, sergeant,' said Anne. 'Give me your notebook. I'll write them down. It'll be easier if I do it.' She scribbled down our landline and mobile phone numbers.

'Anything we can do to help the police,' she said.

'That's cool,' he said, recovering his notebook from her. 'I might be needing to contact you over the next few days.'

On saying that, he walked slowly back towards the main entrance, stopping only briefly to exchange words with Marion and Michael Rigden.

'I wonder what he'd want to talk to us about,' I said.

'Yes,' said Anne. 'I thought all the business about Stephen's death was finished with.'

Later that day, Anne received a surprise phone call from Gemma Sharp.

'Listen, Anne,' she said. 'I need to talk to you. You're a very understanding person. D'you have an hour to come over for a chat?'

'Of course, I do. I'm free now. Shall I pop round?'

'Yes,' said Gemma.

'All right,' said Anne. 'I'll see you in half an hour. Is it all right if Bob comes as well? He's got the day off.'

'Yes, that's fine. It'll be good to see you both.'

Anne changed out of the formal clothes she had worn for the funeral service into a blue patterned dress and fawn coat. I exchanged my white shirt and grey suit for a red check shirt and blue jeans. Then we drove over to the Sharps' two-bedroom, ground-floor flat which consisted of the lower floor of a red-brick semi-detached house.

As we travelled, she reminisced with me about the times she and Gemma had spent together in years gone by - the visits to each other's homes while growing up, the evenings spent listening to music together and the early boyfriends they had known. Marriage had come along for them both and, somehow, sadly, they had lost touch.

Now, at this time of tragedy, events were drawing them back together again.

As I locked the car and we walked towards the flat, I noticed the unpruned roses struggling to thrive in the small front garden next to an unkempt lawn.

Gemma, who was red-eyed and wearing a pair of frayed blue jeans and turquoise blouse, answered the door quickly. She gave Anne a hug and invited us into the light, airy hallway. We then followed her into the main living-room.

She made us some tea and we settled down on a fawn-coloured settee amid the cream-coloured walls.

'I was awfully sorry to hear about Lucas,' said Anne.

'Yes, well,' said Gemma, who was clutching a box of paper tissues. 'I've had Detective Inspector Woods here, asking all sorts of questions. Did you know Lucas was murdered?'

Anne hesitated, looking towards me.

'Er... we'd heard something about that,' she mumbled. 'We couldn't believe it.'

'All they've told me is there was this explosion in the kitchen and he died in seconds - which, I suppose, is some blessing,' said Gemma. 'They think the killer afterwards started a fire in the hope of destroying the evidence.'

'It's so dreadful!' said Anne, moving towards her friend and offering her a hug. 'Who on earth would want to harm your husband?'

'Well, I'm afraid he wasn't flavour of the month with a lot of people. Trouble used to follow him around. He owed money. He got the sack from work. On top of it all, he's been having an affair.'

'You've gone through a lot.'

'Yes, I don't know if you know a Rosie Bennett?'

'No, I can't say I do.'

'He was meant to be meeting the scheming bitch in Chivingden the night he was killed. I call her the blonde floozie. They'd been sending each other emails. The people at the farm have been very good. They've set up a fund for me and the kids. Should be enough to pay for the funeral.'

Anne sipped her tea and pondered for a moment. Then she said: 'You can make a claim for compensation from the Victims' Commissioner. I was reading about it. You can get up to £11,000.'

'I might do that. I've got to do something. Of course, the children have been crying for him,' said Gemma. 'Listen, Anne. There's something you might be able to help me with. D'you know what happened in Lucas's last week at work? Because you work at the farm, I thought you might know more than me. I've been told he was in trouble over some missing money.'

'Well, I'm only there part-time,' said Anne. 'But, funnily enough, we know the lad Lucas accused of taking it.'

'What - you mean the foreign bloke, Yusuf?'

I interrupted to tell Gemma: 'Yes. He lodged with us for a short time. He told us the whole story. Lucas accused Yusuf of taking the money, but the farm investigated and Lucas eventually confessed to it.'

'Oh, I see,' said Gemma. 'Well, thanks for telling me. Are you sure he confessed? Sounds more like a mix-up at the bank. I knew some of that, but it's good to hear the whole story from a different viewpoint.'

Without explanation, Gemma suddenly rose to her feet. She left the room and returned three minutes later. She handed Anne a piece of paper. I looked over Anne's shoulder as she cautiously unfolded it. We began reading it together. It was a love letter from Rosie Bennett.

16

It was a strange feeling to read a love letter sent to Lucas Sharp just days before he was murdered. Rosie Bennett's email said:

'My dearest darling Lucas. I've missed you so much since we last met at your aunt's cottage. It's such a shame we can't see more of each other. But don't worry. Things are gonna change. A time will come soon when we'll be able to spend more time together.

'It was so lovely meeting you at the weekend. I've never made love on a four-poster bed before. It was so thoughtful of you to put that chilled bottle of Chablis and wine glasses on the bedside cabinet.

'Your such a caring lover. You've took me to a few places. We've been in your car, in a caravan and in a hayloft. But your aunt's four-poster easily beats the lot!

'I'll see you on Bonfire Night at seven, but I won't be able to meet up with you on Sunday the twenty-second because my ex is going off caving in Somerset and I've got to have the kids.

'I hope you've done nothing about that plan you were talking about. You were moaning about the office messenger being a little creep and you owed Knight a grand. Do you remember? You said : two birds, one stone. I've been

thinking about what you said and I'm worried you might do something silly. Please be careful, darling. I have spent my life looking for you. I don't want to lose you now.

'Can't wait for Bonfire Night! All my love, Rosie. PS. You're right. I can't spell that posh word for caver. I looked it up online. It's SPELEOLOGIST!!!'

Anne put the email print-out on the table, but Gemma stayed her hand.

'You can keep it. I don't want the bloody thing,' she declared.

'Poor you, finding that,' said Anne, as she picked up the letter and placed it in her handbag. 'Didn't he have any shame?'

'He rushed out the other evening without closing down his laptop properly and I found it among his emails,' said Gemma, tearfully. 'Not a word of a lie -- I wasn't snooping. It was just there. So I printed it out. I'm sure any woman would have done the same.'

A thought suddenly occurred to me. If Gemma had come across this love letter with so little trouble, it would surely have been a simple matter for someone else to intercept the letter - perhaps at Rosie Bennett's home. I thought I might mention this to Anne later.

My wife had been shocked at reading her friend's letter and realised the trauma that details of the blatant affair had caused Gemma. She quickly resolved to change the subject. As Gemma handed tea round, my wife asked: 'What did the inspector want to know?'

'He asked when I last saw Lucas. It was half-past nine on the morning of November the fifth. Lucas told me he was going to work, but we know he'd been sacked - so he couldn't have gone there. The copper also asked about whether I knew the cottage. I said I knew it because it was his aunt's place and I've been there with the kids a few times. Then he wanted to know if anyone had a reason to kill Lucas. I told him Lucas had a knack of putting people's noses out of joint, but I couldn't think of anyone who wanted to end his life.'

Sensing she was about to cry, she reached forward to a small table in front of her, where she had placed the box of tissues.

'I know he could be a bastard, but I loved him, Gem,' she said amid tears.

'Of course, you did,' said Anne, putting her arm round her shoulder to comfort her.

'Look, I know this journalist called Prunella. She'd love to talk to you,' said Anne. 'We need to find out who killed Lucas. You need to get it in the papers.'

'D'you think so, Anne?'

'We need as much publicity as possible so that anyone with information is encouraged to come forward.'

'Yeah? All right. Prunella, you say? Give her my number, or, better still, ask her to call round here. I was telling you about the copper, wasn't I? He was very interested when I mentioned the fireworks through the letterbox.'

'Someone pushed lit fireworks through your front door?' Anne asked.

'Yeah. A few nights ago. It was lucky we was in. I stamped them out on the hall carpet. Not much damage. We've been getting funny phone calls too. You know, silent ones.'

'No words, no threats?'

'That's right. Just nothing. Silence. A bit worrying if I'm here on me own with the kids.'

Just then, while I had been half-listening to the conversation, I glanced up and began studying two large colour photographs on the wall above the fireplace. Each one showed an amateur football team.

'May I?' I asked Gemma respectfully.

'Go ahead. See if you can spot Lucas.' I carefully cast my eyes over the ranks of players.

'Here and, let me see, here?' I said.

'That's right. He played for Broad Oak. He was captain in the second picture. They said he was a useful little player. Scored a few goals. Pity he packed it in. He had to. He got in a row with the manager. Funny you being interested in that picture. The inspector kept looking at it too. He said they're determined to catch the killer before he kills again.'

'Does the policeman think he'll strike again?' asked Anne.

'Well, the inspector said the case was at an early stage and they didn't know precisely what they're dealing with. Then he turned around and said: "Whoever did this to your husband appears to be a very cold, calculating person." There was a long pause. Then he goes: "You never know. He may strike again."

On the morning of Saturday, November the seventh, Prunella Ball called round to see us on her way back from a trip to Canterbury police station. She wanted to thank us for preparing the way for an interview with Gemma Sharp, whom she was planning to visit later in the day. She also brought us up to date with details of the police inquiries.

'They've discovered a warehouse in Cranbrook which was used to store loads of fireworks got broken into last month,' she told Anne. 'Kent and Sussex Business Club kept them there, ready for a big display. More than £1,000 worth were stolen. Catherine wheels and artillery shells reserved for a display in Canterbury were among the haul. The club secretary told police he has heard a rumour they were being offered for sale in pubs and clubs. The mortar that killed Lucas Sharp was a Howling Horace Artillery Shell. Six of those were among the batch stolen. My friend Graham found all this out. He also went round to Finch & Davies, where he asked questions about the row between Sharp and your ex-lodger.

'He has been finding out about the chloroform that was kept at the farm and was asking the farm bosses about a GPS tracking device that might've been delivered there.'

Anne became interested to hear about a tracking device. Prunella disclosed that one had been found attached to Sharp's car. It was thought the murderer might have used it to follow the victim to Lilac Cottage.

Prunella continued: 'The device was ordered online and sent at the end of October to the farm's post-room. No one at the company appears to remember anything about it, but when they checked their register of volatile poisons they found the last person to obtain a five-hundred-millilitre bottle of chloroform was your ex-lodger.'

'Yusuf?' said Anne in amazement.

'Yes,' said Prunella. 'Anyway, things don't look good for your friend because Ted Moreton has now told police about the fight at the Pilgrim's Rest pub. Ted told him - I've got a shorthand note of it here: "Yusuf threw Lucas Sharp against the wall and called him a bastard. Sharp told him to go back to herding camels. Fists were flying. It was quite a punch-up. I had to pull them apart. Then Yusuf screamed: 'Tell any more lies and I will kill you."'

'Yusuf was extremely upset and a little drunk. I'm sure they were just empty words,' said Anne.

'Well, Graham then went to speak to Yusuf himself, He was in his caravan as it was lunchtime. Graham recognised him because he met him a few weeks ago, just after your neighbour's death.'

'That's right,' Anne agreed.

'Well, Yusuf denied everything. He didn't know Lilac Cottage or Sharp's flat in Broad Oak'

'That's right,' said Anne. 'He spends all his time at the farm. He hardly ever stops working.'

'Well,' Prunella continued. 'Your Yusuf claimed he didn't threaten to kill Sharp and said he needed the chloroform to deal with a rat problem.

'But then Graham searched Yusuf's caravan and was he in for a surprise! He came upon a sight that shocked him to the core. Sitting upright, on a sofa, was the effigy of a man. It had been made largely from straw with the aim it should be perched on top of a bonfire. The dummy was dressed in blue jeans, a blue check shirt and a small brown jacket - just like Sharp's clothes. The head had been cleverly crafted from papier mache and sculpted with considerable skill to follow the contours and structure of the face and head.

'The facial features had been painted in flesh-coloured pink and topped with short, brown imitation hair. A firework had been stuffed into the shoulder. It was an exact likeness of the man in a photograph Inspector Woods had shown the sergeant -- the murder victim Lucas Sharp.'

17

After Prunella Ball had said goodbye and walked away down the drive, we closed the front door and stood staring at each other for several seconds.

Why did Yusuf have an effigy of Lucas Sharp in his caravan? And why was a firework attached to its shoulder? Furthermore, why had one of the detectives from the murder investigation team wasted valuable time seeking out Yusuf to interview?

I followed Anne into the living-room. We sat down for a few minutes, mulling over what Prunella had told us.

'Look, he shares the caravan with his three friends,' I said. 'Any one of them could have made the dummy, intending for it to be placed on a bonfire. It's probably got nothing to do with the murder. And it's only Graham Kirwan's personal opinion that it looked like Sharp. '

'Yes,' said Anne, softly. 'Maybe it was just produced as a bit of fun to cheer Yusuf up over the way Sharp had treated him.'

I continued: "It's really puzzling the sergeant should go to the trouble of finding Yusuf's caravan and interviewing him.'

'The police are probably just trying to piece together how Lucas spent his final day. D'you remember what Prunella told me on the phone? The inspector's method is to focus on a victim's life. They are probably just trying to reconstruct in fine detail the final hours of Sharp's time on earth.'

I had to agree with her. But at the back of my mind was a growing realisation that the police might be thinking of including Yusuf on their list of possible murder suspects. Because of our knowledge of the man and our trust in him, I tried to dismiss this from my thoughts. The idea seemed completely preposterous.

However, the mystery of how Sharp met his death continued to intrigue me. I was particularly fascinated by the symbols that had been scratched on the car door.

Over the past few days, on the rare occasions when I had woken in the early hours of the morning and been unable to sleep, I had wondered to myself what these strange hieroglyphics could have meant.

So. a day or two later, it was fascinating to discover the symbols were not, as initially thought, Chinese. They were from a language called Tigrinyan, which is an Afro-Asiatic language mainly spoken in Eritrea and Ethiopia. Together, the letters meant "Devil" or "Satan."'

This new information came to light when Prunella Ball phoned Anne to discuss the interview she wanted to conduct with Gemma.

Prunella disclosed that the police were unsure whether the word had been left on the car door because the killer was associating himself with the devil - implying the devil had struck at Lilac Cottage - or whether the killer was trying to suggest Sharp was the epitome of evil.

We were also privy to new information about the firework. Anne and I had been speculating about how the killer had been able to set off the device indoors without, it seems, damaging the cottage ceiling. But this was easily explained by Prunella.

She told Anne: 'Graham's spoken to an Army explosives expert. He's been shown photographs of what remained of the mortar tube. He believes the firework was a cylinder shell or canister shell which was placed upside down in the cardboard mortar tube. This meant, instead of soaring into the ceiling, the firework exploded at the back of the victim's head. His head received the full force of the explosion and explains why there was no massive hole in the ceiling.'

I listened into the conversation on speaker-phone as Prunella added : 'I don't know if you're interested in the results of the post mortem, but the pathologist, Dr Harryman, has given the cause of the death as severe head trauma. Hang on, I've got the full statement here. He told me: "It's believed there'd have been a struggle in the kitchen for a few minutes before the victim succumbed to the chloroform fumes. The perpetrator's likely to be a strong man. Mr Sharp was 175.26 centimetres tall. He weighed eighty kilograms, which equates to twelve stone eight pounds.

'"When the fuse was lit, the explosion would've blown the plug out of the bottom of the mortar and the blast would then have killed the victim. The victim sustained extensive blast injuries to the head and upper torso that caused death through shock and haemorrhage. Death would have been instant. The victim had to be identified by fingerprints, his wristwatch and his clothing. I'm putting in my report he died from a lethal cranial trauma sustained as a consequence of an explosion."'

There is an old song. It goes: 'No shadow, no stars, no moon, no care, November.'

I recalled those words as I hurried back from school after

an exhausting day. The hedgerows in the lane were brown and bleak with little sticks poking impudently into the cold evening air, while the fields opposite our home were gradually losing their green hue for the russet of winter.

Autumn had finally embarked upon its long holiday, leaving behind as an after-thought just the pink blooms of our camellias, a rare glimpse of colour in the barren garden. I could understand now the negativity implied by the song, but I would suggest an extra verse: 'No light evenings, no break from bitter winds, no visitors, no doctors' appointments, November.'

I remained for a while in a quiet, thoughtful mood. But it did not last long.

Anne arrived back at the cottage ten minutes after me in an agitated state. She had been reading through some local news stories on her tablet computer.

'Oh, Bob. It's awful,' she screamed. 'Police are looking for Yusuf. They think he might have had something to do with Sharp's death!'

'You're joking!' I replied. I struggled for a few minutes to calm her down, then, as she sat down on the living-room settee, she clicked again on the news report.

Unmistakably, there was a photograph which had been taken at the farm of our friend Yusuf on the online news page under the caption 'Wanted.' There was a brief description and then it said he was wearing 'a dark-green check shirt, black jeans and a dark-blue coat.'

'That's the winter coat we bought him,' said Anne, who was close to tears. 'How can they believe Yusuf could've had anything to do with it?'

I had to agree with her. We had grown to know him. He

was gentle. He was kind. He was honest. You couldn't imagine a less likely culprit.

Shortly afterwards, there was a knock on the door. Anne got up and peered through the window.

'It's that detective again,' she said. 'You'd better let him in.'

'Mr and Mrs Shaw,' Sergeant Kirwan said. 'I won't take up much of your time. As you know, we're looking for your former lodger and wondered if you'd any idea where he might be?'

'No,' said Anne. 'You're welcome to search the house, but, as you know, he lives at the farm.'

'We've checked there already. D'you have any idea at all where he might be?'

We both genuinely had no knowledge of his whereabouts - although it gradually dawned on me there was one possible place he might have gone.

As the sergeant stood in our hallway, looking at two blank faces, my wife, calmly but passionately, launched into a detailed explanation as to why -- in her opinion -- Yusuf could not have been involved in any way in the tragedy at Lilac Cottage.

'Yusuf's totally harmless' she said. 'He spends all his time at the farm working or with his girlfriend Kristina. He doesn't even know where Chivingden is. He wouldn't hurt anyone.'

The sergeant responded by saying: 'We know that's untrue. There was a fight at the Pilgrim's Rest with witnesses who say punches were thrown. Anyway, let's not get ahead of ourselves. He's only a suspect at this stage.'

'You yourself would've been upset after someone told lies and put your job at stake with false theft claims!' Anne insisted.

I found it difficult to give any credence to the suggestion Yusuf could have been implicated in the murder.

'Sergeant, I've got to tell you -- you're making a mistake,' I said. 'I've watched him in the garden. If a caterpillar fell off a leaf, he'd help it back on again. If there's no rain and the bird-bath's empty, he fills it. If a crow swoops down to eat bread left out for the birds, he scares it away so the little birds can feed.'

The sergeant told us weeks later that, at this moment, he had quietly reminded himself of the Birdman of Alcatraz. There was a man who had rescued injured sparrows, raised three hundred canaries and learnt how to cure bird diseases. Yet he had brutally murdered a barman and a prison guard, the sergeant recalled to himself. However, because we were so concerned about our friend, he decided this was probably not the right time to point this out to us.

Instead he simply said: 'I'm sure your ex-lodger was a gentle guy. It's very laudable to be in harmony with nature. It's just we need to eliminate him from our inquiries.'

I could see there was little point in trying to take my argument further. The sergeant had apparently already made up his mind Yusuf could have played a part in causing the death of Lucas Sharp.

As he left and walked back down the drive, I believed he and the other senior detectives would eventually manage to find Yusuf. Once that happened, they would interview him and they would come to the same conclusion as Anne and me. Yusuf was no murderer.

However, over the coming days, Anne began to lose confidence Yusuf would be cleared of any involvement. She was beginning to share my deep-rooted suspicion of the police. And she had never had much faith in the traditional concept of British justice. She reminded me of cases in which the wrong men and women had been convicted; she had avidly watched television programmes about the struggles of justice campaigners to gain the release of the innocent.

Meanwhile, I had a quick task to perform. As Anne wanted to carry out more online research into the police investigation involving Yusuf, I left her at the cottage.

I walked down the lane until I reached the entrance to the footpath that leads through the woods. I passed a dog walker amid the trees, crossed the stream and eventually came to the clearing that overlooks a series of fields.

I had half-expected to see Yusuf there, lounging on the bench. But he was not there. No one was sitting on the brown wooden bench. I was alone, standing beneath a canopy of trees and staring across the open ground.

18

As Anne and I gradually recovered from the initial shock of hearing Yusuf was a murder suspect, I quickly realised there might be serious implications for us as well.

If our friend was to face questions, the police would not simply focus on his whereabouts at the time of the murder.

There might also be far-reaching questions covering his past life, his entry into Britain, his immigration status, his accommodation and his job.

Would he tell them he arrived in England clinging to the chassis of our motor-home? If so, would they believe him?

Sergeant Kirwan already realised Yusuf had spent two months lodging with us. Could we get into some kind of trouble because of that? Would they accuse us of harbouring him?

Did our friend have a secret past of which we were ignorant? These were the sort of questions streaming through my mind. I had to talk to Anne about our situation. We needed to get our story straight.

However, at this moment, she was confused and distressed. She had some firm ideas of her own. She took her fawn winter coat from the hall cupboard. She began sliding her arms into it.

'I want to go to the farm,' she said. 'I must find out what's been going on.'

I agreed to drive her there, although the working day had

nearly ended. Within five minutes, the Mondeo had arrived in the car park at Finch & Davies. It was virtually empty, but Sue Wickens' silver Mazda sports car was still in its normal place, next to David Finch's green Jaguar.

Anne rushed into the reception area. She could hear the sound of rattling keys. Mrs Wickens was in the process of locking up and leaving.

'Anne!' she said. 'There's no English class tonight, is there?'

'No, I've come about Yusuf. The police have been round to the cottage. They're looking for him.'

'Yes, I'd been thinking of giving you a call. He's in a spot of trouble.'

'We can't understand why,' said Anne, as I joined her by the counter. 'D'you know where he is?'

'No idea. No one's seen him since this morning. We'd a convoy of police cars here this afternoon. This detective inspector - Woods, I think his name was - was demanding to know where Yusuf was, but no one had seen him since lunch. Someone remembered seeing him in a dark green check shirt, a brown jacket and black jeans.

'Then his colleague, a sergeant, appeared in the office, telling Woods that Yusuf wasn't in the caravan and all his clothes had gone. They checked the cycle shelter and his bike was missing. The inspector shouted: "Damn it! Looks like the bird's flown the coop."

'Then he went onto say they would have to get a message to all units to keep an eye open for him. They were going to contact the media and he talked about issuing an All Ports Warning in case Yusuf tried to flee the country. Then I heard him say: "If this doesn't suggest guilt, I don't know what does."'

'We just can't understand what could've happened,' said Anne.

'Well, the police are looking for someone with a grudge against my nephew. Of course, he'd caused poor Yusuf a lot of distress. But it's rather unfortunate Yusuf was the last person to obtain chloroform from our poisons' cabinet.'

'I've heard this about him getting chloroform. What reason did he give for wanting it?'

'Well, he claims they were bothered by a rat at the caravan, although I've not heard about this from anyone else,' said Mrs Wickens. 'The police also seem to think a tracking device delivered here was used by Yusuf to follow Lucas to the cottage where he was murdered.'

'I know Yusuf was upset at the way Lucas acted, but we can't believe he'd kill someone,' said Anne.

'Well, there's more,' said Mrs Wickens.

'There's more?' I asked.

'Yes. There's a rumour going round the farm the pair were in a fight at the Pilgrim's Rest three weeks ago and Yusuf threatened to kill him. Yusuf then made a Guy Fawkes dummy that looked exactly like Lucas and pushed a firework into the dummy's shoulder.'

'Oh God! So you've heard the same as us,' wailed Anne. I had to admit a mass of potentially damning evidence against Yusuf appeared to be mounting higher and higher.

'Well, we've got to help him, haven't we?' Anne declared, turning first to look at me and then to look at Mrs Wickens.

The secretary was the first to respond. 'Yes, of course. The company will do all it can,' she said.

'We've got to do everything in our power to help him,' I

concurred. 'We all know what kind of man he is. Even if he'd been driven by spite to seek revenge against a man who caused him trouble, he'd not have intentionally wanted to bring about Lucas's death.'

We left Mrs Wickens to lock up the premises and walked to the caravan site in the hope of finding Kristina. As we strode across the car park, Anne was clearly incensed.

'The whole thing's ridiculous,' she asserted. 'Something you said when Yusuf was cleared over the money has come back to me - strangers will always be blamed first. That's what's happened here. The police have just picked on the first stranger they've come across while looking into what happened. There's no way Yusuf would have the nous to track down Lucas to Lilac Cottage - with or without a tracking device. He wouldn't know where to start if he wanted to buy a giant firework either. And I couldn't imagine him fixing it to a man's head with wire and blowing him up.'

I was equally baffled by the police decision to arrest Yusuf. I said: 'I don't think being framed over a theft is sufficient motive for murder. It's Sharp who lost his job at the end of the day and Sharp who was getting a criminal record. Why would Yusuf go to all the trouble of committing murder? He'd seen his rival punished for what he had done. That was surely sufficient retribution. As you say. the whole thing's ridiculous.'

As we approached Kristina's caravan, I recalled there had been little love lost until now between Anne and Kristina. But Anne had clearly decided to swallow her pride. She needed as much information as she could acquire about the events leading up to the police decision to arrest Yusuf.

We found the Romanian girl sitting in her caravan with two

of her fellow countrymen, listening to some folk music.

'Oh, Anne! Bob!' she exclaimed as she saw our distressed faces. 'This is a terrible time. '

Her two friends politely greeted us and then discreetly left.

'Please, sit!' she said.

'D'you know where Yusuf is?' I asked.

'Listen. I know you're Yusuf's good friends. Kristina will tell you what she knows,' she said. 'Yusuf 's doing the run.'

'Gone on the run?' said Anne.

'Yes, but it's not what the police think. They think Yusuf may've done the murder. That's stupid. Yusuf was here with me. But they must think: Yusuf's gone, so he's the guilty man.'

'But he's gone for a different reason - not because of the police?' I asked.

'Yes, different reason,' Kristina confirmed. She explained Sam Tedros and Jaefer Beraki had visited Yusuf's caravan.

'So this big guy Sam, he say: "Great place you've got here, Yusuf. I think I might move in here. Hot and cold running water, and a fridge. Luxury, isn't it, compared with what we all had before." He is demanding: "Have you got our money?"

'Then I hear a cracking sound. This big man break our sofa-bed, he's so big. He say sorry. Then he stands up and pulls it from the wall. It's like snapping matchsticks. I scream at him. I say: "What're you doing? You're not a friend." Then the big man say: "We want what's due. Get me money, Yusuf, or you're dead meat!"

'Yusuf annoys me at first. When the two men are gone, Yusuf say: "I think I can fix it if I get the screws."

I had to smile at this point. I thought: 'That's so typical of our friend.'

Kristina went on : 'I told him to forget about the bloody bed. I say: "What're you going to do about those big bully men?" But Yusuf just say he'll run away. He say: "I think I go to London or somewhere - maybe Scotland. Maybe I look for my mother. They're bad men from my homeland. They want me to give them money and sell drugs."

'I tell him running away's no good. Then he say the police have been to ask him about Lucas. The policeman was very shocked when he saw my bonfire doll.'

'So you made the effigy?' said Anne.

'Yes. I make,' she replied.

'Why wasn't it put on a bonfire?' I asked. Kristina giggled.

'I studied art in my country,' she explained. 'Last month I thought it would be nice to make a Guy Fawkes dummy making fun of Lucas. It made Yusuf and all our friends laugh, We never got round to burning it because, in the end, we had a Hallowe'en party instead of a Bonfire party.'

'Kristina,' I said. 'Did the police speak to you when they visited the farm today?'

'Yes,' she said. 'I tell the inspector Yusuf would never hurt Lucas. Then the inspector say: "He spoke of wanting him dead." I reply: "That was the drink talking. Yusuf was with me when Lucas died. He knows nothing."

'The policeman say: "What about the bloody mannequin of Mr Sharp in your caravan?" I tell him I make the doll. "This is the famous Guy Fawkes guy you English like to make," I said. It was a nice challenge for me. This doesn't happen in my country. We burn the doll of a dictator.'

'Anyway, where's Yusuf?' Anne demanded.

'He cycled to the train and say: "Tell Bob the bike's chained up outside the station,"' said Kristina. 'He's now in London, living on the streets.'

'But it's November,' I said. 'He'll die from the cold.'

'He's done like this before,' she said. 'Yusuf is great survivor.'

19

Yusuf's life on the run did not last for long. Our friend was at large for precisely six hours. As we climbed back into our car, we switched on the radio. The first item on the local radio news was about him.

The news reader said: 'A man sought by police after a farm's accounts manager was found dead at a remote Kent cottage was arrested in the county this afternoon.

'Yusuf Osman, aged twenty-three, was seen boarding the 16.48 London-bound train at Canterbury East station by an off-duty constable.

'The train was held for ten minutes at the station as a search was conducted. Mr Osman was found hiding in one of the front carriages. He was placed under arrest and led away in handcuffs.

'A Kent Police spokesman said a man had been arrested and taken to a police station, where he was assisting with inquiries.'

'Where d'you think they've taken him, Bob?' Anne asked as we travelled towards the cottage.

'I should think they would've taken him to the main Canterbury police station,' I replied.

'Let's go and see if there's anything we can do to help him,' she said. The road was clear of traffic. She spotted a farm gate a short distance ahead. Within seconds, she had reversed into the opening and we began heading back along the road, heading towards the city centre.

When we arrived, we discovered the station closes at five pm, but we called an out-of-hours phone number listed on a board outside. Our supposition was proved correct. An officer in the control room believed Yusuf was being held at the city police station, but we were refused permission to see him. It was suggested we should contact a solicitor.

Anne decided this was an admirable idea. She knew of a woman solicitor in East Kent who had an enviable track record in gaining justice for men and woman who have been wrongly accused.

'I don't know if we can afford to do this,' she said. 'But we must see no stone's left unturned in our efforts to get Yusuf released.'

'I agree,' I said. 'We've got our holiday fund. If necessary, we can forego a few holidays and a few luxuries to make sure he gets the best legal advice.'

Our decision had been taken. As we drove back to the cottage, Anne vowed the following day she would go into see the lawyer Janice Carslake, whose practice, Carslake and Whitter, was based in the city centre.

Early the next morning, we took a bus to Canterbury East station. I had told the school I was unable to come in because I had 'urgent union business to attend to.' I was always reluctant to use this as an excuse, but I felt obliged to help our friend in his moment of crisis.

Chained to railings close to the station, we found the bicycle Yusuf had been using for the past two months. With our duplicate keys, I undid the padlocks on the chains. Then we wheeled the bicycle to the solicitor's office, which was within the city walls, and attached it to a lamppost.

Anne told the receptionist a friend needed legal representation as he had been arrested.

The lady at the desk informed her Mrs Carslake had a busy schedule. Could we return later in the day?

But Anne persisted. 'My friend's accused of murder,' she said.

'Why didn't you say that before?' said the receptionist.

After a brief internal phone conversation with her employer, the lady invited us to climb the stairs to the first floor, where Mrs Carslake would meet us.

Janice Carslake, who was forty-six, had once harboured ambitions to become a high-flying criminal barrister. She had eventually settled for a less competitive environment as a solicitor handling criminal cases in Kent and Sussex, which mainly involved appearing in magistrates' courts - usually defending clients.

But law colleagues from the same generation did not underestimate her abilities. She was renowned for her vast knowledge of criminal law as well as possessing an astute brain. Her skills had led to a TV personality accused of rape being freed from court on a legal technicality. A charge of murder against a man who killed his dementia-stricken wife was dropped after crucial last-minute evidence provided by her was set before the court.

Inevitably, the woman we found standing confidently at the top of the stairs in a grey trouser suit and with immaculately coiffured blonde hair was not a popular figure among the police.

'Mr and Mrs Shaw?' she asked, shaking first Anne's hand and then mine. 'Janice Carslake. Won't you come in?'

She led us into a modestly-decorated room with apricot-coloured walls and a light-green carpet. She seated herself behind a large desk and invited us to sit opposite.

'Now my secretary says this is a murder case. May I know the name of the defendant?'

'Yusuf Osman,' said Anne.

'Why does that name mean something to me?'

'I'm not sure.'

'Is he the man arrested last evening at one of the Canterbury stations?'

'Yes, that's right.'

'Oh, this is the Lilac Cottage case concerning the death of a man called Sharp,' said Mrs Carslake, whose right wrist, festooned with bracelets, rattled whenever she moved it.

Anne nodded. 'It's absolutely ridiculous. The police think Yusuf murdered him.'

'This is a case in which it was at first thought the victim died in a fire and is now being treated as murder. Is that right?'

'The police spoke to me yesterday,' said Anne. 'They're definitely treating him as a murder suspect. There's a strong rumour the dead man was killed with a firework.'

'It's a pretty gruesome way to die,' Mrs Carslake admitted. She then spent several minutes collecting information about Yusuf from us - including details about where she believed Yusuf was being held and the names of the officers in the case.

While we were present, she made a phone call to Kent Police. After a few minutes, she had confirmed Yusuf was being held in the cells at Canterbury police station.

Then she asked: 'How did you become such close friends of Mr Osman?'

'He came to us looking for accommodation after taking a job at Finch & Davies,' said Anne, bending the truth slightly.

'Don't they supply accommodation for their staff at the farm?'

Anne thought for a moment. She did not want to divulge the true details about how Yusuf first emerged in our lives.

'There was some kind of problem,' I said. 'He was reluctant at first to share with Romanians and Bulgarians. Perhaps it's a cultural thing.'

'I see,' said the lawyer, sounding unconvinced.

'Mr Osman's from Eritrea, is he? It's just I've come across someone with a similar name before. They were from the next country, Ethiopia?'

'He told us Eritrea.'

'What's his immigration status?'

'He showed us an Eritrean passport. He said he'd got the right to be in Britain."

'OK. Well, I'll have to look into all that. Have you got his passport?'

'No, he had it with him when he was arrested.'

'So the police'll have it. Where was he going when he was arrested?'

'His girlfriend says he was being threatened by two men from his country. They were demanding money. She says that's why he decided to head off to London.'

'He's not helped himself,' said Mrs Carslake. 'The police now think he was trying to run away from them. All right I'll take the case on. I'll contact the police and go to see Mr Osman. I'll be in touch.'

20

Our solicitor was as good as her word. Later in the day, she phoned the cottage to say she had visited Yusuf in his cell, which she described as measuring about seven feet by eleven feet. He had a hard mattress and a single pillow, but he told Mrs Carslake he at least felt safe for the moment from the bullying thugs Sam Tedros and Jaefer Beraki.

He told her he was confused about the reasons for his confinement. How could the police suspect him of having anything to do with Lucas Sharp's death, he asked her.

He had enjoyed his breakfast - an egg, two sausages, some baked beans and a single slice of toast. They had also brought him some tea.

Mrs Carslake said she told Yusuf that Anne and I had asked her to represent him. He had replied: 'They're my friends - my good friends. They asked you to help me? Then of course.'

She told us: 'Yusuf denies having ever been to Lilac Cottage. He claims he was with his girlfriend, Kristina Petrescu, at the time of the murder. He told me he was born in Asmara, the capital of Eritrea. I stressed to him the importance of him telling the truth. I said: "If we're to get you released, we must provide a cogent, consistent defence." He appeared to understand that.

'He told me, rather than fleeing the police, he had boarded a London train because two men from his past were looking for him. They've threatened to burn down his caravan. I gather they're people traffickers and drug dealers.

'When it came to the end of our interview, he said something that really surprised me. I asked if there was any message I could give you and he said he wanted some pictures of Fiesta. I at first thought he wanted some photographs of a festival. Then he explained Fiesta's a cat he misses very much.

'I thought: here's a young man locked in a police cell who was strongly suspected by the police of committing a serious murder. Two hardened criminals were threatening to burn down his home. Yet his first priority's a pet cat.'

Anne laughed. 'That's our Yusuf,' she said. 'He's a humble, straight-forward guy - almost childlike at times.'

'I see,' she replied. 'Anyway, the police have now spoken to him at Canterbury police station. DI Woods and DS Kirwan conducted the interview. I sat next to Yusuf after warning him in advance not to give any long answers. I said: "The object of the exercise is to find out what they know - to find out the strength of the case against you. So to most questions, answer: 'No comment.'" He agreed with that, but I'm afraid, Mrs Shaw, it now looks to me as if Yusuf 's going to be formally charged with murder.

'Make no mistake. I put our case to them very clearly. I told the inspector, right from the start, it looked as if the police had made a glaring error in arresting this young man.

'But they appear to have a lot of evidence which I'll now have to consider. Not only that. Police believe he may've been convicted of murdering a man in Eritrea. So it's not looking good.'

I had been listening to the conversation on speaker-phone. We were both devastated at hearing these last words from Mrs

Carslake. I dashed to Anne's side immediately and put my arm round her as she burst into tears.

The solicitor went on: 'I'm getting my secretary to type out a transcript of this first police interview. I'll bike it round to you later this afternoon.'

Anne had put the phone down. She was unable to continue talking. I picked up the handset.

'Mrs Carslake, this is Bob Shaw here,' I said. 'Have you got our address? It's Fairview, Hopgarden Lane, Chasehurst. It's the second house along the lane from the Ashford road. You'll send the transcript round later? That'll be fine. Yes, if we've got any points to make afterwards, we'll call you back immediately.'

Three hours later, a courier arrived with a seven-page transcript of the police interview. It began with Detective Inspector Woods turning on some recording equipment in the interview room:

DI Woods: This is Detective Inspector Woods at half-past two on Wednesday November the eleventh. This is our first interview with Yusuf Osman. Also present: Detective Sergeant Graham Kirwan and Mr Osman's legal representative, Mrs Janice Carslake. Right, I need to remind you you're still under caution after we arrested you yesterday. Now I want to begin by asking you where you were going last night when you were apprehended at the railway station.

Yusuf Osman: I'm going to London.

DI Woods: With what purpose?

Yusuf Osman: I'm running from the two men who are making the threats.

DI Woods: So it wasn't you were worried about the prospect of being arrested over the murder of Lucas Sharp?

Yusuf Osman: No comment.

DI Woods: Oh, it's like that, is it? Now I want you to cast your mind back to the evening of last Thursday, November the fifth. Where were you between half-past six and half past seven?

Yusuf Osman: I was at my caravan at Finch & Davies.

DI Woods: Can anyone corroborate this?

Yusuf Osman: What does this mean?

DS Kirwan: Did anyone see you there? Were you with anyone?

Yusuf Osman: I with Kristina, my girlfriend.

DI Woods: Anyone else?

Yusuf Osman: No comment.

DI Woods: OK. Now we understand you were the last person issued with chloroform at the farm. You were given a five-hundred-millilitre bottle in the middle of last week. You told us it was to kill a rat. We've made inquiries and no one else knows about a rat problem.

Yusuf Osman: No comment.

DI Woods: We believe you travelled by bicycle to Lilac Cottage in Chivingden at some time during the early evening on November the fifth. You found out Lucas Sharp had gone there by following a GPS tracker you'd attached to the underside of his car. It was actually a device known as a 'Little Snooper'. You used a mobile phone or computer to track his car's movements. Is that right?

Yusuf Osman: No comment.

DI Woods: Cycle tyre marks were found near the front gate and in the front garden which we believe were left by your bicycle - which we're currently trying to trace. You broke into the back of the cottage and lay in wait for your enemy, Mr Sharp.

You'd got a mortar and artillery shell and some other fireworks with you which had been stolen from a charity's storeroom in Cranbrook. You also had the chloroform. Is that right?

Yusuf Osman: No comment.

DI Woods: You fixed a Catherine Wheel to the kitchen wall and lit it as soon as you heard Mr Sharp arriving. You thought this would be a clever distraction. When he went to examine it, you held some material soaked in the chemical to his face. Is that correct?

Yusuf Osman: No comment.

DI Woods: Then, when he was unconscious, you tied him to a chair and attached the mortar to his head. The shell was placed inside the tube the wrong way round. After it was lit, it exploded at the back of Mr Sharp's head and he was killed. D'you have anything to say about that? It may look bad later if you refuse to comment now?

Yusuf Osman: No comment.

Mrs Carslake: I'm not sure whether Mr Osman totally understood what you've said. Have you, Mr Osman?

Yusuf Osman: I'm understanding. No comment.

DI Woods: After the murder, you scratched an African word meaning 'Devil' on the passenger door of Mr Sharp's Vauxhall Astra. Our forensic team also found a fingerprint of yours on the driver's door of the car.

Yusuf Osman: No comment.

DI Woods: Well, our murder investigation team have been hard at work Mr Osman. I thought you might be interested to know we've found out a few things about you.

For one thing, the immigration authorities have no record of you. We also believe you've killed another man in cold blood in your homeland in a very similar way - with a bomb strapped to their body.

Yusuf Osman: No, this is somebody else. This not me.

DS Kirwan: Are you all right, Mrs Carslake? You seem to have dropped your notebook. I can just reach it. There you are. D'you need a glass of water or anything?

Mrs Carslake: No, I'm OK. Thank you for asking.

DI Woods: It's a bit stuffy in here. Anyone mind if I open the window? Yes, this has come as a bit of a surprise to all of us - not only you, Mrs Carslake. We're now more certain than ever our Mr Osman was involved in the murder. He may not have acted alone, but we're convinced he was concerned in some way.

Mrs Carslake: So you're saying, are you, Mr Osman is an illegal immigrant?

DI Woods: We're not sure. Inquiries are on-going as we speak.

Mrs Carslake: Is it your intention to charge my client with any offence?

DI Woods: Not at this juncture, Mrs Carslake, but we're considering applying to the magistrates for a warrant granting more time to question Mr Osman. Is there anything either of you wish to say?

Yusuf Osman: I didn't kill Lucas. I'm innocent.

Mrs Carslake: There's no need to say any more, Yusuf. Inspector, you'll keep me informed of any major developments in the case, won't you?

DI Woods: Yes, of course. This is DI Woods. First interview with Yusuf Osman terminated at two forty-five pm.

21

Yusuf looked haggard and unwell when Anne and I were finally allowed to visit him on Thursday, November the twelfth. He had always been an outdoors man who relished the fresh air and being at one with nature.

The ordeal of being locked in a cell for the best part of twenty-four hours a day appeared to have crushed his spirit.

He had been allowed to shower and change into a grey shirt and brown trousers. But he was downcast. Even his enigmatic smile was absent when we squeezed into his small cell for our visit. We had only gained permission to see him after Mrs Carslake made a personal request to the chief superintendent.

As Yusuf had requested, we had brought along two photographs of Fiesta the cat. One pictured the pet walking gracefully towards the camera with a proud look upon his face. The other showed Yusuf holding the pet outside the front door of our cottage.

We had brought a small container of poster adhesive with which he managed to stick them onto the wall beside his bed.

'The police have been talking to you about the murder then?' I said after he stood back to admire the pictures.

'Yes. They think I tied Lucas to a chair and blew off his head with a big firework. They're crazy!'

'Mrs Carslake has told us everything and we are going to do everything possible to get you out of here,' Anne assured him.

I could tell from Anne's face she was distressed to find our friend in such a predicament, but she was hiding it as best she could for Yusuf's sake. We both realised there were aspects of his life which were closed off to us. He had no doubt crossed swords with some unsavoury characters, including some criminals - in his efforts to reach the safety of Britain.

We were also aware Sharp left our friend deeply upset by blaming him for the theft. However, we were equally convinced our friend could, by no stretch of the imagination, have carried out the horrific murder.

I tried to cheer him up as best I could.

'Fiesta's been chasing birds in the garden again,' I informed him. 'Sometimes she sits on the mat outside the front door. She looks up whenever a cyclist comes by. She's probably looking out for you.'

'I miss Fiesta,' he said. 'I miss everything about your cottage and the garden. Are there still foxgloves growing in the lane?'

'Yes, along with some daisies and there are some hollyhocks as well now!' I said with a laugh.

We said our goodbyes. I shook Yusuf's hand and Anne kissed him on the cheek. We promised to visit him again soon.

But, as we drove slowly home, I began to realise we would have to put our normal lives on hold.

'Bob, we have to help Yusuf. We are probably the only people who know for sure he couldn't have carried out this murder' she said. 'The police appear to be increasingly convinced Yusuf is guilty, so even though neither of us has ever been faced with a situation like this before, we have got to do something. D'you know what? I'm going to have to find out myself who the real perpetrator is.'

'Would you like me to buy you a magnifying glass and deer-stalker?' I quipped.

'This is not a time for joking,' she insisted. 'You always make a pathetic attempt to introduce humour. It's not helpful.'

When we got home, Anne decided she would make her introduction into the world of private sleuthing by visiting Lilac Cottage. It was now a week since the murder. She hoped, since it had not rained much, the cycle tyre tracks would still be visible. We did not know Chivingden very well, so I printed off a map of the area from the internet and we set off.

'Is it a reasonable map showing The Street?' Anne asked.

'Yes, it's not bad,' I replied. 'Only a few bits are missing.'

Anne stopped the car on the Ashford Road so she could study it.

'It resembles a sort of pictorial Morse code,' she said. Then she reproached me. 'Why didn't you mention the printer was running out of ink?'

We eventually managed to find the cottage and parked a few yards back. She wanted to examine carefully the grass verge outside.

The lane was still and peaceful. Although it was the second week of November, it was mild. Now and then we could detect the sound of distant birdsong. How chilling to think, just a few days earlier, some evil force had been at work, snuffing out the life of poor Lucas Sharp.

Anne set to work. She found a bicycle tyre mark which was about a metre long in the mud close to the wooden gate. She had expected more of them - much more. She photographed the solitary remaining track.

She then entered the garden and found signs of more tracks

on the left, beside the hedge. She photographed those as well.

'Look at these, Bob,' she said. 'These don't belong to our bicycle tyres. They've got a far more pronounced pattern consisting of black rubber nodules. What d'you think?'

I studied the marks in the cold, moist November ground. I then examined the photographs she had taken on her digital camera, enlarging them for a clearer view.

'I'm thinking mountain bike,' I said. 'I think, if we went to a cycle shop, we might even be able to work out which brand of cycle's made them.'

'That's what I think - mountain bike,' said Anne. 'But I think we'll have to take some casts with plaster of Paris if we want to produce evidence that could convince either the police or a court.'

We next went round to the back of the cottage in the hope of finding the shoe-mark near the back door that had been mentioned to us, but we could not find any trace of it. Perhaps it had been trampled over too frequently by beleaguered scenes of crime officers.

When we returned home, Anne went online. She found an American website that explained how to make casts of tyre marks. All she needed was a container of water, plaster of Paris, a serving spoon, a bucket and some tiny twigs or wire mesh to strengthen the casts.

Following the instructions, she returned to Lilac Cottage with her equipment. Mindful that police forensic officers had performed a similar task already, she mixed the plaster in a bucket and meticulously spooned the mixture into the two tracks in the earth.

She came home and allowed more than three hours for the

plaster to set fully. Then she returned to the scene of her handiwork, carefully removed the casts and placed each one inside large empty cardboard boxes before driving back.

Anne made some tea before examining the casts upstairs in the spare bedroom.

She called out to me: 'Could be an American tyre.'

'I'm sorry?' I replied from my comfortable seat in front of the television. I climbed the stairs and looked over her shoulder at the fragile cast she held in her hands.

'I'm thinking of the WTB Nano tyre we saw in the cycle shop,' she said, referring to an American cycle tyre that has a distinctive pattern incorporating tiny rubber nodules.

'Could be,' I said. 'Maybe your next move's to find someone who rides a mountain bike.'

'I suppose so.'

Over the next two hours, we sat in the living-room deliberating about the case.

'I'm going to have to go back to the school next week,' I said. 'They were very good in letting me have today and tomorrow off, but my services are sorely missed.'

'That's all right,' she said. 'But I'm going to carry on with this as long I need to.'

She took a notebook from a drawer and found a pen on the mantelpiece.

'Bob,' she said. 'Who d'you think might've murdered Lucas?'

It was a question that had clearly been on both our minds since the moment we heard murder was involved. But hearing the words emerge from her lips at this time still took me unawares.

'I - I don't know. I've thought about it. There must be a few possible suspects.'

'I'm going to make a list,' she said. 'If I write them all down, it might lead us somewhere. Something might leap out at us.'

'Well, obviously someone who owns a mountain bike might go to the top of the list,' I suggested.

'I'm leaving that until tomorrow,' she said.

I remarked: 'You'll have to put Gemma Sharp near the top of the list.'

'Gemma?' said Anne. 'D'you think so?

'Well, Lucas was clearly having an affair. She can't have been overjoyed about that.'

'Gemma told us Lucas's affair was with a Rosie Bennett from Sturry,' said Anne. 'I don't suppose that woman's husband would be all that happy with Lucas for carrying on with his wife - so he's got to go near the top as well,' she insisted.

'You can also add the man from our village called Knight,' I told her. 'Prunella and Miles Benton have both told us about him. It seems this man was pursuing Lucas for a drugs debt. According to Miles, Knight's meant to have said something like: "Just you wait till I get my hands on that Lucas." D'you want me to go over to the pub and see if I can find out anything more?'

'If you want, but don't worry too much. I'll ask Gemma about it when I see her. Bob, the list of suspects isn't very long at the moment.'

'Let's have a look!' I said. I read out the names she had written down: Rosie Bennett's husband; Gemma Sharp; a friend or lover of Gemma Sharp; Mr Knight.

'D'you know for sure Gemma Sharp has a lover?' I asked.

'No,' she replied. 'But I thought I'd put it down because it's a possibility. I'm in contact with her. I can easily find out.'

'I think you're being a bit optimistic. I'd have thought most people would keep schtum if they've got a secret lover.'

'Don't worry. I have my methods!' said Anne with a grin.

I suggested, if it was possible for Sharp to have had a rival for his wife's affections, Rosie Bennett could equally have had another admirer -- apart from Sharp.

'If someone lost Rosie Bennett to a sneak like Lucas, I should think they'd be mad with rage - possibly mad enough to kill him,' I said.

'Yes. We've got to look at all the options,' she admitted. 'I'll make a start by calling on Gemma this afternoon. I just hope she's around.'

22

Gemma was delighted to receive a phone call from Anne. I had the distinct impression the mother-of-two did not have many friends.

Anne arranged for us to visit her at two o'clock. We drove into the city and arrived a couple of minutes early.

Gemma hugged Anne when she opened the front door. 'It's nice to have company at a time like this,' she told us.

'You seem in a better frame of mind now. Are you feeling better in yourself?' Anne asked.

'It's all superficial,' said Gemma, who was wearing frayed jeans and a pink blouse. 'I'm still completely torn up inside.'

She led us into her bright, sunny living room where we both sat on Gemma's settee. She remained standing.

'This is a lovely flat, Gemma,' Anne remarked.

'It's all right. The garden needs sorting,' said her friend. 'You wanted to see me urgently?'

'Yes,' said Anne. 'I've taken a big decision today. I'm on a one-woman mission to find your husband's killer.'

'What d'you mean, Anne? Aren't the police doing that?'

'I don't trust the police. They've arrested our ex-lodger, Yusuf.'

'Oh my God. I didn't know. They said they was going to keep me informed.'

'See what I mean?' said Anne. 'There's some circumstantial evidence pointing to our ex-lodger, I must admit. But he's the sweetest, kindest man and I've decided I have to help him. I just know he wouldn't have committed such a heinous crime. And I have to help you as well, Gemma. I owe it to you, as a friend, to find out who did it.'

'Well, I'll help you, of course. D'you want some tea, by the way?'

'No, thanks. We can't stay long. I've so much to do. Could you just tell me a few things?'

'I'll tell you anything you want to know.'

'D'you know why Gordon Knight had the hump with Lucas?' asked Anne, taking her notepad out of her handbag.

'I don't know precisely, but I think it was to do with money. I think he owed the guy over a grand.'

'D'you know what the money was for?' said Anne, as she began taking notes.

'Look, I'm only telling you this because I see you as my friend. I don't want anyone else to know - especially not the police. Lucas bought some drugs from him - just cannabis and a very small amount of cocaine. Just for recreational use. I don't approve of drugs myself. I'd a massive row with him when I found out he'd bought them. I was concerned about the kids. I made him promise it was the last time. He tried to pay the money back, but he never earned enough. He kept giving the bloke excuses. '

Anne asked: 'D'you think Knight was annoyed enough to want to kill Lucas?'

'It's hard to believe someone would kill another person over a relatively small amount of money,' Gemma admitted. 'But I suppose anything's possible.'

I interrupted to ask: 'Could it have been a lot more than £1,000 that he owed the man? Could the debt have run into several thousand pounds?'

'I suppose it's possible.'

'Can you tell me a little more about Rosie Bennett? What's her husband called? How long's she been married?'

'Rosie's husband's called Neil. He's about thirty-six. He's a supermarket manager. The blonde floozie kicked him out and he went to live with his brother Luke in St Stephens. They've been married for about eight years.'

'D'you know how he spends his spare time? Is he out looking for a new girlfriend? Is he a member of any sports clubs? I'm trying to build up a picture of the man.'

'His family come originally from Sissenden. I'm told he sometimes goes for a drink at the Pilgrims. You'll never guess what his hobby is - potholing.'

'Potholing?'

'Yes. People have told me he's taken the split from Rosie very badly. He's trying to behave himself, so he can get back into her good books. The gossip is he's trying very hard to curry favour with her - but she just don't want to know. I think there've been a few times when he's got a bit rough with her after a night's drinking.'

'Oh, one of those,' said Anne. 'How d'you know so much about the Bennetts then?'

'I've made it my business to know. I wanted to know as much as I could about the woman trying to smash up my marriage. It does help, mind, someone I used to work with lives a few doors away!'

'Who's that - Judy Scott?'

'No, Jennifer Campbell.'

'Was her maiden name Harvey?'

'Yes, that's right.'

'Thin face, good at running?'

'That's her.'

'I think I was at primary school with her,' said Anne. Then she paused for a moment. She remembered from watching police dramas on television the wife or husband of a murder victim was often one of the main suspects in the case. It was now time to ask her friend a difficult question. She had to phrase it in a delicate way to avoid offence.

'Gemma,' she began. 'Could I ask where you were on Bonfire Night? Did you take the kids out to a display or party?'

'No, I was here. The kids went to a friend's house where they had some fireworks. Why?'

'Oh, I just wondered. Most people try to watch fireworks, don't they?' She quickly added a lie: 'We did, didn't we, Bob?' I nodded, happy to support her claim. 'So you were here at seven o'clock that night?'

'Yes, having tea. Baked beans on toast, if you must know.'

'Gem, d'you know anyone who's got a mountain bike?'

'Funny question, out of the blue.'

'It's just we've found tracks made by a mountain bike on the ground near the gate at Lilac Cottage.'

'Lots of people have mountain bikes,' said Gemma. 'I've got one meself.'

Anne contemplated asking her friend if she could show her the bike so she could examine its tread. But the Gemma she recalled from her past was prone to mood swings. In addition, she had only just lost her husband. Anne did not want to risk an argument since she would no doubt need further information from Gemma as her career as an amateur detective progressed.

But as we left the flat, she assured me she would return at some point to inspect the tyres.

Anne had only been inside the Pilgrim's Rest three times before. She enjoyed having a social drink, but the former coaching inn with its beamed ceiling and dark wooden panelling would not be her choice of venue for an evening out.

However, she put this to the back of her mind when she paid landlord Bernard Couchman a visit with me at ten o'clock on the Friday morning.

'We're not open yet!' called a voice from the cellar as she pushed open the main door and stepped inside onto creaking floorboards. I remained outside, convinced the landlord would be more forthcoming when addressed by a lady on her own.

However, I kept my foot in the door to stop the light wind from blowing it shut and was able to hear the full conversation.

Mr Couchman, a balding, heavily-built man of fifty-four, clambered up the cellar steps to speak to Anne.

'We don't open till eleven, young lady,' he said as he hauled himself up into the bar.

'I didn't want a drink,' said Anne. 'I wanted a chat with you.'

'It's been a good few years since an attractive young lady like you said that to me!' he said.

'I'm making a few inquiries about a local family,' she said.

'Not press, are you?' he said. 'We've had them all here - Kentish Gazette, KMFM radio, the Sun, the Mirror. '

'No, I'm not from the press.'

‘They all want to know about Lucas Sharp and Joseph somebody,’ said Couchman, who was shabbily dressed in a crumpled white shirt and dark trousers. ‘As if I haven’t got enough to do.’

‘I just wondered if you knew the Bennett family?’

‘For what reason?’

Anne quickly needed to conjure up a convincing excuse as to why she was asking questions about his customers.

‘I’m making some discreet inquiries on behalf of a local solicitor,’ she said - aware this was only partly true. She was about to suggest it involved a criminal case, but Couchman for some reason jumped to the conclusion her inquiries concerned a matrimonial matter.

‘Oh, say no more. I’ve been divorced myself,’ he said. Anne was relieved he had made a wrong assumption and she did not rush to correct him.

‘Is this strictly between you and me?’ he asked.

‘Yes, of course.’

‘All right. What d’you want to know?’

‘I’ve heard Neil Bennett and his family are regular customers and just wanted to confirm that,’ she said.

‘Yes, I’ve known them all the time I’ve been landlord here, which is seven years.’

‘Do they come in on a Thursday night? I was wondering about Thursday of last week, November the fifth.’

‘Yes, they’re here every Thursday for quiz night.’

‘So they were here on Bonfire Night?’

‘That’s right. They never miss a quiz. They were here last night as well. They’re as regular as clockwork. You know all these teams have quirky names, don’t you? The Gordon Bennetts -- that’s what they call themselves. If you saw how fast the gin goes down when they're around, you'd know why.'

Anne smiled. 'Who were in the team here on November the fifth?'

'Well, there was Ryan and Judith Bennett - that's the father and mother. Then there was Neil. Let me think. Ian MacDonald, Shauna McCarthy and Ted Moreton, I think.'

'Has Rosie Bennett ever been part of the team?'

'Once or twice, but she's not really a drinker and doesn't like going in pubs. That's fair enough. Some of you girls are like that. But her friend Shauna's a keen quizzer. Ian's Rosie's ex-boyfriend. He's regarded as a friend of the family - there are no hard feelings.'

'Ted Moreton works at Finch & Davies, doesn't he?'

'You're very well informed, young lady. Yes. He's a pub regular who fills in when the Bennett team are short of quizzers.'

'Who's the quizmaster?'

'The role of master of ceremonies and quizmaster's one that falls to me.'

'You arrange the whole thing - you set the questions, who hand out the quiz papers?'

'Yes, with a little help from bar staff. It's good fun. You should come along. You'd enjoy yourself. You could sit up the front, next to me.'

'Thank you. I- I might come along some time. What time does the quiz begin?'

'We kick off at about half-past seven, but you've got to be here by about seven to make sure you get a table.'

'So the Bennetts were here that night at seven o'clock. What time did they leave?'

'They were here till about eleven o'clock, closing time.'

'Neil was definitely here with his family and friends?'

'Definitely. He had about six pints of lager, like he usually does. If you're interested, I might even have the quiz papers. It was only a week ago so I don't think I've thrown them out.'

He rummaged around behind the bar. Within a few minutes, he had found a stack of quiz sheets, which he placed on the bar counter.

'I've got the list of questions typed out as well. Here we are - the Gordon Bennetts. Ooh, they didn't do as well as they normally do. I don't know why, but Neil wasn't really on form that night. Perhaps he overdid the drinking. They only got eleven out of twenty. They're usually among the high scorers.

'Last night, Ian MacDonald couldn't make it, so another friend of the family joined them, a man called Chad who's staying with the Bennetts at the moment. They did much better, scoring eighteen. They just got pipped by the team known as Don't Upset The Apple Cart, who scored nineteen points.'

Anne asked: 'D'you mind if I take their sheet from Bonfire Night? I'd like to show my husband the kind of questions and answers that come up.'

'Here you are, young lady. Take their quiz sheet and here are the questions and all the correct answers. And when you come along to take part, don't worry about your husband. You can leave him at home! He wouldn't enjoy it.'

'Thank you very much,' said Anne. 'You've been very helpful.'

'Couchman's the name - Bernard Couchman. And you are?'

'I'm Anne,' she said. 'It's been nice to meet you.'

'It's been very nice meeting you, young lady,' he said. 'I thought you wanted to talk about the fight between Lucas Sharp and the migrant when you first came in.'

'You witnessed the fight?'

'I came in at the tail end of it,' he recalled. 'I heard the Eritrean man - I think his name's Joseph or something -- shouting in poor English: "You're a complete bastard." Excuse my French. Then Lucas, whom I knew quite well, said something like: "You should be at home, peasant boy, caring for your camels!" They traded blows and it was all over in seconds. Ted and one of the regulars pulled them apart. The Eritrean went off shouting: "Tell more lies and I kill you."'

'Sounds frightening.'

'Oh, it's the kind of thing you get used to in the pub game, young lady. Bye then. Nice to see you!'

23

As I drove Anne away from the pub, I couldn't resist teasing her a little.

'Why don't you come to my pub quiz, young lady! Come and sit on my knee, young lady!' I said, mocking Couchman's rich country accent.

'Stop it, Bob. We've work to do,' she snapped.

After leaving the Pilgrim's Rest, Anne wanted to call in at the farm. Her main intention was to speak to Kristina, but when we entered the pack-house we chanced upon Ted Moreton as he hurried towards the exit door with a clipboard.

'Hi, Mr Moreton,' she called out as he went to rush past her.

'Oh, hello. Sorry, I'm in a bit of a rush. We're all very sorry to hear about Yusuf. We'd never have expected it of him, but I suppose you never know.'

'I've promised to try to help Yusuf,' she said. 'Could I quickly ask you about the night Yusuf and Lucas were fighting. You were there, weren't you?'

'Yes, I had to break up the fight.'

'You go to the Pilgrim's a lot and I gather you were at the quiz on Bonfire Night?'

'Yes, that's right. '

'So you were with Neil Bennett?'

'I was on the other side of the table and didn't say much to him. I was talking to a guy called Ian all evening. But he was there all right. Why's that?'

Anne began floundering for an explanation.

'Oh, I just wanted to clear up a possible misunderstanding. That's all,' she said. Her claim appeared to lack logic. He looked at her in a way that told her he did not believe her.

'Anyway, nice to see you both again, but I've got to go,' he said, disappearing through the door into the yard.

As Anne looked round for Kristina, she received an urgent text message on her mobile phone from Janice Carslake, asking Anne to call her. Since she was preoccupied at the farm, she decided she would phone the solicitor later and she continued trying to find Kristina.

Eventually we spotted the Romanian's long black hair bobbing up and down behind some machinery.

'Kristina!' she called. The hard-working girl looked up, put down a container of apples and walked towards Anne.

'Hi Anne!' she said. 'Any news about Yusuf?'

'He's bearing up. Bob and I went to see him yesterday. He's fine. Look, I wanted to have a word with you.'

Kristina said: 'I'll just see if my supervisor can let me have a short break.'

Moments later she returned. 'Yes, I can have ten minutes. Shall we go to the caravan?'

The three of us left the pack-house and entered the caravan park.

'I just wondered if you caught that rat?' Anne asked.

'Yes,' said Kristina. 'But I threw it in the bin.'

'Is it possible to retrieve it? I'd like to take a photograph of it.'

'You want to take a photograph of a dead rat?'

'Yes, it's important. Also d'you still have the bottle of chloroform Yusuf obtained?'

''No, the police took it, but I've got the cardboard box it's coming in.'

'Could you bring that as well? I'd like to have the box and the rat in the same photograph.'

Kristina continued to look puzzled.

'The police say Yusuf used chloroform to knock Lucas out,' Anne explained. 'Yusuf says it was to kill the rat. If we have proof...'

'Oh I understand now,' said the girl, picking the rat out of the bin by its tail and collecting the box from the caravan.

Anne took out her camera. Then, as the rat swayed from side to side in the gentle breeze, she took a timed and dated photograph of the dead creature alongside the box that the chemical had been stored in. She made sure the easily-recognisable Finch & Davies building, a red-brick former farmhouse with three prominent chimneys stretching into the sky, appeared in the background.

When Anne returned from her visit to Sissenden, she received a second text message from Mrs Carslake, repeating the request for Anne to contact her.

Anne quickly called the practice, apologising profusely for the delay in responding. But she found the solicitor was furious with her. I listened in after switching on the phone's loud speaker.

'Didn't you realise Yusuf should have made an asylum claim?' Mrs Carslake demanded. 'Didn't you realise there's a question over his right to remain here?'

Anne had been totally unprepared for the lawyer's diatribe.

She tried for a minute or two to keep her temper. But eventually she had to react.

'We'd no idea he had no right to stay,' said Anne. 'We're not bloody immigration experts. He came to us as a lodger. As we got to know him, we realised we ought to contact the asylum screening unit in Croydon for him and sought out his status. We were going to call them at the beginning of October, but this was then overtaken by events.'

Gradually, the temperature of their heated exchange began to cool. Mrs Carslake was at least not threatening to withdraw her services. In fact, she made it clear she was still keen to proceed in defending our friend.

But she warned, whether he was prosecuted or not for the murder, it was important she made an asylum claim on his behalf. We were still rather surprised he had not done this already of his own volition. Perhaps it was Yusuf's ignorance of how the system works or perhaps he had applied some time before and been turned down. We simply did not know.

The solicitor told Anne: 'Eritrean nationals are usually fortunate in being able to gain refugee status because their country's been called the "North Korea of Africa." Conditions there can be harsh with arbitrary detention and torture. Human rights don't exist there.'

She added: 'Anyway, I'm sorry if I lost my temper earlier in the conversation, Mrs Shaw. I suppose part of the problem was I was annoyed after twice failing to reach you by phone.'

'I'm sorry as well,' said Anne. 'I should've called you back when I received the first message, but we were at the Finch & Davies farm. I've been working hard, Mrs Carslake. I've been collecting information about the case which I eventually aim to share with you.'

'That's good, so long as you don't cause any problems for the private detective I've hired myself to make inquiries. By the way, I think it's a little encouraging so many days have now passed and Mr Osman's not been charged. I think there's a good chance now they might let him go. Anyway, as I've just mentioned my private detective, I suppose there are a few other things I should tell you. We've traced Mrs Taylor's solicitors. In the event of Mrs Taylor's death, Lilac Cottage was to have been left to Lucas Sharp. He was her only nephew and she'd no nieces. Her sister Martina had a son years ago, but he was killed in a road crash.'

'So who inherits the cottage in the light of Sharp's death?'

'The will says, in the event of Lucas predeceasing her, the cottage will go to Lucas's wife, Gemma. In the event of Gemma's death, the cottage passes to the three remaining sisters equally - Andrea Sharp, who's Lucas's mother; Martina Moreton; and Sue Wickens.' There was a pause in the conversation.

Anne asked: 'Are you still there, Mrs Carslake?'

'Yes, dear. I was just looking for... ah, here we are. I'd a call earlier from Detective Sergeant Kirwan and I've found the note of the conversation. We've had an apology from the police. You know they suggested Osman killed another man with a bomb a few years ago? They admit making a mistake about that. It was another man with a similar name.'

'Oh, God!' said Anne. 'What blundering idiots!'

'He'd been asked to call me and explain how the murder investigation team made a dog's breakfast of it.'

'It doesn't give you much confidence in them, does it?' Anne concluded.

24

My wife could be very artful. I have learnt this to my cost on a few occasions. This skill of hers came to the fore in the next stage of her quest to prove Yusuf's innocence - finding out who had ordered and paid for the GPS tracking device sent to Finch & Davies.

We had learnt the model found attached to Lucas Sharp's car was a 'Little Snooper' device, which is sold by a company in Yorkshire.

Anne decided to use our home phone and speak to the firm's customer service department. During the conversation, she would claim the device had still not been delivered. Could they double-check to whom the item had been addressed? In that way, she hoped to bluff out of the firm the name of the person who had ordered it. She decided to put the landline call on speaker-phone. She then pressed the record button on her mobile phone's voice recorder, so she would have a full recording of the conversation.

With some trepidation, she dialled the number. Eventually, one of the staff answered, saying he would be only too happy to help. He apologised for the delivery problem.

'What's your name, love?' he asked with a strong Yorkshire accent.

'Sue Wickens. I'm from Finch & Davies in Sissenden, Kent,'

said Anne without hesitating. 'We ordered a tracking device about two weeks ago for our farm's technical department. Despite lengthy inquiries, we can't trace it.'

'Can you hold on? I'll check the computer,' the man said. After two minutes, he returned to the phone.

'Well, I can see the record of the order for Finch & Davies. It was ordered on October the second. Is that right?' he said.

'That's it!' exclaimed Anne with mounting excitement. 'It was ordered so we could monitor one of our lorries.'

'But we don't have the name Wickens here. Have you got the order number?'

'No, I'm afraid I haven't,' said Anne. There was a pause. 'It's on a file document I can't access at the moment,' she hastily added.

'Well, I'm not sure I'm allowed to give you any details. You could be anyone phoning, couldn't you?'

Anne mounted one last desperate attempt to trick the information out of him.

'Look, this is ridiculous!' she said, raising her voice. 'We have given your firm a lot of business over the years. We are very annoyed about this missing item. If you don't give me the delivery date right now and details of the order, I will recommend to the managing director that we take future business elsewhere.'

'Sorry, love,' the customer service assistant replied. 'Don't be hasty. There's no need to fly off the handle. I've got the details in front of me. Can I just ask how you believe the tracker was paid for?'

'Company credit card,' she said without stopping for breath.

'All right. I can tell you we sent an email giving a delivery date of October the thirteenth and someone signed for it with a squiggly signature on that date. On the address line it said: "For attention of Tech." That fits in with what you said, doesn't it? Tech Department. Oh, hang on. No, I'm misreading my colleague's writing. It's not Tech - it's Ted. Do you have someone on your staff called Ted?'

Anne retained her grip on the phone with her left hand, she told me later, but she waved her right fist in the air in triumph. She had made a giant leap forward in her hunt for the truth. So the device had been ordered by Ted Moreton!

'Are you still there?' said the man.

'Yes, that's right. It's my colleague Ted. I'll make further inquiries this end,' Anne declared. The Yorkshireman was still chatting away on the line.

'Sorry to have taken up your time,' Anne added. 'If there's still a problem, we'll call back. Thank you!'

Excited by this new discovery, she urged me to get the car started and we set off back to the farm. Ted Moreton sometimes went home early on a Friday. She hoped she would be in time to confront him before he left for the weekend.

As we travelled, she recognised our mission might be putting us at risk. Here we were, about to confront a man who was thought to have surreptitiously ordered the tracking device used to follow Lucas's car - probably used on the very night he was murdered. She was glad I was accompanying her. I suppose my presence gave her more confidence and made her feel safe.

Was Ted Moreton - who was one of Lucas Sharp's uncles through marriage -- involved in the murder in some way, we wondered? Although she had some personal fears, she knew she had to go on. She had to find out.

Anne discovered him in the pack-house, changing out of

his blue work overalls. Fortunately, none of the other staff were around and it appeared to be an appropriate moment to tackle him.

'It's young Anne!' he said by way of a greeting, unaware I was just outside the open door, eavesdropping. 'Twice in one day! You're starting to make me feel important. You've lucky. I was just off. What can I do for you this time?'

As I stood watching from the doorway, concerned for her, she told Moreton: 'I'm sorry to bother you again, but there's something else I'm mystified about.'

'Well, we can't have that. What is it?'

'I'll be straight with you, Mr Moreton. One of the police accusations is Yusuf took and used a GPS tracker that was delivered to the farm.'

'Yeah, I'm with you so far, Anne.'

'Well, we both know that's not true, don't we?'

We noticed the colour draining from Moreton's cheeks.

'I don't want my friend Yusuf being blamed for something he didn't do,' she persisted.

'All right. I'll come clean,' he said. 'I can see you know. Yes, it's true. I ordered the device. But it never came to me. I checked the post-room at the farm every day and never saw it. I phoned the company. They swore they'd sent it. I was going to phone again today, but never got round to it.'

'You never fixed it to Lucas's car?'

'No, I never laid my hands on the bloody thing, even though I paid for it. Why would I want to find out where Lucas was? I had his home address. He's only a short distance from me. I could see him any time.'

'Can I ask why you wanted a 'Little Snooper'?'

'You can ask, whether I'll tell you is a different matter.'

'And why involve the farm? Couldn't it have been sent to your home address?'

'All right. I admit it might seem a little fishy. Look, if I tell you, will you promise to keep it under your hat?'

'Of course.' He lowered his voice and his next words were lost to me. But Anne related to me later that, he claimed, he had ordered the device 'for personal reasons.'

He explained his marriage had entered a 'rocky patch.' He had wanted to 'keep tabs on someone.' Then their conversation became audible again.

I heard Anne say: 'Look, I'm not concerned about your personal circumstances. I just want to clear Yusuf's name. Did you tell anyone about the tracker?'

'I haven't mentioned it to anyone. Why would I? I never saw the bloody thing. Someone stole it from the post-room at the farm before I even knew it had arrived.'

'Why would someone take it?'

'Well, I suppose it's possible someone overheard me ordering it and was looking out for it. Or maybe someone spotted it and guessed what it was. It doesn't take a lot of guesswork if the sender is advertising on the packaging, using words like "tracking and surveillance," which these firms do.'

'Who's got access to the post-room?'

'In theory or in practice?' he said. 'In theory, only Sue Wickens, Yusuf and me.'

'But in practice?'

'All the world and his wife. Anyone going into the reception area could nick an item of mail. So could virtually any member of staff drifting about behind the counter.'

'That's not a very secure system. All right, well, thanks for trying to help.'

'You're welcome, young lady!' said Moreton. 'Don't forget -- silence is golden!'

25

Two pale, elderly faces peered out from the leaded light window of their home into the foggy night. A strange woman was knocking at their door.

One face belonged to an old lady dressed in a long, pink floral dress with a white cardigan haphazardly fastened at the front. The other face was that of her husband, who announced loudly: 'It's a small blonde woman in a fawn coat.'

His wife demanded: 'Well, go and see what she wants. Hope it's not the bloody press again.'

Joshua Tolhurst, who was seventy-eight, hobbled along the dim hallway to the glazed front door. As he turned on the outside lamp, he could distinguish through the misted pane the outline of the woman standing alone in the dark lane.

I had driven Anne to Chivingden so she could visit Jane Taylor's next door neighbours. She knew she had more chance of being admitted if she called upon them on her own, so I waited in the car a short distance away.

'What d'you want?' he demanded. An out-of-date neighbourhood watch sticker on the outside door frame indicated the householders were wary of strangers.

The retired financial services consultant had also ensured a security chain was in place.

'I'm inquiring about Mr Sharp's death,' Anne explained. 'I'm working for Carslake & Whitter, solicitors.'

'Have you got ID?' said Mr Tolhurst.

'Only my driving licence,' she said.

'What's she say?' came a voice from the living-room.

'She says she's only got her driving licence,' yelled Mr Tolhurst, as he stood, slightly trembling, in his brown cardigan and pale green trousers by the door.

'Tell her to push it through!' said the voice.

Anne held the letterbox in the door open with her left hand and passed the plastic licence through with her right hand. Her name was just legible to him.

Mr Tolhurst opened the door and handed back the licence.

'You can't be too careful these days,' he told her. 'You'd better come in.'

'My husband's outside. D'you mind if...'

'We can't have him hanging about outside in this weather, can we?' he replied.

Anne waved to me from the doorway and I quickly joined her. We then followed Mr Tolhurst along the hallway of the cottage, which was called Hunter's Moon.

'This is Anne Shaw, dear,' said Mr Tolhurst, introducing the visitor to his seventy-six-year-old wife. He turned to me. 'And you, sir?'

'I'm her husband, Bob. Pleased to meet you.'

'I'm fairly pleased as well,' he muttered.

'How can we help you, dear?' Bridget Tolhurst asked Anne.

'I'm carrying out research on poor Mr Sharp,' she replied.

'I guessed as much,' said Mrs Tolhurst, who was sitting with some knitting on a green three-seater settee in the oak-beamed living-room.

'You've had a few people here before me, I'm assuming?' said Anne.

'You're quite right, dear,' said the solemn-faced Mrs Tolhurst, who was clearly the one in charge in the marital relationship. 'We've had the police and all the papers. Anyway, what d'you want to know?'

Anne, who accepted an invitation to sit at the far end of the settee, asked: 'I'd like to know, if possible, what happened round here on Bonfire Night.'

'D'you want to tell her or shall I?' Mrs Tolhurst asked her husband as I joined Anne on the settee. 'You tell her, if you like.'

Mr Tolhurst, who had sat down in an armchair across the room, recalled: 'All the fireworks round here started at about half past five and they went on for hours. We've got a little dog, Mimi, so we had her in here with us. She gets frightened, you know. She's a chihuahua.

'Well, at about seven o'clock, I heard a car draw up outside. I recognised it as Lucas's. He often goes to Lilac Cottage. It belongs to our friend, his Aunt Jane. Anyway, it was a red estate car - don't ask me what make. Soon after that I was making tea in our kitchen when I noticed light coming from the kitchen next door.'

'From Lilac Cottage?' asked Anne.

'Yes. It was a flickering light. We've read in the local paper police believe a Catherine Wheel was set off in the kitchen - so we reckon that's what it must've been. Strange I know. They're meant for outside. Then a short time later there was this almighty bang.'

'It was like a car backfiring,' Mrs Tolhurst interjected.

'No, it was louder. It was like a gun going off. Boom, it

went. Mimi went mad. She was barking non-stop for a couple of minutes.'

'You didn't think to go next door and see if Lucas was all right?' Anne asked.

'Well, I'm sorry I didn't now,' he admitted. 'But the noise was immediately followed by a succession of rockets, which soared into the night sky from somewhere round here. We assumed maybe Lucas was having a few fireworks. We didn't know what to think.'

'He's seventy-eight, you know!' said Mrs Tolhurst.

'Yes, I'm seventy-eight. I know I don't look it, but I've got to think of my health. Anyway, you get bangs on Fireworks Night, don't you? We just thought Lucas was having a small party.'

'You didn't see anyone arrive or leave the cottage that evening apart from Lucas?' said Anne.

'No, except the fire brigade, obviously. They turned up very quick because they'd been on a job nearby. Jane was lucky. The whole place could've gone up. That's what the firemen said, wasn't it, dear?'

'Yes' Mrs Tolhurst confirmed. 'They told us it might be arson. Someone piled a load of dirty washing on the table next to the kitchen curtains. Then whoever it was set the whole lot on fire.' Anne mentioned to the couple that police believed an intruder had broken into the cottage at around seven pm.

'You didn't hear a pane of glass being smashed in the back door at about that time, did you?' she asked.

'No, dear,' said Mrs Tolhurst, picking up her knitting. 'As we've told you, there were lots of bangs and flashes that night. It's hard to tell them apart.'

Anne continued: 'And the intruder would've had to bang a

nail into the back wall to hold the Catherine Wheel.'

'We were in here, dear. We've got secondary double glazing. We didn't hear it,' Mrs Tolhurst said.

'I've just remembered something,' said her husband. 'I did hear someone ride by on a bike some time before seven. Is that of any use to you?'

'That's interesting. Any idea what kind of bike?'

'It sounded like a push bike, but I didn't see it, dear. It was just before seven. It was starting to get dark and my eyesight is not what it was. But my hearing's still OK. There was a sort of clattering. I knew it was a bike. And I can tell you something else - it had a squeaky wheel. Crying out for a drop of oil. I was putting some rubbish out. The sound stopped after a few seconds. I went back inside at that point because I was getting cold. There's a boy called Riley Craddock who lives round here. He's thirteen and he's always riding up and down the lane on his bike, so I just thought it might've been him. Maybe I should've mentioned it to the policeman.'

Anne was pleased. If the old man was correct in his assessment of the time when he heard the bicycle, that fitted in with her conclusion the killer had arrived by that means.

'All right. Thank you very much for your time,' said Anne.

'I'm afraid we haven't been of much help,' Mr Tolhurst told her. 'We feel very sorry for Jane. She loved that boy.'

'Is she still in hospital?' Anne asked.

'Yes, as far as we know,' said Mrs Tolhurst. 'This can't have helped her - knowing her nephew was killed in her own house.'

Anne replied: 'No, definitely not. Anyway, thanks once again. We can see ourselves out.'

After we drove back to Chasehurst, I left Anne to her own

devices and spent an hour in the company of Miles Benton, the landlord of the Merry Friar. I amused myself listening to the light-hearted banter he exchanges with his customers while slurping down a couple of pints of his finest ale.

Before venturing out into the cold November night, I had a quiet word with Miles. I needed to prise some information from him on Anne's behalf. I said: 'Miles, d'you recall seeing Gordon the roofer on Bonfire Night?'

'Gordon Knight?' he said. 'He was here all evening. We'd a few fireworks in the garden. He was lighting them.'

'OK, that clears that up then,' I said.

'Look, Bob. There's something I've been meaning to tell you. It's just I haven't seen you. You know your Anne was interested in the fireworks murder? Well, I was at a meeting of the local branch of the licensed victuallers. I was having a chat with some of the guys. There's been a bloke going round selling industrial fireworks on the cheap - the kind used for displays.'

'He's been going round the pubs?'

'Yes, trying to sell them to customers just before Bonfire Night. I gather he's sold a few.'

'Any idea which pubs?'

'I know two of them - the White Hart at New Heath and the Red Lion at Isley Green.'

'What did the man look like?'

'Generously built, like me,' said Miles. 'Over six foot. Athletic type. Uses the name Don.'

'That's his first name. I take it?'

'Search me. But here's how you contact him.' Miles handed me a small piece of paper with a mobile phone number on it. 'Don't mention you got this from me, by the way,' he added.

26

I returned from the Merry Friar to find Janice Carslake had phoned and wanted us to meet her at ten am the next day. There was a note of urgency in the lawyer's voice.

Anne could not wait to see her. I don't know why, but my wife thought the solicitor might have some good news for us. During the short time she had spent on her research, Anne had discovered several flaws in the police case. She could not believe our friend had been kept in custody for so long already. She was confident he would be released at any time.

I dropped Anne off outside the offices of Carslake and Whitter and drove off to find a parking space.

Anne was to be quickly disillusioned when she met the lawyer. Yusuf's plight now was even worse than before. We were stunned to hear that, the previous evening, he had been charged with Lucas Sharp's murder.

Mrs Carslake dropped the bombshell as soon as Anne walked through her office door.

'There's no easy way to tell you this. He's been charged with murder and will appear at Canterbury court on Monday after nine-thirty am,' she said.

Anne had to sit down at once. She shook her head several times. She found it hard to assimilate the appalling news.

'Why? I can't understand this at all?' said Anne. 'Have they received some additional information? You led me to believe he might be released.'

'Unfortunately, it's not turned out like that. I've heard on the police grapevine forensic tests on various items have come back with some important findings. Tiny fibres from the front of Mr Osman's coat passed onto the front of Mr Sharp's jacket, showing there was interaction between the two men. What's more, several fibres from the coat attached themselves to the rope used to bind Mr Sharp. The police seem to think it conclusive proof your friend was at Lilac Cottage when the murder was committed.'

As I joined Anne in the solicitor's office, my wife furiously denounced the police over their assumptions. She told Mrs Carslake: 'That's absolutely ridiculous. Of course, there were particles from the front of Yusuf's coat on the front of Lucas's jacket - they'd been involved in a punch-up at the pub. That's no evidence he went to the cottage. The main physical contact at the cottage happened when the murderer came up behind Lucas and forced chloroform into his nose and mouth. We know they must've struggled like that for several minutes. That's the time when any loose fibres would have been transferred. The forensic people should have examined the BACK of Lucas's jacket for DNA evidence - not the front.'

Mrs Carslake was clearly impressed by the logic of Anne's remarks and also by the impassioned way she expressed them.

'What you say has a ring of truth about it,' she said. 'Are you sure you've never worked for the police yourself or had legal training?'

'No, but I went to the School of Common Sense. It's a shame the police didn't get on the same course,' said Anne.

'But what about the rope?' Mrs Carslake asked. 'Some microscopic fibres from the coat were evidently found embedded in the rope that tied Mr Sharp to the chair. Surely the rope wasn't present during the fight in the gents' toilet, was it? So how d'you explain that?'

Anne paused for a moment. 'That's easy to explain as well,' she insisted. 'A few of the coat fibres which became lodged in Lucas's jacket in the pub fight must've dropped off the jacket and attached themselves to the rope when he was tied up.'

Mrs Carslake leaned back on her black leather armchair. She said: 'I'm not sure if that could've happened. What you're saying, in essence, is some fibres got onto Mr Sharp's jacket in the pub. When he was tied up, some of them left the jacket and got onto the rope. Is that what you're saying?'

'Yes.'

'I'll have to call a forensic expert and see if what you're suggesting is feasible. Meanwhile, I'd suggest you write a nice letter to Mr Osman with words of encouragement. As you can imagine, he's feeling at a very low ebb right now, since he was charged last night.'

Anne asked: 'Did he say anything after being charged?'

'He simply denied carrying out the murder. Will I see you at the court on Monday?'

'Definitely,' said Anne. Mrs Carslake then passed onto her some minor details about the case which she had gleaned from Sergeant Kirwan.

In return, Anne began to reveal some of her own findings.

'I'm not really meant to be working today, as it's Saturday,' said Mrs Carslake. 'But fire away, anyway.'

Anne explained how she had made casts of the bicycle tracks, which indicated the killer had used a mountain bike. Yusuf only used a road bike. Yusuf's explanation for the use of chloroform had been verified - a rat had been caught near the caravan. She showed the photograph she had taken of the rat. Ted Moreton had admitted ordering the tracking device, which he claims vanished from the farm. The effigy of Lucas Sharp was made by Kristina - not Yusuf - and it had been Kristina's idea, by sheer coincidence, to place a firework close to its head.

She added that we had just discovered a man had been selling dangerous fireworks round East Kent pubs - and Anne suspected the one that killed Sharp may have come from the same batch.

'My, my! You've been busy, Mrs Shaw,' said the solicitor. 'In due course, I'd like you to give me this evidence you've accumulated so I can study it in detail.'

'The plaster casts, the photographs and all the documents I've collected have all been stashed away in a desk at our home,' Anne explained. 'But since he's been charged, I'm going to redouble my efforts. There are other inquiries to be made. I'm determined to clear our friend's name, Mrs Carslake.'

'I can see that!' she said.

That weekend became one of the most dispiriting weekends I can recall. Anne spent much of the time crying. It was as if a telegram had only just arrived bringing news the Titanic had sunk or we had only just seen the headlines revealing a school in the Welsh village of Aberfan had been engulfed by a slurry tip.

In an effort to keep her mind occupied, Anne spent some of the time neatly filing in alphabetical order the documents and photographs she had acquired over the previous days.

She had begun to show how weak the evidence against Yusuf was proving. But it was gradually dawning upon her, as she had researched the various clues, none of the evidence pointed to any one individual being responsible for the murder instead.

This line of approach was not going to help free Yusuf. The only sure way of getting him released was to find the real killer, she thought. Only then would police be forced to drop their flawed case. Anne decided to take a fresh look at her list of suspects. This time she added some details beside each name:

Gemma Sharp: No alibi; eating beans on toast at home alone. Last person to see Sharp alive. Mrs Carslake says she'll inherit Lilac Cottage on Aunt Jane's death. Male suspect more likely.

Friend of Gemma Sharp: Alibi uncertain. Gemma has been visiting the Northgate area of the city, where she may have a secret lover. More information required.

Neil Bennett: Alibi: Couchman and Moreton vouch for him being at the quiz at Pilgrim's Rest.

Gordon Knight: Alibi: lighting fireworks in the Merry Friar pub garden.

She decided to add some fresh names to her list:

Ted Moreton: Alibi: Couchman vouches for him being at the quiz at Pilgrim's Rest.

Rosie Bennett: Alibi: Uncertain. Present at the scene of the fire at half-past seven; no evidence of her whereabouts at seven pm; claims to have received a phone call and visited school; claims not yet verified. Male suspect more likely.

Ian McDonald: Rosie's ex-boyfriend. Alibi: Couchman and Moreton vouch for him being at the quiz at Pilgrim's Rest.

Random killer: Possibility of Lucas Sharp being killed by burglar he disturbed.

27

It was a relief when the sun streamed through our bedroom window on Monday morning, giving hope the bright new day would bring us better fortune.

We feared our friend was about to be moved from his police station cell to a prison cell. But I tried to remain upbeat as I washed and dressed.

The national newspapers were describing the full horror of Lucas Sharp's murder for the first time. Previously, the police had been treating it as a suspicious death in a fire.

'Murder by firework' ran the banner headline in one red-top tabloid. The front page of a rival paper screamed: 'Murder by mortar,' while a third paper carried a news story inside headlined simply: 'Shell shock.' Kent and Essex Serious Crime Directorate received plaudits for the efficient way they had acted in the case and for arresting a suspect so swiftly.

Anne and I took a bus to the court because of the difficulty in finding a parking space in the city centre. Although the building does not open until eight-thirty am, we arrived half an hour early in order to be sure of securing seats in the public gallery.

It was just as well we did. The court may be an unattractive grey concrete building on a busy main road which could easily be mistaken for a disused supermarket. But dozens of people were falling over one another to get inside on that cold Monday morning in the middle of November.

We were among the first to pass through the entrance of the nondescript two-storey building, built in the 1970s on the site of an old brewery. After being searched, we found a seat at the back of the courtroom and waited for proceedings to begin.

A large crowd of people gathered outside in the hope of catching a glimpse of the man accused of the Lilac Cottage murder. Several other bystanders sitting beside us in the public gallery were there for a similar reason.

But the British courts work in a mysterious way. The magistrates insisted on following the schedule of cases that had been set out by the listings clerk.

We all had to sit through the case of a man who stole two sandwiches worth four pounds seventy pence from a corner shop. He was eventually ordered to carry out community service. We also had to watch as a motorist was banned from the roads for two years for drink-driving. Then came a succession of cases which were all adjourned.

During a break in proceedings when the lawyers had all left the courtroom, I noticed Prunella Ball waving to us from the press bench.

'You go and have a word with her,' said Anne. 'I don't feel up to it.'

I slipped out of the public gallery, entered the courtroom below and strolled over to the press bench, trying not to look too conspicuous.

'Hi, Prunella! You OK?'

'Yes, fine, Bob. I didn't realise you'd hired Janice Carslake to defend your friend. You know she's a well-known character in the courts, don't you? She's known to the guys in Kent CID as "Jangling Janice." DI Woods can't stand her. He always says : "We don't want that bloody Carslake woman here, jangling her bloody necklace and bracelets and cavorting round the court."'

'I can only think that must be sour grapes because she's found flaws in some of his cases,' I replied.

'Oh, there's no doubt about that,' Prunella agreed.

Finally, at around midday, Yusuf was called into the dock. He looked different - as though he had lost some weight. He was wearing a white T-shirt and brown trousers which we had not seen him in before. He glanced round at us and smiled. We tried to smile back. But this was difficult as it was upsetting to see him there, flanked on either side by a custody officer.

'Are you Yusuf Osman?' asked the court clerk, who was sitting just in front of the three magistrates. Janice Carslake was seated behind a long wooden desk a few feet in front of the dock. She turned and indicated with gestures he should stand up and confirm his name.

'Yes,' he said.

'Is your date of birth August the sixth 1993?'

'Yes.'

'What's your nationality?'

'I'm from Africa.'

'I have a note you're Eritrean. Is your address: The Caravan Park, Finch & Davies, Ashford Road, Sissenden?'

'Yes.'

'Yusuf Osman, you're charged with the offence of murder. The particulars of the offence are, on November the fifth, 2015 in Chivingden in the county of Kent, you did murder Lucas Arnold Sharp, contrary to common law. How d'you plead?'

Mrs Carslake was by now leaning over the dock, whispering to Yusuf. A few minutes passed.

'Come now, Mrs Carslake,' said the chairman of the bench, Michael Humphreys. 'This is taking a lot of unnecessary time. Does your client understand the charge?'

'Yes, he does, Your Worship,' she said.

'Then how does he plead?' asked Mr Humphreys, clearly becoming agitated.

Mrs Carslake stretched over so she could whisper in Yusuf's right ear.

'Not guilty!' he said loudly.

Mr Humphreys was a stern, red-faced man with grey hair and a beard who, for some reason, I guessed might be a farmer. He nodded towards each of his fellow JPs.

The court clerk, after ordering Yusuf to sit down, pointed out, in view of the seriousness of the charge, the case would be transferred to the crown court. Then a lawyer from the Crown Prosecution Service indicated police were opposing bail. Mrs Carslake confirmed she would not be applying for bail in any case.

The clerk's voice boomed out again across the courtroom.

'Mr Osman, please stand!' he said. 'Their worships are transferring your case to the crown court. D'you understand? Take the prisoner away.' Our friend glanced over his shoulder towards us. Then he disappeared from view into the bowels of the court.

Anne cried. I put my arm round her, trying to console her. I managed to say: 'We must redouble our efforts,' although I must admit I found it hard to articulate the words. It was an emotional moment.

Outside the courtroom, a few remaining defendants waited with their friends or relatives, eager to learn what fate might befall them. As we emerged from the building into the cold, fresh air, we were surprised to find a small throng of spectators had gathered.

They were waiting for Yusuf. We had learnt from Mrs Carslake he was likely to be held on remand at one of three prisons on the Isle of Sheppey. It appeared the dozens of onlookers wanted to watch the murder suspect being driven away.

We overheard murmurs. The Kentish man had been killed by a firework attached to his head. Where was the monster who had done this?

An hour later, Yusuf was brought out through a side door with a blanket over his upper body and bundled into the back of a prison van. At first, only a few eagle-eyed press photographers had noticed. They busily snapped away. Then the horde surged round the van. There were shouts of 'Murderer!' and 'Foreign scum!'

Three zealous bystanders began thumping upon the side of the van as five police officers - completely overwhelmed by the numbers -- tried to forge a way through the crowd for the driver.

I learned later among those who rushed forward were Rosie Bennett; a frequent companion of hers, Shauna McCarthy; and Chad Draxfield, a close friend of the Bennett family who was staying temporarily at Luke Bennett's house.

Police pulled them away from the van. The driver headed off towards Monastery Street with Rosie, Shauna and Chad in hot pursuit, along with four national press photographers.

Suddenly Chad, who was slim, six feet two inches tall,

covered in tattoos and wearing a grey shirt and black slacks, hurled a stone which struck the back of the van. A portly policeman, who witnessed the incident and took exception to this conduct, grabbed him by the arm.

I was too far away to hear exactly what was said, but I could see he was giving the stone-slinger a stern reprimand.

The near-riotous scenes only added to Anne's distress. We drove home with her vowing to find the real perpetrator of the crime while I began thinking of ways in which I could raise her from the state of melancholy into which, I feared, she was rapidly sinking.

However, Anne had greater strength than I had realised. Within a few hours, she had partly recovered from the depths of depression. She took on a determined attitude. She was not going to let an innocent man suffer injustice. In the black tunnel of despair there sometimes flickers a firefly of hope - and, in this case, it emerged in the form of the mobile phone number of a man who appeared to have a ready supply of illegal fireworks.

She suddenly remembered I had given her this phone number. She hatched a plan. She would phone it, pretending she had been tasked with arranging a fireworks display to celebrate a friend's birthday. Someone from the Red Lion at Isley Green had passed on the number, she would claim. Did he still have some rockets and mortars at reasonable prices?

She recorded the call. It was answered by the deep voice of a man with a Kentish accent. Yes, he had some fireworks left. 'They're mainly Category Three and I've got a couple which are Category Four,' he said. 'They're meant for displays. You need to have gone on a course to use the more powerful Category

Four ones.'

'That's all right. I've a friend who's been on a course and used to do displays for the council,' said Anne.

'All right. It's going to cost you a bit, but I've got some good stuff. You'll definitely want to buy from me. I won't give my address for obvious reasons. We can meet outside a pub, if you like. How about the City Tavern in Northgate? What time can you get there?'

Anne said: 'I'm free now. I can see you at five o'clock.'

'Good. Don't forget to bring your money.'

'What name shall I ask for?'

'You can call me Don.'

Two hours passed. The pedestrianised streets were still bustling with shoppers. Anne's bus took thirty-five minutes to reach the city centre. She just had time to walk across the city for the meeting.

The City Tavern was a popular student pub located at the junction of two streets. The hubbub of conversation could be heard over the sound of pop music.

Anne told me later she carefully chose to stand in a shop doorway twenty yards away. From there she had a clear view of the pub entrance. She waited for several minutes.

Eventually, just as the historic cathedral clock chimed five, a muscular man wearing a long black coat appeared on the pavement outside the tavern. He was holding a large, black plastic sack full of bulging items. Anne had been distracted for a moment by some passers-by. She did not notice the direction from which he had come. Perhaps he had been inside the pub, she told me.

The man appeared to be becoming impatient. He kept

looking at his watch. After more than five minutes, he must have decided the lady on the phone had changed her mind.

He walked slowly up the street in the direction of the ring road. Anne walked to the corner. She watched his every step.

After about a hundred yards, he crossed the street and continued walking. Anne followed him at a distance, trying not to look conspicuous in her fawn coat. She told me she could not recall a time when she had ever felt so nervous. She was worried at any moment he might turn round and spot her. She wished she had asked me to accompany her - just in case the man realised she was stalking him and became aggressive.

Finally, the man reached a block of flats, she told me. There was a short woman with long, brown hair standing outside wearing a dark-blue jacket. He spoke to her. He kissed her tenderly on the left cheek. He drew out some keys. He opened the door. Anne caught a glimpse of the woman's face. It was Gemma Sharp.

28

A week after Yusuf had been taken to Elmley Prison on the Isle of Sheppey as a remand prisoner, I was woken at eight o'clock by a knock on the door. I peered through the curtains into the garden below. It was the postman.

I at once assumed he had a package or parcel he had been unable to post through the letterbox. Slipping into a dressing gown, I came downstairs and answered the door.

'I'm Tom, your postman,' said the young man in Royal Mail uniform. 'You've got a letter from Yusuf.'

I thought this servant of the Royal Mail was being a little over-enthusiastic.

I said: 'Why didn't you push it through the letterbox?'

He replied: 'Well, I know he's a guest of Her Majesty at present and thought you'd want to receive his letter straight away.'

'How d'you know Yusuf?'

'I used to see him working in your garden in August and September. We always passed the time of day. Then, when he was put in charge of the post at Finch & Davies, I used to see him every day there. I was shocked when I heard he had been arrested. No one thinks he did it.'

'All right,' I said. 'Well, thank you for the letter. I'll let you know what he says later in the week.'

'If you would,' he added. 'Everyone at the farm is anxious for news. Please tell him Tom the postman sends his best wishes.' With that, I closed the door.

'He's got some cheek!' I thought. 'Perhaps he wants to update his Twitter account and be first with news of Yusuf's prison life.'

Anne had overheard the conversation. She came downstairs in her nightgown. She noticed that the letter, which was addressed to her, bore an Isle of Sheppey postmark.

She had visited the modern prison, built in 1992, a few days after Yusuf arrived there. She discovered from warders the jail had been designed for nine hundred and eighty-five men. Yet it housed more than one thousand two hundred. She had spent ten minutes talking to him across a table in a crowded room, but it seems he had been reluctant at that time to upset her by revealing the poor conditions in which he was being kept. He had spent most of the visit asking her about Fiesta and events at the farm.

She opened the letter eagerly and then read it out loud. This is what it said. I have tidied up the English where necessary:

> *'Dear Anne and Bob, I hope I'm finding both of you well. Life here continues to be the nightmare. The only happy moment since I arrived was your visit on Thursday, Anne.*
>
> *'I'm still sharing a small cell with an English guy called Lee. The cell is built for one person. There's two beds and not much room. I've not had much sleep. The food is horrible. The prisoners say we're on the Elmley Diet. I think this is the English humour. I'm hoping to be at Maths classes. The prison chaplain spoke to me. He said this would be good idea.*
>
> *'But the warders keep saying no staff. We stay locked in*

a lot of the time. Some days we're locked up twenty-three hours.

'I had association for two hours the other evening. This is when you mix with other prisoners on the block. A friend of Sam Tedros told me I was to be punished on Sam's orders.

'When I got back to my cell, my mattress had been set on fire. It was quickly put out. When I complain, a warder called Pete said I must have done it. I'm now sleeping on the floor. Inside the cell the smell of the burnt mattress is in the air. Lee says I'm lucky to sleep on a blanket on the floor because his mattress has bed bugs.

'I'm missing everyone so much. Please try to get me free. When I was in my country, I heard of the British justice, but I don't see the justice. I never was in the Lilac Cottage. Please help me to make people understand.

'Please say Hello to my Kristina and ask if she'll write. Also give Fiesta a cuddle from me. Your friend, Yusuf.'

We sat looking at each other for some seconds in stunned silence. I thought of remarking about how much his English had improved but decided this would not be the right moment to make such a comment.

I then thought about the terrible plight Yusuf was in. To my mind, it was shameful that he was facing such harsh conditions inside a British jail. Furthermore, it was disgraceful that, somehow or other, African criminals from Yusuf's past life were able to pursue their feud against him inside a British jail.

It was Anne who broke the silence. She said: 'My God! I can't believe people are treated like that in our prisons - especially remand prisoners, who are meant to be treated as innocent until found guilty. They are meant to have more rights, so God knows what sort of conditions the normal inmates are facing!'

'I don't know what to say,' I admitted. 'It's shocking, truly shocking!'

'It's all wrong, Bob. We have got to do something.'

'But there isn't much we can do,' I told her. Then, for some reason, she suddenly snapped.

'For God's sake, Bob. You just sit there, twiddling your pen and rustling the envelope. Can't you be more dynamic?'

'Don't have a go at me,' I retorted. 'I'm as shocked as you, but it's hard to see where we go from here.'

Anne continued: 'Yusuf shouldn't be having to sleep on the floor. It's inhuman. Bob. We have got to do something. How can these criminals operate INSIDE a prison?'

'Well, I suppose all we can do is take our complaints to Mrs Carslake,' I said. 'I mean, what are we paying her for, for Christ's sake? She should try and sort this out. Or we take up these complaints with the visitors' centre at Elmley.'

Anne replied: I've got a feeling we'd be banging our heads against a brick wall there.'

Anne appeared to calm down. She decided to follow my suggestion. She would raise the issue of Yusuf's prison ordeal with our solicitor.

As I drove to school, Anne took a bus into the city in order to see Mrs Carslake. She brought Yusuf's letter with her and thrust it in front of the lawyer.

'I'm afraid we've had lot of similar reports about the conditions inside some of the prisons,' Mrs Carslake told Anne. 'I'm not surprised to hear he's being forced to share a single cell and is being locked up for long periods. The prison reform groups have been trying to address this. But what's very alarming to me is some vendetta is being played out and someone's set fire to his mattress, forcing him to sleep on the floor.'

'Can anything be done about this?' Anne asked.

'Well, actually, yes, it can. I'm going to speak to the governor, whom I know privately. I believe I may be able to get this sorted out fairly quickly.'

However, despite Mrs Carslake promising her best intentions, nothing was done to ease our friend's prison ordeal. He remained sleeping on the floor of his cell. Sam Tedros's friend continued to intimidate him. Anne noticed on her next visit he looked pale and exhausted. Over the coming weeks, his health declined further.

29

That evening Anne sneaked up the concrete path beside Gemma Sharp's uncut front lawn. Instead of approaching the front door, she crept along the side of the house until her eyes rested upon her friend's mountain bike. I watched her from the warmth of the car.

Pulling a chrome torch from her pocket, she carefully examined the tread on the front tyre. It was similar in design to the pattern left in the mud at Lilac Cottage, but Anne was unsure whether it was an exact match.

She was wondering how she could take an impression of the tyre when she heard a sound behind her.

'Oh, it's you!' said Gemma.

'Sorry!' said Anne. 'I heard a tinkling sound as I reached your door. I thought I'd dropped some money.'

'If it's a two-pound coin, it's mine!' said Gemma. 'You didn't say you was coming round.'

'Bob and I were just passing,' said Anne. 'Can we come in for a cuppa? It's freezing cold out here.'

'Yes, of course,' replied Gemma, suddenly noticing me walking slowly up the path towards her. 'It's good to see you both.' We followed her into the ground-floor flat.

As we waited for our hostess to make tea in the kitchen, Anne was unsettled. She had been carrying out some research into the man who had promised to sell her the fireworks and who lived in a block of flats in Northgate. Earlier she had spent time in one of the libraries, examining the electoral roll to see who inhabited the ten flats.

She had eliminated from her inquiries all the female tenants and all the tenants with foreign names. She had been left with just two names -- Gregory Smith and Brandon Hill. She wanted to ask about Gemma's association with the fireworks man. She was uncertain how her friend would react.

After a few minutes, Gemma entered the living-room, where we had made ourselves comfortable on the beige settee.

'Just one sugar for me, Gem, and one for Bob, please,' Anne said. Her friend spooned in the sugar, stirred the steaming brews and handed each of us a cup and saucer.

'Can't beat a cup of tea!' said Gemma.

Anne decided to seize the moment and confront her friend directly.

'D'you know a man called Gregory or possibly Brandon?' she asked.

Gemma nearly dropped her drink. 'I know a Brandon. Why?' she asked.

'Bit of a long story,' said Anne. 'You know I'm looking into the murder? Well, someone's been going round local pubs, selling the kind of firework that killed Lucas.'

'What on earth are you talking about?'

'Look, I got a phone number given to me by a pub landlord for a man selling fireworks on the quiet. I phoned it and pretended to be interested in buying some. I arranged a rendezvous with the man outside the City Tavern on Monday evening. Then I watched to see who'd turn up. I followed him.

He went to some flats and I saw you meeting him.'

Suddenly Gemma's welcoming attitude was gone.

'I don't know what planet you're on, Anne,' she said. 'Brandon's a friend of mine, but he don't sell fireworks. He's a builder. It sounds like you've been snooping on me.'

'I haven't been snooping on you,' Anne insisted. 'I never expected you to turn up. Is Brandon a boyfriend, a relative or what?'

'It sounds to me like you've got your lines crossed somewhere,' said Gemma. 'Sounds like someone was playing a joke on you and gave you Brandon's phone number. Anyway, I've been thinking good and hard about what you've been up to. I'm not very happy about it.'

'What d'you mean?'

'Why're you trying to undermine the police case against this Osman character?' Gemma demanded. 'The inspector came round to see me. They seem to be doing their job properly. Why don't you trust them to get on with it?'

'Because sometimes in this world mistakes are made and the wrong people get accused. That's what's happened here.'

I interrupted Gemma to say: 'Gemma, Anne's only trying to help. She wants to make sure there isn't a miscarriage of justice.'

Gemma started to become agitated. 'I'll talk to the pair of you about justice, if you want. Doesn't Lucas deserve justice for the horrific way his life was cut short? Shouldn't you both be helping instead of hindering the police? Are you doing this because you're soft on refugees and think the country should be flooded with illegal immigrants?'

Anne stood up. 'I think perhaps we should be going,' she said. 'I'm sorry you see things that way. I just really wanted to ask if Brandon is a friend of yours or a relative?'

'You can mind your own bloody business!' our hostess yelled. 'I'm not telling you about Brandon. It's just between me and him. I don't need someone coming here and prying into my private affairs.' Anne walked into the hallway and opened the front door.

'I'm sorry, Gem,' she said.

'Yes, and I'm sorry too!' shouted Gemma, as Anne and I walked slowly away down the path.

A few days later, on Thursday the nineteenth of November, a horrifying incident happened at the farm. When Anne arrived to hold her class that evening, Kristina was absent. One of her Romanian friends explained why.

Ted Moreton, a man unaccustomed to running, had sprinted into the pack-house just after two pm that afternoon with a look of panic on his face. He had shouted: 'Kristina, come quick! Yusuf's caravan's on fire!'

A small number of Romanians and Bulgarians had been kept on at the farm. As the apple season had ended, they had been gradually switched to general husbandry work.

Moreton informed Kristina he had dialled 999 for the fire brigade, but the flames were quickly taking hold and there might be no caravan left if they waited for the fire crew.

Kristina and several of her Romanian friends ran to the caravan park, Anne was told.

As they feared, flames were appearing at the back of the caravan where Yusuf had been staying with three other farm-hands. Kristina had sometimes shared the sleeping quarters with Yusuf. Many of her personal belongings were inside.

The flames danced and flickered in the misty Kentish air,

sending a pall of black smoke into the winter sky.

Kristina's woman friend informed Anne that Kristina and two other workers knew where to find buckets. They each filled two from the water butt by the pack-house door. They then rushed with them towards the blaze.

While they ran, they met a man in a grey, hooded top and black trousers hurrying in the opposite direction.

Anne was told that, as they passed him, they fleetingly heard the words: 'This is for Yusuf!' spoken in a malicious voice. There was no time for anyone to chase after this man. All their attention was on stopping the blaze from taking hold, but their efforts were to no avail. They splashed the contents of their buckets onto the fierce flames. But the fire roared like a blacksmith's furnace, unleashing noxious fumes and ever more acrid smoke into the atmosphere. Within a few minutes, two fire engines from Kent Fire and Rescue Service arrived. But it was too late. The caravan was almost completely destroyed.

Kristina was seemingly left in tears. Colleagues tried to console her, but she could not be pacified. Some of her clothes and many of her treasured possessions had been devoured by the flames, along with those of Yusauf's three Romanian friends. The only comfort - if it could be so described -- was their passports and money had been safely locked away in a farm safe. Luckily for Yusuf, his belongings had either been placed in Anne's care or were being held at the prison.

Kristina is said to have told her fellow-labourers: 'This is all because Yusuf has bad friends. They want him to give them money or work for them. They're crazy! He's in prison. He can't do nothing. I sometimes wish Yusuf had never come here.'

‘You can’t mean that,’ said one of her friends, with his arm round her.

‘But I do!’ she screamed.

30

I must have fallen asleep while marking some history essays because I woke with a jolt. Some unexpected noise downstairs had roused me. I think it may have been the sound of Anne entering the cottage through the front door.

It was a quarter to ten in the evening. I had dozed off across my desk in an upstairs bedroom I used as a study. I could hear Anne moving about in the kitchen.

Poor, troubled Anne had returned from the farm. She looked exhausted. I found her slumped in an armchair in the living-room, staring. Her arms were hanging loosely by her side. Her handbag had been discarded on the floor.

'I've got a good idea who might've killed Lucas Sharp,' she said, turning her head towards me as I stood in the doorway.

'Who?' I asked.

'Gemma's been visiting a man named Brandon Hill - the man who was selling fireworks,' said Anne. 'I've been racking my brains. I don't like saying this about a friend, but I think Gemma may have killed her husband. Or Brandon might've done it without involving her. Or they might be in it together. But I just don't see how I can prove any of it.'

I walked into the room and sat on the settee. I told her: 'If Gemma and Brandon are in a relationship, that does question the strength of Gemma's marriage and provides a possible motive.'

Anne sighed. 'Oh, I don't know. It's so frustrating. I'm starting to feel I shouldn't have started all this. Maybe I should have left it to the police.'

I was disappointed to see she had become disillusioned again. I tried to encourage her.

'You've made great strides,' I said. 'Don't give up now. Perhaps you should look through all the paperwork again. You might find you've missed something.'

This suggestion appeared to revive her interest in the case slightly. She went upstairs to our study, where I had left a pile of history exercise books. First, she carefully put the school books in a pile on an empty shelf out of the way. Then she collected from a drawer the documents and photographs she had assembled during her week of research. She spread them out across the desk.

Half an hour passed. I was watching a television programme downstairs when I heard a noise upstairs. Anne must have had a sudden moment of inspiration, I thought.

She came rushing downstairs clutching the quiz sheets she had been given by Bernard Couchman, landlord of the Pilgrim's Rest.

'Who did we think had the strongest motive for killing Lucas right at the beginning?' she cried. 'Who did we think was the most likely candidate?'

'Rosie's Bennett's husband Neil was at the top of your original list of possible suspects, but we decided he had a cast-iron alibi,' I said, turning the volume down on the television.

'Well, look at this,' Anne said. 'On Bonfire Night, we were told by two people he was at the Pilgrim's Rest quiz as part of his family's team.'

'That's right. You mentioned they received a poor score when they're often one of the top teams.'

'OK. Well, how come they got a question about caving wrong? Surely if Neil had been there - one of the keenest cave explorers in the country - they would've got that question right?'

'Let's have a look!' I said.

Fortunately, Anne had kept the sheet of twenty answers the Gordon Bennetts team had given during the quiz night.

The fourteenth question asked: 'Underground potholers sometimes come across a tall, narrow passage formed by a stream eroding downwards. What do we call this passage above the water table - phreatic, vadose or littoral?' The team had written down 'phreatic.' But the correct answer should have been 'vadose,' according to the list of answers Bernard Couchman had given Anne.

I looked at the sheet in some confusion since I could not recall coming across any of the three words before.

'Don't you see?' she continued. 'If Neil Bennett had been taking part in the quiz, he would've known the correct answer immediately.'

'Perhaps he was at the bar when the question came up or in the toilets,' I suggested.

'But surely someone would've run to get him?'

'I see what you mean, but the fact remains the landlord and Lucas's uncle both confirmed he was there.'

Anne could not be dissuaded. She was convinced there was something odd about the make-up of the Bennett family team that night.

She began considering various possibilities. Were Couchman

and Moreton lying for some reason? Had someone bearing a resemblance to Neil Bennett taken his place? Did he perhaps have a brother who looked like him? Had he only been at the Pilgrim's Rest for part of the evening and been absent when the fourteenth question came up?

These options - and numerous others - were swirling round her head when we both went to bed. By the Friday morning, she had devised a plan. She would carry out research on the Bennett family.

Anne paid for a subscription to a genealogy website. She discovered Neil Bennett had been born in Chatham on June the twenty-eighth, 1977. His mother had been Judith Spillett before her marriage to Neil's father, Ryan Bennett, in 1976. Another child, Luke Bennett, was also born in 1977.

She decided to travel to Rochester, where Chatham birth records were kept, so she could obtain a copy of Neil Bennett's birth certificate - still unsure where this would lead her.

I took a bus to the school so Anne could have the car. It took her nearly an hour to drive to the register office, which was 33 miles away. Then she had to wait an hour for the document to be written.

She was glad she had taken the trouble. The certificate showed Neil Bennett was one of twins. As she had read online, he was born at Medway Hospital, Chatham on June the twenty-eighth, 1977. What was unusual was it stated the time of birth, which was "two thirty-six am." She asked the register office staff whether this held any significance as she had never seen a time of birth given on a certificate before. They told her this meant the child was a twin.

Anne immediately asked if the staff could provide her with

the other twin's birth certificate. After a further wait, they presented her with a certificate showing the birth of Luke Bennett at the same hospital twenty-seven minutes later.

We discussed the implications that evening when I got back from school.

'We all know about identical twins who've fooled people down the centuries,' said Anne. 'I wouldn't be surprised if Luke took his brother's place at the quiz that Thursday evening. If so, Neil's got no alibi. He would've been free to follow Lucas to Lilac Cottage.'

31

I was secretly pleased Anne was showing renewed interest in the mystery of Lucas Sharp's death. By becoming engrossed in this latest theory involving the Bennetts she was distracting herself from worrying about Yusuf. But I felt she was not being completely logical.

'Your idea about someone taking Neil Bennett's place would only work if they're identical twins - and we don't know that,' I told her. 'We've got to find out if they're so alike it often leads to confusion.'

'Yes, you're right,' said Anne. 'I could ask Ted Moreton at Finch & Davies, but I don't entirely trust him since I found out it was he who ordered the GPS tracker. Oh, I know - Jennifer Campbell. She'd know.'

'Who's Jennifer Campbell?' I asked.

'She's someone Gemma Sharp knows. She lives a few doors away from Rosie Bennett in Sturry and knows the family well. I know Jennifer vaguely myself. I went to primary school with her.'

'So you're planning to contact a woman out of the blue you haven't seen for twenty years, are you?' I said. 'Then you're going to say: 'Are Neil and Luke Bennett identical twins?''

'Well, it won't be quite like that,' said Anne.

'It's going to be an awkward conversation.'

'I know. But I can't see any other way of checking the brothers out - short of standing outside their house and watching them come in and out.'

'D'you know where their house is?' I asked.

'Yes, I checked the electoral roll for St Stephens. There's a Luke Bennett living at 41 Summoners Close. It seems Neil's staying with him after being thrown out of his own house by Rosie.'

'Well, all you can do is try Jennifer. If that fails, it's option two,' I said, switching on the television.

I am pleased to say Anne easily found the neighbour's phone number and her call to the woman was beneficial. Jennifer, whom Anne had remembered for her thin face and running skills, recalled Anne from their early school days. She was happy to hear from her. She found it a little strange to be asked whether the Bennett brothers were identical twins.

However, many people had asked her the same question over the years. She was glad to confirm they were indeed identical twins. Even their own parents, Ryan and Judith, had been confused by them at times.

Friends would have described Jennifer Campbell as a keen conversationalist; others might have used less kind words such as 'gossipmonger' or 'blabbermouth.' When she started talking, it was hard to stop her.

I could clearly hear the conversation because Anne turned on the speaker-phone switch on our landline phone. Jennifer told Anne how the twins' mother, Judith, had dressed them differently as children because even she found it hard to tell them apart.

'It was blue and green for Neil, while Luke tended to wear

red and yellow,' said thirty-two-year-old Jennifer. 'As they went through school, stories about the brothers passed into legend. They made fools of so many teachers.

'Once Neil won a prize for woodwork. He was skiving off, despite it being school prizegiving day. Luke went up to accept the prize. Many of the kids laughed because they could tell them apart, but the teachers couldn't. The staff were mystified by the laughter.

'There was a rumour going round Neil went for the interview that led to Luke getting his current job with Associated Carpets. Neil passed the interview with flying colours sixteen years ago, but he's never been back. Luke turned up for work in his place and he's held the position ever since.'

Anne interrupted to ask: 'What about Rosie? I hope she could tell the brothers apart.'

Jennifer continued: 'Luke twice went out with Rosie when Neil was unavailable. The story goes, on one occasion, Luke took her to the pictures. On another, they went stock-car racing. Rosie was totally shocked when she found out - but they didn't tell her till years later.' She was in full flow now.

'Rosie eventually learned how to tell them apart - Luke's got a mole behind his right ear. That was the only clue she had. Once she married Neil, she spent a lot of time checking behind his ear, I can tell you!'

'What about twin telepathy?' Anne asked. 'You know, they're meant to be able to transfer thoughts between themselves.'

'If it happened, they never spoke about it. But Neil made me laugh one day. I asked him about whether he had the same thoughts as his brother. He looked at me with a grin on his face. He said: "When Luke won £5,000 on the horses, I'd a sudden compelling urge to see him. Does that count?" They were always larking about. Life was never dull with them around. I was only thinking the other day...'

'Oh sorry, Jennifer. I've got to go,' said Anne, quickly thinking of an excuse to end the conversation. 'My other phone's going. But it's been lovely talking to you.

Bye.'

'Oh, well, goodbye. Lovely talking to you too,' said Jennifer.

Anne told me, if she had not brought the call to a halt at that point, she had a sense Jennifer Campbell could have talked about the Bennett twins for the rest of Friday evening.

Anyway, we now knew Neil Bennett's alibi for Bonfire Night was in tatters. His twin brother Luke, who had been adept at changing roles with Neil almost since the day they were born, had almost certainly taken his place in the quiz team.

So where had Neil Bennett been at the time his wife was preparing for a lovers' tryst with accounts supervisor Lucas Sharp? Where had he been at the moment Lucas was attacked and killed and Lilac Cottage set on fire? Anne was now more determined than ever to find out.

A short time after her conversation with Jennifer Campbell, she approached me in the living-room as I watched a comedy programme. I turned the volume right down. I could see she had a serious matter on her mind.

'Bob,' she said. 'I know what I must do now, and I'd like your help. I've got to get inside the house where Neil Bennett lives.'

I was lounging on our brown leather settee at the time. If I had not been so well ensconced, I fear I might have fallen off on hearing her suggestion.

'What?' I yelled.

'I've got to do it. We know the police have bungled the case. Someone's got to find out who the real killer is for Yusuf's sake. I've got to get inside that house to find evidence.'

We had managed to avoid any major arguments during our marriage, but it appeared we were about to break with tradition.

'I absolutely forbid it!' I said. 'I have my reputation as a teacher to think of. There must be some other way.'

I paused for a moment, staring down at the beige carpet.

'How about if you used a little subterfuge?' I suggested. 'For instance, you could make a badge and pretend to be a meter reader. You could come up with some genuine-looking ID. While pretending to read the meter, you could have a look round - "case the joint," as they say in America. Or you could talk your way in as some kind of door-to-door saleswoman - you know, offering some kind of bargain. I could make a phone call at the same time to distract them and that would give you a chance to snoop round.'

Anne smiled at me. 'Don't you think I've already considered all those options? I've estimated I'll need at least ten minutes to make a proper search. None of those options gives me enough time.'

'Here's another idea,' I said. 'I knock on the front door and pretend a child's ball's strayed into their garden. Of course, it helps if I've got a cute four-year-old child with a cheeky smile. They leave the front door open as we search the garden. Meanwhile you sneak in and look around.'

Anne shook her head. 'There are all sorts of problems with that. For one thing, I believe the houses in Summoners Close all have side alleys leading to the rear. The most likely outcome is you'll be directed along the side alley into the back garden. We won't even get a chance to get into the house. Another thing is both brothers could be at home. One might be distracted, but it's unlikely they'd both be. On top of which -- we don't have a cute four-year-old child with a cheeky smile.'

I acknowledged the wisdom of what she was saying. I calmed down a little. It occurred to me, provided I did not actually trespass in anyone's house myself and left that side of the operation to Anne, the consequences to my teaching career might not prove so severe.

'What kind of evidence are you expecting to find?' I asked.

'I won't know till I find it.'

'You must have a vague idea -- a box of fireworks, a bottle of chloroform, a mountain bike and some matches?'

'Well, I'm probably not going to find all that. But to find some of those items would help.'

'And how're you hoping to get inside?' I said with a hint of sarcasm creeping into my voice. 'Are you going to smash a window?'

'I haven't decided yet,' she said. 'I'm still working on my plan.'

Anne went into the kitchen to make some tea. I turned the volume up on the television quiz programme and tried to concentrate on it. It was not easy. I could not clear my mind of the rash suggestion she had made to enter the Bennett house.

The more I thought about it, the more I knew it would be a foolhardy enterprise. I comforted myself with the notion Anne had, twice before in our marriage, conjured up some zany ideas. They had been considered for a short time and then forgotten. I convinced myself the same would happen on this occasion.

32

In an attempt to raise Anne's spirits and dissuade her from any reckless course of action, I suggested we go shopping in Canterbury on the Saturday morning and buy her a new dress. I am sure she recognised at once this was a crafty ruse on my part. But the prospect of acquiring a new dress is nearly always a great temptation for a woman and she fell in line with my plan.

Just as we entered one of the department stores in the city centre, a strident greeting from the women's lingerie section -- the words 'Hi, Anne! Hi, Bob!' -- alerted us Prunella Ball had also gone on a shopping spree. The journalist, who was wearing a smart grey trouser-suit covered by her light-brown coat, rushed over and hugged Anne.

'Great to see you both!' she said. 'I've got to thank you for passing on that love letter from Rosie Bennett, Anne. Did you see my story in the Mirror? It made almost the whole of a page.'

'No, I missed that, Prue,' said Anne. 'Sorry!'

'Rosie Bennett was hopping mad. We had to contact her to give her a chance to comment and she went through the roof. She slammed the front door on me. She has written a furious letter to the editor.'

'Did you receive your birthday card from Anne?' I asked.

'Yes, it arrived last week. Thank you. I had a marvellous

birthday. I was taken to London as a special treat and my boyfriend bought me a diamond ring.'

'That's brilliant,' I said. 'My friend Miles was boasting in the pub the other day that his wife once asked him for "something with diamonds." He ended up buying her a pack of playing cards!'

Prunella smiled, but quickly changed the subject. She was eager to tell us of a new development. In a hushed voice, she revealed that the activities of Sam Tedros and Jaefer Beraki had come to the attention of Kent Police.

'DI Woods may have little time for your Janice Carslake, but he's got an intense aversion towards people traffickers and extortionists and when she informed him about what's been going on, he went straight into action,' Prunella told us. 'These two men are believed to run a gang from a car wash in Canterbury and are up to all sorts.'

Looking around her to ensure we were not being overheard, she went on: 'They've got a detective who's half British and half Romanian, and I gather he's gone undercover. Woods realises the gang have been threatening your friend Yusuf inside Elmley. They've also had a report from the fire service about suspected arson at Yusuf's farm caravan. I don't think it'll be long before those two thugs are caught.'

'That's good news,' said Anne. 'Yusuf will be relieved when I tell him. We're going to be seeing him later today.'

Anne's mood improved after I had parted with more than a hundred pounds for a black tulle fishtail evening dress in which she looked stunning. We then returned home and, after a quick lunch, we prepared for our journey to the Isle of Sheppey.

Anne was in some ways reluctant to go. Seeing Yusuf inside

a prison was a heart-breaking experience for her. However, she knew how much visits meant to prisoners. She told herself she could not let him down.

We brought with us some of Yusuf's clothing that had been left behind in the cottage, some magazines and sixty pounds in cash.

Then we set off in the Mondeo for the thirty-mile trip to Eastchurch. We crossed the bridge to the island in good time and arrived after around fifty minutes for our two pm visit.

As soon as we had parked the car, we gazed around at the prison buildings. It looked as if some crazy architect had set to work on a scheme to build dozens of interconnecting supermarket buildings behind high walls. Beyond the walls there were nothing but fields.

Anne had been here once before, but she stated the system never changed. We showed our driving licences at the reception desk, read out our booking reference number and signed in.

We were shown how to place the money in Yusuf's personal cash account. This would allow him to buy small luxuries from the warders. We left the bag of clothing with one of the prison officers. We had to place our mobile phones and Anne's handbag in a locker.

After being searched, a drug patrol dog approached and sniffed us along with other visitors in case any of us had fallen prey to temptation and brought drugs in.

As we were led into the visitors' hall by a burly warder, we suddenly became aware of a commotion at the far end of the room. We could see two warders grappling with an overweight man. He was shouting and screaming at a middle-aged male visitor.

'Don't worry,' said our escort. 'That's Vinnie. He's taken a sudden disliking to his visitor. We're having him transferred to a psychiatric hospital next week. We'll miss him. He's a bit of a character.'

Anne was not really listening. She was conscious of her growing excitement at seeing Yusuf again.

Finally, we saw him being escorted past groups of other inmates' friends and relatives. His head turned left and right in anticipation of seeing us. At last our three sets of eyes met. He gave us a smile that reminded me of his first smile when he emerged from beneath our motor-home. It began with a sparkle in his eyes, a wrinkling of his nose and then it spread across his face, ending with a widening of the mouth.

'Anne! Oh, Anne! It's nice for seeing you,' he said. 'And Bob. Nice for seeing you' as he was directed to a seat in front of a small square table. Anne took his hand and smiled broadly back. His pallor told us he was still unwell. He still appeared to be losing weight. He was normally clean-shaven, but now he had stubble on his face - a sign perhaps of self-neglect, I thought. A sign perhaps of a growing despondency.

As we sat down opposite him, he grinned and asked: 'Are there still foxgloves growing in the lane?'

'Yes, they were still flourishing when I last looked,' Anne laughed. 'How've you been these past few days? Are things any better?'

'I survive,' he said. 'I have new mattress, so I sleep better. The burning smell is no more. Anne, I have to go.'

For a brief moment, we misunderstood him. We thought he meant he was returning to his cell immediately.

'You're going?'

'No. I have to get free. A man is trying to kill me in here. He's called Mehari. He works for Tedros. He cuts me.'

He pulled up his dark-blue casual shirt - one of the shirts we had bought him in a charity shop three months earlier. We were at once appalled to see a slash wound running down his right neck and shoulder. 'A doctor give stitches,' he said.

We were horrified at this injury, although glad it was not readily visible.

'Didn't you report this to the staff?' Anne asked.

'Yes, but they don't care. They say: "What did you do to him?" They don't have time to look at prisoners' arguments. Anne, it's- how d'you say in English? - it's the jungle in here.' He then broke into tears as if he had been battling to control his emotions and was no longer able to sustain it. He bent forward over the table with his head in his hands. I had not seen him like this since his emotional outburst at our kitchen table when he first arrived in England.

'To be accused of a crime when I know nothing about it is very harsh,' he sobbed.

'I feel I've travelled across desert and sea to find new life. I've lost my best friend to the sea. I've tried to prove myself. But I'm to be cheated. My cellmate says I'll be found guilty and locked up for ever.'

'Don't be silly, Yusuf,' Anne begged him. 'I've got an idea who murdered Lucas. I believe I can find the proof. Just hold in there. You won't be locked up forever.'

'I'm in dark place,' Yusuf continued. 'I sometimes think my life isn't worth living.'

'Of course, it is,' I insisted. 'You've made such a success of your time in England. Keep your chin up. This won't be for long. Mrs Carslake's working her socks off for you. She's also using a private detective. You'll be out of here in no time.'

'I'm hoping, Bob. I'm hoping.' With glistening eyes, he asked: 'How's Fiesta?'

'He's fine,' said Anne. 'He brought a field mouse into the house two days ago. It was barely alive. I tried to catch Fiesta, but he ran away. I found the mouse later. It was dead.'

'Fiesta can be naughty,' Yusuf acknowledged. 'I miss him so much. I have his pictures on my wall. Kristina's been here.'

'Kristina's been to see you at last?'

'Yes, she came on Wednesday. She didn't stay long. She doesn't like me being in here. '

Something about these words took Anne by surprise. She asked Yusuf: 'Surely she doesn't doubt you?'

'She says I'm not guilty,' Yusuf said. 'But I can see in her eyes she's not certain. She's just a young girl from a poor Romanian family. She hasn't got much thought of the world.'

'You mean knowledge of the world.'

'Yes,' continued Yusuf. 'Knowledge of the world.'

Ann asked: 'Is she going to visit you again?'

'She said she would. Anne, I have this letter. I show it to you.'

Yusuf took a folded piece of paper from his pocket. One of the warders noticed his action and walked towards them, eyeing his every movement. He handed the letter to Anne. The warder approached them. He took the letter from Anne and glanced at it. It met with his approval. He handed it back to Anne without a word.

The letter, from Janice Carslake, simply informed Yusuf a preliminary hearing in front of a judge had been booked for November the thirtieth, which was in nine days' time.

'What's it meaning?' he asked.

'It means things are moving onto the next stage in the legal process,' said Anne, who had been reading books about court procedures. 'The lawyers meet at the Crown Court. You and Mrs Carslake'll be there. A timetable is agreed.'

'What does this mean -- a timetable?'

'It means times and dates are arranged. The prosecution and defence have to provide their evidence by a certain date. Try not to worry. This day, the last Monday in November, could be the day we get you freed.'

'I'm hoping, Anne,' he said. 'To go on - it's hard.'

33

It was five o'clock on Sunday evening. As we drove to Summoners Close on what I still regarded as a hare-brained venture, I noticed some families must have spent the weekend festooning their homes with Christmas lights.

Their colourful handiwork shone out from among the drab streets of modern red-brick houses built in the 1970s -- little havens of light amid the winter gloom.

After twenty-five minutes, we arrived near the Bennetts' home, number forty-one, an address we had found through a library search of the electoral roll. I parked a few yards away, round the corner in the next street.

The semi-detached house was deserted. No lights were on and no car was outside. It appeared we were in luck, if that is an appropriate word to use in the circumstances.

I asked myself: Are we going mad? We are planning to break into somebody's house because of an inkling one of two brothers may have murdered an accounts supervisor. Had we finally lost our minds?

I made it clear from the outset I would not be venturing inside myself. I had too much to lose - my job as a teacher, for one thing. My salary was our main means of financial support. If I lost that, through some madcap scheme, our lives could be ruined. However cowardly my attitude appeared, I was not prepared to trespass inside someone else's property. I was, though, prepared to keep watch outside for Anne.

Our first step was to ring the doorbell and check whether any occupant was inside the house. We walked the short distance to the white front door, past the small front garden laid to lawn. I pressed the doorbell. We waited for three minutes.

If anyone had come to the door, I would have used the excuse I believed a child's ball might have landed in their garden. The absence of any child at my side might have stretched the imagination of any householder, but it was the best possible answer I could devise. Fortunately, there appeared to be no one in.

Anne wondered whether people still kept a spare door key under a flowerpot or beneath the doormat. We checked, just in case, but it seems people don't do that anymore.

She did become excited though at spotting a mountain bike at the end of an alley by the side of the house. She ran down the passage and examined its tread under the light of a torch.

'Bob!' she said quietly. 'It looks like the same tyre pattern as at the cottage.' I ran after her. I had to agree. The front tyre appeared to have the same range of different-sized rubber nodules. There were also clear signs the bike had recently been ridden through mud. She wheeled it a few metres along the alley. It made a regular squeaking noise as if it urgently needed lubricating. We looked at each other without a word being spoken. We were instantly reminded of the words of old Mr Tolhurst.

'I've got to get in,' she whispered.

'Count me out. But I'll keep cavey,' I replied.

Anne, who was wearing a grey pullover and blue jeans, had thoughtfully planned for the event. She had brought with her, in a black council refuse sack: her torch; a three-foot-long stick with a wire loop attached to the end for opening windows; a pair of thick gloves; some clean plastic carrier bags in which to place any evidence; and a navy-blue beany hat to cover her head. She had also brought her mobile phone so I could alert her to anyone's sudden arrival.

'Did they teach you all this in the Girl Guides?' I joked.

'Don't make fun of me,' she said. 'This has just got to be done. Come on. No more talking.'

I waited by the front door in case anyone came while Anne walked round to the back of the house, looking for any open windows.

As she had half expected, a fanlight window on the ground floor at the rear of the house had been left partly open.

She hauled a green metal garden chair over to the window, clambered up and fully opened this fan light window. Then she deftly poked her stick through and caught the handle of the main side-hung casement window with the wire loop. She eased the handle up and then pulled the window back.

Her years of cycling and keep-fit classes had kept her body supple. With just a small amount of effort, Anne -- who was clutching her black bag -- was able to kneel on the worktop next to the sink, crawl through the opening and enter the kitchen.

As I watched through a side window, I noticed Anne put her bag down on the kitchen floor. Gingerly, by the light of the torch, she crept into the spacious living-room. She appeared unimpressed by its plain, light-green walls and beige, mottled carpet. The state of the room, she told me later, reminded her of a disorderly menswear department at the height of the January sales.

Coats and jackets were strewn all round the room. A mobile phone and a portable lantern rested on a coffee table, alongside books on caving and engineering projects. A pair of fell boots, a miniature stove, two caving helmets and a sleeping bag were stacked next to a folded wire caving ladder by the front door. A tablet computer, some DVDs and some magazines had been tossed onto the floral-patterned three-seater settee.

She stopped still in her tracks for a moment. We could hear the sound of a car approaching. Light from the vehicle flashed around the room. Were the Bennetts returning? She stood for what felt like an eternity behind the white net curtains in the bay window, peering out into the darkness. After a while, we realised the driver had parked and gone into another house in the close.

Returning to her task, she began to rummage through the pile by the door. Then, at last, she realised her efforts had not been in vain. Lying on the floor beside a pile of neatly-folded clothes she spotted somebody's right shoe. Examining it under the torchlight, she discovered it was a size twelve walking shoe made from brown leather. On its sole, trapped among the narrow grooves, there were tiny fragments of glass.

The left shoe, which she found beneath a black coat nearby, was free of fragments. She placed the first shoe in one of the carrier bags. Then she made an even more crucial discovery - a black cotton balaclava, folded in two among a batch of outdoor clothing, and a pair of black leather gloves.

'I immediately thought these could've been used at Lilac Cottage,' she told me later.

Anne was excited, but also nervous. She realised there might well be other important finds to be made. But, at the same time, she was concerned she should preserve the evidence she had already obtained.

She cautiously opened the front door in the hope of finding me. At first I was not to be seen. I had become worried I might be spotted by residents. When the neighbour had driven up, I had slipped behind some bushes. I was still there, partly concealed by leaves and branches, when Anne emerged.

After a few seconds, she saw me. She handed me two carrier bags - one containing the shoe and one with the balaclava and gloves.

'Put them in the car boot and then come back,' she whispered. 'I've got to go back in.'

Anne, who had left the front door ajar, then returned to the living-room, where she found several more pairs of footwear. But this time they were all size tens. These included two pairs of size ten leather boots - similar to fell boots - which Anne realised may have been used for caving. They most likely belonged to Neil Bennett, she thought. Even if they in fact belonged to Luke, she would have expected the twins to have similarly-sized feet.

The mystery was deepening. She then found Army correspondence relating to a British soldier who had been born in Dresden in 1984.

She spent a few minutes reading through the letters. Then headlights flashed around the room. Another car had arrived in the close. Anne's mobile phone rang out as I tried to warn her.

Anne knew it was time to leave. She quickly pocketed the letters and hurried to the door.

As she did so, a man parked a small silver Toyota Aygo directly outside. He stepped onto the pavement. He walked up the concrete path towards the house. It was Luke Bennett.

34

The home owner probably wondered at first whether his imagination was playing tricks. He had no doubt spotted rays of light from Anne's torch beam darting across his bay window.

Someone - an intruder - was inside his house. Any fear he might have had of the unknown was quickly overtaken by rage - anger that someone appeared to have breached his privacy and broken into his domain. He stormed up the path and was shocked to find his front door open. His fears were confirmed. Someone had got inside.

Then he spotted Anne in the shadows, standing in the living-room close to the door.

'Who in God's name are you?' he demanded.

'I can explain,' said Anne, who felt like a startled hare caught in the headlights of a car. 'I've just realised I'm in the wrong house. This is 41 Summoners Close, isn't it? I'm meant to be at 41 Summoners Gardens.'

She was unsure of the man's identity. She knew from all her research the house belonged to Luke Bennett. But his brother Neil also lived there - and the pair looked exactly alike. Was it Luke? Or was it Neil?

As I watched and listened in trepidation from my hiding place in the nearby bushes, events took an even more disastrous turn. Luke had noticed the pile of belongings next to the door had been disturbed.

'You've been going through our things!' he declared. As he stood defiantly in the doorway, blocking her exit, he took out his mobile phone and dialled 999.

When a distant voice asked which service he required, he announced: 'Police!' Seconds later his call was diverted to a police operator who asked the nature of his inquiry.

'I've been burgled. The woman's still here. If you come straight away, you'll catch her,' he said. 'Yes, 41 Summoners Close, St Stephens, Canterbury. No, Summoners Close. That's it. You will? Fine. Thank you.'

Anne moved towards the door in an effort to squeeze past him, but Luke, who I later discovered was normally an amiable man with a relaxed approach to life, was determined to use his body to impede any escape attempt by her.

'Oh no, you don't!' he said. 'You're staying here till the police arrive. I want this sorted out properly.'

I was in a quandary. Should I step forward and tackle him? I was averse to the use of violence, particularly after my unsuccessful brush with the law at the London march. Imaginary newspaper headlines flashed before me: 'Burglary plot teacher thumped homeowner' and 'Teacher on assault charge.' But my wife was in trouble. Surely I had a duty to assist her? I decided, if the police came, they would certainly find me. My best course of action was to emerge now, in my wife's time of need. I could attempt to divert Luke's attention, thereby giving Anne a possible chance to flee.

'Look, we can explain everything,' I said loudly, stepping out of the bushes. My idea of surprising him appeared to work to begin with. Luke spun round.

'So there's two of you. Yeah?' said Luke, who regularly trained in a gym. 'Don't try anything with me.'

I gesticulated for Anne to use this moment to escape, but it was no use. She tried to slip past him as he was momentarily distracted. But he soon recognised her game plan. He swiftly grabbed her arm as she tried to run and refused to let go.

'What are you looking for? We've got no money. I suppose you just take anything you can and sell it,' he sneered.

'Can I ask you a question?' she said out of the blue. 'Why was there a balaclava in your living-room?'

'A what?' he said. 'I don't know what you're talking about and, in any case, what bloody business is it of yours?'

The minutes passed. I tried to placate him. We had made a simple mistake. We were in the wrong street. If he let Anne go, we would apologise for our error and be on our way.

As I spoke, I could faintly hear the wail of a police siren in the distance. The sound drew nearer and nearer. Finally, a blue light could be seen among the neighbouring trees and houses. The police had arrived.

Two officers leaped out of their vehicle.

'Right, what's happening? Who called us?' asked the first constable to stride up the path.

'It was me,' said Luke.

'And your name, sir?'

'Luke Bennett. I live here. I caught these two breaking in,' said the aggrieved householder.

'Breaking in or trying to break in?'

'This woman was inside my house when I arrived. This man was hiding in the bushes.'

'If this guy would let go of me, I can explain,' Anne insisted. 'We're meant to be in Summoners Gardens. Right number, wrong street.'

'That's nonsense,' said Luke. 'She's been rummaging through my things.'

'I'm not sure there is a Summoners Gardens in Canterbury. How did you get inside anyway?' the officer demanded of Anne while he removed a notebook from his top pocket.

'It's a long story,' she replied.

'Sounds like one you'd better tell us down the station,' he said as he began taking notes with a pen. Turning to me, the officer asked: 'And what about you, sir?'

'I've travelled here with my wife. As she just told you, we've just made an honest mistake.'

The officer did not seem to believe our presence at the house had been the result of an error. After writing down our names, ages and address, he told us we were both under arrest on suspicion of having been involved in a burglary.

He said: 'You don't have to say anything. But it may harm your defence if you don't mention, when questioned, something which you later rely on in court. Anything you do say may be given in evidence.'

We both declined to comment. 'Right,' he said. As his pen quivered across a page in his notebook, he declared: 'Both suspects made no reply.'

A second police car roared into the close and parked nearby.

The constable announced: 'You two are coming with us. Mr Bennett, I'll take a brief statement from you, sir, if you don't mind.'

We were handcuffed, each led into separate cars and, after

the statement had been taken from Luke Bennett, we were driven away. I imagined the police wanted to keep us apart for good reason, although I could not appreciate why at the time. I suppose, if we were both in the same vehicle, we might make a joint escape attempt.

My feelings were at a low ebb. I had tried to dissuade Anne from going to the house. It gave me little satisfaction to say my attitude towards the whole venture had been vindicated.

Anne, however, did not share my misgivings. Even though we were under arrest, she believed the evening's work had been totally worthwhile. She believed she was close to unmasking the real killer of Lucas Sharp.

35

It had been without a doubt one of the worst times of my life. I had been forced to sleep on a bed in a draughty cell at Canterbury police station. It was possibly the same cell Yusuf had occupied just twelve days before. And for what? Because I had allowed my well-intentioned wife to set out on an ill-judged errand.

The more I considered our plight the more I regretted having agreed to it. However, Anne was not a woman who could be easily dissuaded from a course of action once she had set her heart upon it. I recalled someone had once told me you can't bring a drifting boat back to harbour till the storm abates. I had begun to understand what that meant.

The cell measured only eight feet by eleven feet. I had slept fitfully on the hard mattress with just a single pillow to rest my head upon. My neck was aching.

At an ungodly hour - it felt like five o'clock, but it might have been seven - the custody sergeant woke me. He came with a barely-passable breakfast of partly-burned sausages, cold beans and congealed egg, which I was able to wash down with a cup of coffee. I believe it was coffee. It may have been tea.

Then I spent some time pacing around the cell in my sloppy, unfastened shoes - the custody sergeant had removed my laces as well as my tie - wondering what would happen to us.

However, unknown to me, legal wheels had been set in motion. Janice Carslake had been notified of our arrests. As soon as she had realised the circumstances, she had contacted Sergeant Kirwan in CID. They were both, in their individual ways, battling to secure our release.

Just before ten am, I heard a knock on the hatch in my cell door. I looked up to see the smiling face of the custody sergeant.

'Mr Shaw,' he said. 'You've got a visitor.'

'Oh, if I'd known someone was coming, I'd have tidied up, put out the rubbish and vacuumed the carpet!' I said, trying to make light of my situation.

The rattle of bangles and a chunky necklace in the corridor outside heralded the arrival of Mrs Carslake, who was smartly dressed in a grey jacket, matching skirt and an orange blouse.

'Good morning, Mr Shaw,' she said, depositing a heavy, grey handbag upon the white, tiled floor. 'I'm so sorry to find you in this predicament. I've had a word with your wife...'

'How is she? Is she all right?' I asked anxiously.

'She's fine - bearing up, you might say. Obviously, full of regret she's put you through all this. I don't think you'll be kept here long. I've explained the situation to Sergeant Kirwan, whom I understand you know.'

'Yes, that's right.'

'The arresting officer was treating the matter of last night's suspected illegal entry of a house in Summoners Close as a criminal offence. He was considering burglary charges. However, I think I've persuaded them no major harm's been done. In fact, your wife appears to have secured some valuable evidence that may well help us get your friend Yusuf released.'

'We really hope so,' I said.

'Sergeant Kirwan is not here yet. But when he arrives, you and your wife will be summoned. We'll have a chat with the arresting officer. Hopefully, we can get this quickly resolved and get you both released.'

Mrs Carslake's words had a soothing effect. I had been concerned about the possibility of being charged with burglary or assisting in a burglary.

I had imagined in a dream during the night I was facing an interview in the headmaster's study. He was saying: 'Shaw, you've been charged with aiding and abetting a burglary.' I heard myself confessing: 'Yes sir.' Then the headmaster again: 'What're you alleged to have taken in this burglary?' I heard myself replying: 'A shoe and a pair of gloves.' Then I imagine a cackle of laughter as pupils outside heard the words and they spread like wildfire around the playground.

Mrs Carslake's voice brought me back to reality with a jolt.

'Mr Shaw,' she said. 'I'm sorry if a night in a police cell's been a shock for you, but don't worry. I don't think you'll remain here for long. I'll just go and have a chat with the officer now.'

'Thank you very much for all you've done,' I said. 'For both of us.'

Mrs Carslake was clearly a force to be reckoned with. In the coming hour, Anne and I were brought upstairs from our basement cells and reunited in an interview room on the first floor. I hugged Anne and kissed her on the cheek, reassuring her that I had suffered few ill-effects after my night as a guest of the Chief Constable.

Anne had spent the night in a similar condition to me, trying to sleep on an uncomfortable mattress. The constable who had arrested us informed us on the first floor landing there would be no further action, but warned us to be sure to keep within the law in future. We assured him we would. We were happy to accept his caution.

Then, at about ten am, Mrs Carslake led us into an interview room where Sergeant Kirwan was sitting behind a small table, staring out of a window at the car park below.

'Ah, Mr and Mrs Shaw!' he said. 'When I heard you'd been arrested, I thought: "Graham, what's happening to the world?" A more unlikely pair of burglars I'd find it hard to imagine now.'

We sat on two chairs facing the sergeant. Mrs Carslake took a seat next to him.

'Anyway, that's all finished with,' the sergeant went on. 'I have to say I was very impressed with the results of what you've found, Mrs Shaw. It turns the whole investigation on its head. Is it right, inside 41 Summoners Close, you found a balaclava, a shoe with glass embedded in the rubber sole, some black leather gloves and some Army letters?'

'That's right,' said Anne. 'Most of the items were among a pile of clothing, shoes and caving equipment by the front door.'

'I've heard brief details, but could you tell me again -- why did you visit Mr Bennett's house?'

'I've been playing detective because we know Yusuf Osman is innocent and we thought the police were on the wrong track. The most obvious suspect was Neil Bennett because his wife was having an affair with Lucas Sharp. I initially ruled him out as he appeared to have a reliable alibi. We were told he'd been at a pub quiz in front of dozens of people. But, a few days ago, I realised he couldn't have been at the quiz after all.'

'How's that now?'

'Because they'd a question about caving. His team gave the wrong answer. If he'd been there, they'd have got the answer right.'

Sergeant Kirwan still failed to grasp the full implication of what Anne was saying. I decided to try and help.

'Look, there are two Bennett brothers,' I said. 'They're identical twins. One of them, Neil, is one of Britain's most experienced potholers and cavers. The other twin, Luke, knows little about the subject.'

'Oh, I think I see what you mean now. So Luke the twin turns up to the quiz. Everyone thinks he's their normal team member. Neil's able to be at Lilac Cottage or somewhere and no one's any the wiser.'

'Precisely!' I said.

Then Anne took all three of us by surprise.

'I'm not entirely sure what role Neil Bennett had in the murder,' she stated.

'What d'you mean, Mrs Shaw?' asked the sergeant. 'I thought all your efforts pointed to him having the motive, the opportunity and the knowledge.'

'Oh, I'm certain he had some role in that terrible event,' she said. 'But I believe it may've been only a minor part. I believe he had an accomplice who played a much greater role. Most of the footwear I found in Summoners Close were size ten fell-boots and shoes. But the shoe that had the glass in the sole was a larger shoe - a size twelve. I'm convinced glass got into the sole when its owner walked around the kitchen at Lilac Cottage. I understand, of course, it could just be coincidence. The shoe could've trampled on broken glass somewhere else.'

'What you're saying may or may not be true, but it's an

interesting theory and our forensic people may well be able to tell whether the glass fragments come from the cottage,' said the sergeant. 'So, to sum up, you believe the killer has size twelve feet? And all we have got to do is find Cinderella?'

'In a manner of speaking, yes,' said Anne. 'The fell-boots, I imagine, were used by Neil Bennett when he went caving. So his feet are too small. As Neil and his brother are identical twins, we can assume their feet are a similar size.'

'They probably both take size tens. Yes, I can see where you're coming from,' the sergeant admitted. 'Sounds like we may well be looking for a big guy with size twelve feet who's got some kind of association with the Bennetts. Anyway, you've mentioned this key evidence. What I need to know is: where is it? When you were searched and rather unceremoniously thrown into the cells of Canterbury nick last night, you only had a handful of typed letters with you.'

'I locked the other things in the boot of our car,' I explained.

'So they're all in a place of safe-keeping?'

Anne nodded. 'Yes, provided our car is still where we left it. You see, I was concerned, if we were caught with these items, the brothers might've disposed of them or the police might've filed them away. That evidence is vital, as far as I'm concerned. We need it desperately to clear Yusuf's name.'

'Well, you're very resourceful, I have to say,' said the sergeant. 'Wouldn't you agree, Mrs Carslake?'

'Yes, I certainly would,' the lawyer said. 'Where's the car exactly?'

I explained how we had left the Mondeo in the next street to Summoners Close in St Stephens.

'Well, I think the next stage is for me to drive you back to your car,' said the sergeant. 'I need to take your evidence away and get our forensics team to give it the once over. I will also have to take statements from you both at some stage. I have to say you've done a brilliant job, Mrs Shaw. My inspector thought the case against Yusuf Osman was cut and dried, but since you became involved, everything's changed. When I mentioned to him what you'd done, he called you a "plucky lass." That from him is quite a compliment. But one thing we've been wondering about is how anyone can tell the twins apart?'

'Luke's got a small mole behind his right ear,' said Anne.

'Well, let's hope he doesn't go to hospital and have it surgically removed,' said the sergeant.

'I've also been doing some library research on the Bennett family. Six years ago, Neil Bennett was in a bad road accident. He was in hospital for three months and had to have a metal plate inserted in his leg. So one sure-fire way of telling which twin is which is to use one of those portable metal detectors. So your inspector might want you to take a metal detector with you when you visit him - to make sure you have the right man!'

'That's one of the craziest things I've ever heard,' said the sergeant. 'Anyway, we're not totally convinced by your suggestion that a second man was involved. The inspector appears to think Bennett acted alone. He thinks it's more likely the killer drove to the area himself, hid the vehicle, took the bike out of the boot and cycled for the remaining part of the journey. He can't think why the killer would involve another person. He says there's enough suspicion for us to pull Neil Bennett in and question him. You'll be pleased to know he also wants me to set the wheels in motion to get the charge against Mr Osman dropped.'

36

It was a cold, misty morning when we left the police station. Sergeant Kirwan drove us back to our car and we handed him the two carrier bags from the boot.

Then we set off on the four-mile journey home in the Mondeo. I had not expected temperatures to plunge so low - our barometer at home was struggling to reach four degrees Celsius. But Anne did not seem bothered by the cold. She was elated following her discoveries the previous evening.

After parking in the driveway shortly after eleven am, my first concern was to attend to the cat. Fiesta had entered the house through our new cat-flap and was parading round the kitchen with his tail twitching in anticipation of being fed.

'Shouldn't you contact the school?' Anne asked as I spooned cat-food into Fiesta's bowl.

'I've just phoned them and apologised for being held up this morning,' I said. 'They got another teacher to stand in, but I've got to go now. I'll see you later.'

While I began holding a series of History classes, Anne devoted the rest of the day to further research on the murder. She visited the library, returned to Summoners Close to make inquiries with the Bennetts' neighbours and spoke to a retired Army colonel whose name and details she had obtained from Prunella Ball.

She was delighted when, two days later, we received an early evening phone call from Sergeant Kirwan because, by then, she was convinced she knew the identity of the main perpetrator and wanted to pass her findings to the police.

Turning on the phone's loud speaker so I could overhear the conversation, Anne told him: 'You know Neil Bennett didn't kill Lucas Sharp, don't you?'

'How can you be so sure?' he asked.

'He doesn't take size twelve shoes and, in any case, he's not big enough,' she said. 'Someone else has been living at 41 Summoners Close apart from the twins -- a British soldier called Chad Draxfield. I have seen his identity tag. He is a muscular, heavily-tattooed man who's six feet four inches tall. Neil Bennett may be into outdoor pursuits, but he's shorter. He'd have had a struggle overpowering Lucas, but not this man.'

She revealed Draxfield was attached to a unit of the Royal Engineers. He had a record of distinguished service in Afghanistan. He had been granted Army leave for most of the month, but was due to return to his base at Catterick on November the twenty-seventh - just two days away.

'Do you understand he has spent his entire leave with the Bennetts?' said the sergeant.

'Yes, it looks that way, according to neighbours,' said Anne. 'It seems he's not married - well, if he is, he's divorced or separated. He appears the most likely person to have killed Lucas.'

The powerful words hit home with me. I remembered our visit to the remote Lilac Cottage. I thought of its white-washed walls and thick, brown thatch standing in its tranquil rural setting. The thought that an act of such savagery could have taken place there still filled me with alarm. Could her words be true? Could a soldier on leave have snuffed out the life of poor Lucas Sharp? Anne was still talking.

'The two men were drawn together through their love of extreme sports. Draxfield is an expert mountaineer and caver who has gone potholing all over Europe with Neil Bennett. The pair have gone white-water rafting in Africa and mountaineering in the Himalayas. On top of that, Draxfield is an expert in the use of explosives, according to his former commanding officer.'

'That's most useful, Mrs Shaw,' said the sergeant. 'I have made a note of all that. I have got a lot to tell you as well. Could I call round tomorrow evening to see you both?'

'Yes, that'll be fine, won't it, Bob?

'Will seven o'clock be convenient?'

'That should be ideal,' said Anne.

'By the way,' said the sergeant. 'Did you know Yusuf Osman is due in court next Monday? We won't be offering any evidence and the case is expected to be struck out.'

'That's fantastic news!' said Anne. 'Right, we'll see you tomorrow evening.'

Over the past three months, my attitude towards Sergeant Kirwan had gradually changed. On his first visit to our cottage, he had appeared quiet and reserved. He was suspicious of us and treated us coldly.

When he called round the following evening, three days after Neil Bennett's arrest, the tall, overweight sergeant appeared more sociable. He was less guarded in what he said. It was as if we had been finally accepted into his circle of trusted acquaintances.

I suppose he had been impressed by the way Anne had found the weak link in Neil Bennett's alibi and been so focussed on solving the mystery of Lilac Cottage.

'I promised to keep you updated,' he declared as I opened the front door. 'I'm a man of my word.'

'Would you like to come in? I can offer you tea, coffee -- or something stronger?' I said.

'Tea is fine now because I'm still on duty,' he replied. 'Oh, good evening, Mrs Shaw!' he said after noticing Anne pottering about in the kitchen.

I led our visitor into the living-room, where he at once made himself comfortable on our leather settee.

'You go into see him,' I whispered to Anne in the kitchen. 'I know it's you he really wants to see. I'll make the drinks.'

Five minutes later, we were sitting drinking tea with the sergeant as if we were old friends.

'Well, I've a lot to tell you,' he announced after we had exchanged pleasantries. 'First you'll be pleased to know Neil Bennett's been arrested. Of course, he's been flatly denying any connection with Lucas Sharp's death and implying we're a bunch of idiots.'

We were delighted to hear of the arrest. It was a sign all Anne's efforts were about to be rewarded. I was proud of her. She had followed her gut instinct that indicated the police were following the wrong path. She had worked hard, refused to compromise, taken chances and it all appeared to have paid off.

Over the next half hour, the sergeant described how Bennett had been rigorously interviewed at the city police station. He had personally taken charge of a raid on the Bennetts' house.

Most residents in quiet, tree-lined Summoners Close took no

notice as Sergeant Kirwan's light-blue Volkswagen Golf drew up outside the home, he told us.

His car was closely followed by two police cars containing two detective constables, a trainee detective and three uniformed constables. Four forensic officers inside two vans parked nearby moments later.

Here and there, he recalled curtains twitching as a few anxious householders strove to catch a glimpse of the unexpected visitors.

The sergeant had learnt Neil Bennett drove a battered, gold-coloured Toyota Land Cruiser. He was delighted to find one parked right outside the house.

It had crossed his mind he could have made his arrest at the Supremo Save supermarket where the suspect worked. But, after consulting with CID colleagues, he decided to wait until Bennett had returned home. He did not want to embarrass the man in front of his staff and customers. He needed him to be in a compliant, cooperative mood, if possible, in the hope of obtaining answers to some of the myriad of questions running through his mind.

Flanked by the two detective constables, the sergeant strode up the path to the front of the house and rang the bell. A man who opened the door confirmed at once he was Neil Bennett.

'At first he thought we were there to investigate the burglary,' he told us. 'But the smartly-dressed man's carefree manner soon vanished when we informed him he was under arrest. After our DC Tariq Khan cautioned him and mentioned he was suspected of having committed murder, he replied: "What murder? What are you talking about?" When we mentioned the name Lucas Sharp, he said : "Don't be so ridiculous. I was at the

Pilgrim's Rest all night. There were dozens of people with me."

'Then, just to make our job a little challenging, Luke Bennett suddenly walked up the garden path and DC Khan made some comment along the lines of: "Suddenly I'm seeing double." We had to bar Luke Bennett from going into his house as the boss had asked for the forensic team to give the place a thorough search.

'We drove Neil Bennett to the station, while DC Khan took a statement from the brother.'

Anne had been listening to every word, but she was desperate to ask a question.

'Sergeant, I was wondering if any results had come back from the forensic tests?' she said.

'I was just going to come onto that. You'll be pleased to know the pieces of glass found embedded in the shoe were definitely from the broken pane in the back door. They were composed of the same obscure glass pattern known in the glazing trade as stippolyte. In addition, tiny traces of a wheatgerm bread spilt on the kitchen floor in the cottage were also found ingrained in the sole.'

He explained the partial shoeprint scenes of crime officers had found in the mud just outside the cottage door appeared to have been created by exactly the same shoe.

The sergeant added that tread on the Bennetts' mountain bike matched the tracks discovered at the cottage.

'We've made checks with the Automatic Number Plate Recognition system for the twins' cars,' he said. 'Both vehicles were in the Sissenden area at the time of the murder, but we've no information about whether either car travelled to Chivingden.

'CCTV cameras picked up Neil's gold Toyota Land Cruiser when it was travelling in St Stephens, but we couldn't get a clear enough image of anyone inside.

'Then we interviewed Neil Bennett. He was a cool customer to begin with, I must say. He was represented by his solicitor, Rashid Chowdhury.

'Bennett confirmed he is separated from his wife. He said he returned from work on Bonfire Night just after six thirty. He drove to the Pilgrim's Rest at about seven and claimed he was there all evening. We were getting nowhere. He was denying everything. Then suddenly we had a breakthrough.'

37

Sergeant Kirwan's face broke into a smile as he recalled how the interview with Neil Bennett suddenly began to produce results.

He said : 'We began making headway when I asked him the names of his quiz team that evening. He could recall his parents and Ted Moreton being there but couldn't remember anyone else.

'Then Inspector Woods intervened to say: "How come you didn't know the answer to question fourteen?"

'He said: "What d'you mean, question fourteen? Am I expected to remember every single question asked that night in numerical order and the answers we gave?"

'I told him: "You'd remember this one all right. It concerned caving. You're a bit of an expert in that subject, aren't you?" He admitted he was. Then I pointed out the fourteenth question asked: "Underground potholers sometimes come across a tall, narrow passage formed by a stream eroding downwards. What do we call this passage above the water table - phreatic, vadose or littoral?"

'He snapped back at us: "That's right. The answer's vadose. What's the problem?" We then revealed the team gave the answer as "phreatic." He tried to deny it, which was ridiculous. The inspector really let rip at this point.

'He said: "We've got the quiz sheet filled in by your team. Your brother stood in for you at the quiz, didn't he? You were somewhere else, weren't you? We've had a long chat with Luke. Eventually he confirmed the pair of you swapped places. No one noticed because you're identical twins. It's the kind of prank the two of you have played all your lives."'

Anne interrupted to say: 'He must've been shaking in his boots then.'

'Yes, he asked for an adjournment at that point. He said he wanted to speak to his brief.'

'Had Luke Bennett really confessed to standing in for his brother?' Anne asked.

'No, we were bluffing,' said the sergeant. 'But it did the trick. Ten minutes later Neil Bennett and his solicitor resumed their seats. Then Mr Chowdhury told us words to the effect: "My client would like to make a statement. He'd like to inform you he's not been totally honest with you. The reason was he wanted to protect his child and try not to involve his family in view of his estrangement. The fact is you're correct, gentlemen, in your assumption Mr Bennett was not present at the quiz that night. He was with his son Mark, who's twelve. He took him for a drive to show him the fireworks." That was the gist of what the solicitor said.

'Well, we were making progress. But the inspector felt this statement didn't have the ring of truth about it. He looked Bennett directly in the eye and said: "We'd like you to tell us whereabouts you drove to show your son the fireworks?"

'Bennett looked uncomfortable. He looked towards his lawyer. He said: "I don't mind telling them. We drove to Herne Bay. There was a big display on. We watched from a distance."

The inspector said he didn't believe him because one of our detective constables had checked mobile phone records for the area. This had shown that, on Bonfire Night, the phones used by both Bennett brothers had been solely in the Sissenden area throughout the evening.

'All he could come up with was the lame excuse he might've left his phone with his brother. Then the inspector established both Bennett brothers take size ten shoes and questioned him about the brown size twelve shoe found at the house. Bennett couldn't explain why it was there and denied anyone else had been staying with them.

'The inspector was really beginning to lose his temper now. He warned Bennett: "You're accused of premeditated murder. Whichever precise charge you eventually face, it remains a fact the more you hold back, the worse it'll be for you in the long run." But Bennett still refused to cooperate and said simply: "No comment."

'We were becoming concerned the twelve hours we'd been granted to hold Bennett in custody were nearly up. But shortly afterwards some fresh information came in and we were able to convince our boss, Chief Superintendent John Packham, we deserved a twelve-hour extension.

'The new information came from Rosie Bennett's mother, Sandra Fagg, who confirmed her grandson Mark remained at Rosie's Sturry home for the whole evening on Bonfire Night.

'Our forensic team at the Bennetts' house yesterday afternoon found more military correspondence in the loft at Summoners Close. Along with the letters you found, Anne, they all referred to the soldier Chad Draxfield. Microscopic fibres from a military-style jacket in the loft matched fibres found on the back of Lucas Sharp's jacket.

'We knew we were on the home straight then. We even received a report from DC Khan by email which supported the information you gave us earlier in the week, Anne, about Lance Corporal Draxfield. Khan confirmed he's been fighting in Afghanistan as a member of the Royal Engineers.

'In a third interview, we questioned him about his links to Draxfield, along with details about the tyre tracks from Luke Bennett's bicycle.

'The inspector demanded: "Are you going to play around with us or tell us the truth? The maximum sentence for murder is life. Did you realise that? It means you won't see Mark and Cheryl growing up." This appeared to do the trick. The son's name had cropped up previously. But Bennett had not realised the inspector knew the name of his seven-year-old daughter. That came as a shock. Tears welled up in his eyes.

'He suddenly said : "I've been a fool. I must tell you the truth." His brief nearly fell off his chair. He tried to intervene, but Bennett said: "No, I can't take no more of this. I'll tell you what happened."'

'Did he explain his precise part in the murder?' asked Anne.

'Of course, he's tried to downplay his role. It appears he got Ted Moreton, an old family friend, to order the tracking device. They got it sent to Finch & Davies to avoid awkward questions. Neil attached it to Sharp's car and used it to trace him to the cottage.'

'Just as I thought. Ted Moreton lied to me,' said Anne. 'He told me he ordered the device for himself and the package was stolen from the post-room.'

The sergeant went on: 'We don't believe Moreton knew

the real reason Neil Bennett wanted the tracker. Anyway, this is how we now see it. On the night of the murder, Luke Bennett lent Neil and his friend Draxfield his mountain bike, which they put in the back of Neil's car. Neil drove Draxfield - known among the squaddies as 'Mad Chad' -- to the hamlet of Chivingden.

'When they reached the start of the lane called The Street, they unloaded the bike and Draxfield cycled off to the cottage. After the deed was done, Draxfield tried to destroy all evidence by setting fire to a pile of clothes. Luckily that failed, as you know, because the fire brigade were nearby and acted quickly. Afterwards he cycled back down the lane and met up with Bennett. They placed the bike back in the car and drove off.

'Neil denies Draxfield was his hitman. He claims he was against the whole scheme. He never thought Sharp would be killed. He thought he'd just be scared off.'

I interrupted to say: 'What? When they had a deadly firework, rope and a hammer?'

'Well, that's his story. He says it all got out of control and he's put all the blame on his friend Draxfield. He says the soldier was devoted to him and could see Neil was heartbroken at Rosie's affair. Draxfield was determined to get rid of Lucas. He couldn't purchase any explosives without causing suspicion, but managed to buy some industrial fireworks being sold by a man he met in a pub.

'He knew how deadly it would be if the shell was upside down. He also mastered how to write "Devil" in Tigrinyan and scratched the letters onto the car to cast blame on Osman. I'm pleased to say our Mr Bennett will be appearing in court next week charged with murder.'

Anne asked: 'Who d'you think made the mystery phone call to Rosie Bennett to delay her going to the cottage?'

'We think Draxfield made the call, putting on a foreign-sounding voice - possibly in another attempt to implicate the Eritrean. If Bennett had made the call, Rosie would've recognised the voice - however much he tried to disguise it.'

'Have you had any luck in finding Draxfield?' I asked.

'We're hoping to arrest him tomorrow in North Yorkshire,' the sergeant said. 'If we'd launched a nationwide manhunt with full publicity, we feared he could've gone to ground.'

'So he's no longer in Summoners Close?' I said.

'No. We're not exactly sure where he is right now.'

Anne declared: 'Bob - he's a caver, a mountaineer, a parachutist and a sailor. He's a survival expert, a woodsman, a denizen of the outdoors. No roof? Not a problem. He builds a shack in the woods. No heating? Not a problem. He lights a fire. No food? Not a problem. He kills a deer and roasts it on the fire.'

'Once again,' said the sergeant. 'You seem remarkably well-informed, Mrs Shaw.'

'I've just made a personal study of the man, sergeant,' she explained. 'I'm sure, if he says he's returning to Catterick tomorrow, he'll be there.'

'I know and, when we slap a pair of handcuffs over the big hands that wore those leather gloves we found, I'll be one happy man,' he said. 'But I'm not counting the chickens. As my mam used to say, you don't toot your trumpet while you're stirring the porridge.'

The sergeant then told us he also wanted to discuss a matter close to our hearts - the future of Yusuf.

'As you may know, there's a preliminary hearing booked for

next Monday. The inspector's decided to have a word with the Crown Prosecution Service and we plan to offer no evidence.'

'What does that mean precisely?' I said.

'It means the murder charge against Mr Osman is dropped and no further action will be taken. Of course, that doesn't mean he'll be released from custody. Because of his illegal status, I'd expect him to remain in prison for a time and then be transferred to a detention centre. '

'Is there no way he can be released?' asked Anne anxiously.

'Well, this is what I was coming to. Your Mrs Carslake should file an application for him to be granted leave to stay in Britain. Migrants from Mr Osman's country have more luck than most asylum seekers because the government there is one of the world's most repressive regimes and human rights abuses are rife.'

Anne assured him, early the following day, she would visit the solicitor and urge her to do all she could to allow Yusuf to stay in England.

'He might be given temporary leave to remain while his situation is considered by the Home Office,' the sergeant said. 'He might be allowed to live with yourselves for a while, providing he wears an electronic tag.'

'That would be tremendous, if that could be arranged,' said a delighted Anne.

'Well, no promises now. It's just my thoughts after dealing with a few of these migrant cases myself from time to time. Well, I'd better go, but it's been nice to see you people again.'

We both shook the sergeant's hand warmly.

'Thank you so much for coming and bringing us up to date,' I said. 'We definitely won't be tooting our trumpet until we know that squaddie is safely locked up!'

The sergeant walked slowly back to his car, deep in thought. I watched him from the window and waved as be began to drive away. We knew we had been lucky. We could have landed in court for harbouring Yusuf. We had acted foolishly, I suppose. Months later we discovered from Prunella Ball that, at one stage, the two detectives had been extremely suspicious of Anne and me.

But when their inquiries began into the Lilac Cottage case, the two officers found there was no time to worry about us. It was such a high-profile case their focus had been principally on solving the murder. Woods and Kirwan had also believed, according to Prunella, Yusuf might have conned us in the same way he had possibly conned many other people.

DI Woods had on one occasion claimed: 'I want to get the murder case done and dusted before we deal with the minor matters.' But there was more to it than that, Prunella insisted. She disclosed senior officers had later elected to take no action over our conduct to avoid any embarrassing revelations about police blunders emerging in court.

Over the weekend, Anne received a mobile phone call from Gemma Sharp. She told Anne: 'I want to apologise. I said things to you I should never have said. I accused you of trying to undermine the cops and prying into my personal life regarding Brandon, who genuinely is just an old friend. I'm sorry. I've been through a lot over the past four weeks. Could you forgive me?'

'Of course,' said Anne. 'I realise you've had a tough time.'

Gemma went on: 'I've heard the floozie's husband's been arrested over the murder, so it looks like the cops got the whole thing wrong. I should've trusted you in the first place when you spoke up for the immigrant. I hope we can be friends again.'

'Don't be silly! Of course, we're friends,' said Anne. 'I'll call round and see you and the children during the week, shall I?'

'Yes. That'd be nice. It'd be good to see you. It's a great relief for police to catch the bastard who killed my Lucas. I know he'd got his faults, but I never stopped loving him. He was a great father to my children. Even though William was his stepson, he treated him just the same as his own son, Richard. I really miss him, Anne.'

38

We arrived at the crown court in good time on the morning of Monday, November the thirtieth. It was a bitterly cold day, but neither of us was aware of the icy wind. This was expected to be a day of triumph, a day when all Anne's efforts would be rewarded. It was the day Yusuf was due to be acquitted of the murder.

However, we knew in advance it would be something of a hollow victory and our celebrations would be muted. Yusuf was to remain in custody because of his illegal status in our country. Mrs Carslake had already informed us of that.

I had not been to a crown court before. Canterbury's is a distinctive cathedral-like building on the city's edge with two impressive turquoise-coloured box windows at first floor level - one on either side of the towering glazed entrance. A giant roof gable overshadows the double doors, which are reached by a sweep of ten steps.

Inside the main courtroom, a Royal Coat of Arms hangs from the wall above the judge's bench. The clerk and lawyers sit at benches beneath him while the defendant sits in the "dock" - a glorified wooden box at the rear of the court.

Anne and I took our places in the public gallery at the side. We waved to Yusuf, who was sitting in the centre of the dock, flanked by two women custody officers. He looked more gaunt than before but managed to smile and wave back.

Just after ten o'clock, a court usher in a black gown entered through a side door. As judge Philip Hayden-Jones began to emerge in his wig and violet robe, the usher's voice boomed out: 'All rise. All persons having any business before my lords, the Queen's justices, in the jurisdiction of this court draw near and give your attendance. God save the Queen.'

'Good morning, Mr Pennycook!' said the judge as everyone sat down. Giles Pennycook, who represented the Crown Prosecution Service, rose to his feet. 'Good morning, Your Honour.'

'I gather this is going to be over fairly quickly this morning. Is that right?' said the judge, who appeared to be in a hurry to get away. Perhaps he had lined up a round of golf, I thought.

'Your Honour, yes.'

'Good.'

The clerk of the court ordered Yusuf to stand up.

'Yusuf Osman, you're charged with the offence of murder. The particulars of the offence are, on November the fifth, 2015 in Chivingden in the county of Kent, you did murder Lucas Arnold Sharp, contrary to common law. How d'you plead?'

Mrs Carslake, who was sitting on a bench close to Mr Pennycook, mouthed the words 'Not guilty' to him, which Yusuf repeated out loud.

'You may sit down,' said the clerk.

'I understand this is a pre-trial hearing to set out the prosecution's reasons for wanting to bring this defendant, Mr Osman, to trial; to discuss the serving of evidence; and to arrange various dates,' said the judge.

'Your Honour, yes,' said Mr Pennycook. 'I represent the

Crown in this case. My learned friend Mr Gideon Fanstone's here on behalf of the defence. Your Honour, I've to inform you the Crown will be offering no evidence against Mr Osman. The prosecution takes the view there's no merit in continuing the action against this defendant. Another man's made a confession and it's anticipated, in time, he'll be brought to trial. However, I've to inform the court Mr Osman's understood to be an illegal immigrant with no status in this country. We've been asked by the Home Office that he should be referred to them while inquiries continue.'

The judge asked: 'Is that right, Mr Fanstone?'

'Your Honour, yes. As I understand it, Mr Osman somehow arrived in Kent earlier this year and inquiries are being made as to his status. However, I've several testimonials I can submit to the court as to his excellent character.'

'Mr Fanstone, as you know, this is not the time nor the place to discuss these matters,' said the judge. 'My hands are tied. He must be handed over to the proper authorities. Mr Fanstone, I imagine you'll be making an application for travel costs?'

'Yes, Your Honour.'

After a discussion with the clerk, the judge agreed the costs should be reimbursed from central funds.

'Mr Osman!' said the judge. His deep voice echoed round the courtroom. Mrs Carslake gestured Yusuf should stand in the dock.

'Mr Osman, it's not in the public interest this case against you regarding the alleged offence of murder should be continued. However, you'll remain in custody and be placed under the authority of the Home Office. Is that understood? Yes?' Yusuf nodded in agreement before the judge added: 'That's all.'

The usher's voice bellowed out: 'Court rise!'

Everyone stood as the judge left the court. Yusuf was led back to the cells. Then the lawyers and court officials began to depart.

We encountered Mrs Carslake in the corridor outside. Anne was in tears.

'Come, come, Mrs Shaw,' the lawyer said, putting her arm round Anne's shoulders. 'You've done so well in getting that ridiculous murder charge dropped.'

'I just can't bear to think…' were the only words Anne managed to mumble. I helped out for her.

'She's upset he's still locked up,' I explained.

'I know,' said the lawyer. 'But I'm making progress on that score. We've made a proper asylum application and I don't believe he should be subject to what we lawyers call "administrative removal." I've been discussing the case with Sergeant Kirwan. We think he may be at high risk from Tedros's gang if he's returned to Eritrea. They pose a threat to his safety. There are also concerns about his human rights, were he to return. On top of that, his mother's believed to be in this country and that'll no doubt help his case.' She added : 'He'll be able to stay in England in detention while his asylum claim's processed.'

'Is there any chance at all he might be set free?' Anne asked.

'There's a small chance. While his application to remain is being considered, we might argue he should be allowed to remain with yourselves at your cottage - provided he keeps in regular touch with an immigration reporting centre.'

'That'd be wonderful!' said Anne.

'It's early days. But I'll do my best to see if we can achieve that,' Mrs Carslake added.

At daybreak the following morning the atmosphere was so cold I was reluctant to haul myself out of our soft, warm bed. But I had a great deal of school work to do after taking so many days off - exercise books to mark and lessons to plan.

I glanced through the partly-frosted window over the fields that lay on the other side of the lane. The barren ground appeared to have been covered with a light sprinkling of glistening white frost. The dark trees swayed gently in the distance, starkly pointing up into a grey, misty sky.

My sombre mood was interrupted at around ten am when we received an unexpected phone call from Prunella Ball. She had some encouraging news for us. She had discovered the two thugs who had been plaguing Yusuf's life for several weeks had been arrested in the city at the end of a successful police undercover operation.

'Graham Kirwan asked me to pass on his best wishes to you and to inform you his colleague, Detective Constable Alex Kovacs, has managed to con his way into Sam Tedros's gang,' she told me.

'They employed him at a car wash in Herne Bay and he managed to record on his mobile phone Tedros talking about blackmailing Yusuf and his girlfriend into handing them five hundred pounds as part of their cash demands.

'The secret recording picked up the African's voice clearly - including the gang master's chilling words: "You'd not believe the efforts we've gone to so as to make him see sense. We even had to set fire to his prison bed.'

I interrupted to say: 'So it was definitely Sam Tedros's gang behind that prison arson attack?'

'Yes,' said Prunella. 'The officer pretended he had collected some money from Kristina which he was going to give to Tedros and his henchman Jaefer Beraki. Then he got the two men to agree to meet him at their Canterbury car wash on the western side of the city at just after six pm. He switched his mobile phone to record mode underneath his clothing. Then he approached the two men. You've got to remember Kovacs is only five feet nine inches tall and Tedros towers over him.

'Well, Kovacs handed over a brown envelope containing money and Beraki began to open it. For a brief moment, it looked as if the whole operation might go wrong because suddenly the Goliath-like man grabbed Kovacs' shoulders and slammed him against the railings. He revealed they had been watching Kristina's caravan and he knew Kovacs had not visited her at the time he specified. They accused him of being connected with the police. Beraki then opened the packet and found it filled with folded pieces of plain, white paper.

'As Tedros released his grip upon Kovacs, the officer threw his hands in the air in a gesture of amazement as if to say: "I don't understand - the money should be there." This was the signal his police colleagues had been waiting for. Within seconds, a team of ten uniformed officers in peaked caps - including four firearms officers with Heckler and Koch submachine guns - ran from nearby hiding places.

'Beraki was quickly overpowered and handcuffed. But arresting Tedros proved a different matter. He had been taken wholly by surprise, but he was averse to the prospect of spending the rest of his evening in a police station cell.

'Two officers were punched by him before a sergeant authorised use of a Taser. A constable fired the 50,000-volt stun gun towards the eighteen-stone bodybuilder and Tedros merely winced. He was obliged to strike him with two more bursts of the Taser -- as well as pepper spray in the face -- before he and the sergeant were finally able to slap handcuffs on him.'

'Yusuf will be so relieved to know they've been caught,' I remarked. 'I'd think that detective constable must have been over the moon to see them arrested.'

'Yes, he's done well since he switched to Kent Police from the Met. I wouldn't be surprised if he's promoted soon,' said Prunella. 'Old Tedros is in big trouble. He was cautioned on the spot and faces a whole string of charges -- human trafficking, assault, supplying drugs, conspiracy to commit arson and demanding money with menaces.

'As he was about to be led away, he told Kovacs: "I'll make you pay for this. You see if I don't." Kovacs at once responded: "Thanks for that. We'll add threatening behaviour to the list."

39

A few days passed. Then, on the evening of Wednesday the second of December, as Anne and I sat watching television in our front room, we noticed Sergeant Kirwan's light-blue Volkswagen Golf pull up in the lane outside.

I went to open the door to the sergeant, who was wearing his customary brown suit and yellow tie. He was carrying a black briefcase.

'I thought I'd just bring you up to date with events,' he said, as I invited him into the living-room. Anne greeted him and turned the television down.

'Well, quite a lot's been happening,' he said, making himself comfortable on the settee. 'D'you know Catterick camp at all?'

When we both shook our heads, he said : 'It's a major Army base three miles south of Richmond in North Yorkshire. The place is like a concrete housing estate, vast and impersonal. Anyway, that's as maybe. I went up there on Friday to grab a word with our Mr Draxfield.'

'Did you arrest him? Has he admitted anything?' asked Anne, who was ebullient and eager to hear of any police progress on the case.

'Well, it was all very bizarre,' the sergeant admitted. 'I displayed my warrant card at the gates and my three constables and I were directed to the single storey guardroom. There we were kept waiting for fifteen minutes.

'Eventually, a major from the Royal Engineers came to see us - and we were in for a shock. He told us : "I'm awfully sorry, gentlemen. We don't seem to be able to locate Lance Corporal Draxfield. He may be off the base." I was furious. I had travelled nigh on three hundred miles.

'This major went on: "He was required to return to barracks last night. Someone here's seen him, but it's just we can't locate him at present." We went off to have a meal and came back three hours later, but there was still no sign of our Mr Draxfield.'

'D'you think the Army are trying to foil the investigation and are hiding him?' asked Anne.

'I doubt it. The Army are usually very helpful and want any possible criminal matters involving their squaddies sorted out quickly,' said the sergeant. 'But you can imagine how annoyed I was. So I called DI Woods in CID. He was even angrier than me, and he'd been stuck in the office. He said something like: "They've got a bloody cheek, those barrack-room boneheads!" Hang on! Perhaps I'd better not tell you the rest of what he said! I don't want to get myself into any bother.

'Anyway, he promised to have a word with the chief super and get back to me. It ended up with me and my three constables having a relaxing evening in Richmond and the next day I got called back to Canterbury. DI Woods said we should leave it to the local boys. He said something like: "I'm sure Draxfield will turn up in a day or two. When he does, the officers at Richmond are perfectly capable of making the arrest and you can travel back as soon as that happens."'

But Draxfield did not reappear at the barracks, the sergeant revealed. Richmond police made continual approaches concerning him, but all their inquiries were in vain.

'Then something really strange happened,' said the sergeant. 'The next morning, DI Woods received an email from Chief Superintendent Packham. He'd received a phone call from some civil servant in Whitehall about Lance Corporal Draxfield. The civil servant wanted to hold a meeting with the inspector and the chief super at the Ministry of Defence building up in town. He claimed he wanted to give them some background information about Draxfield but refused to go into any further details over the phone. Well, the DI immediately phoned Mr Packham and asked: "Why can't he travel down to Canterbury? I could meet him at the station." But this was out of the question, according to the chief super. He told the inspector: "Whatever he's got for us is hush-hush."

'Well, the meeting was held on Monday.' The sergeant rummaged around in his briefcase for a few seconds before producing a twelve-page typed document.

'This, Bob and Anne, is a print-out of an email the chief super sent to our Assistant Chief Constable following the meeting.'

'It looks very detailed,' I said. 'It's nearly half a book.'

'Yes, you're right. I'd better explain. The chief super was a court liaison officer early in his career and he's got excellent Pitman's shorthand - you know, the speed-writing system. Well, he took notes and this is a transcript of the entire meeting.'

As he handed the A4 document to Anne, who was sitting on a dining chair near the television, I asked: 'Sorry, Graham. I'm a bit confused. This is a transcript of a conversation your inspector and chief superintendent held while on a visit to the

Ministry of Defence earlier this week, is it?'

'That's right, Bob,' he confirmed. 'Unfortunately, I can't let you keep a copy. They're in short supply. It's been sent to the Assistant Chief Constable and he hasn't responded yet, so we don't know quite yet what is going to happen with this report. But the inspector thought it was only fair, in view of Anne's contribution to this case, you should both be allowed to glance at it.

'We may also be letting Gemma Sharp have sight of it eventually. No decision's been taken yet. Anyway, I can certainly give you a few minutes to have a quick look at it. Some of the wording's had to be redacted because of the Official Secrets Act.' The pair of us sat down together at the dining table to read through the report:

From: jdpackham@kentconstabulary.police.uk

To: acc@kentconstabulary.police.uk

Subject: MOD meeting re Lance Corporal Chad Draxfield.

Monday, November 30 11.00 GMT. Confidential.

Present at meeting : Chief Superintendent John Packham, Kent Constabulary; Detective Inspector Russell Woods, Kent Constabulary; Mr Wilberforce, Joint Corps Research Branch.

As chief superintendent (East Kent Division), I received a call from a verified MOD office phone number in Whitehall late on Friday, the twenty-seventh of November, in relation to a murder case. Officers from one of our murder investigation teams had expressed a wish to interview a Lance Corporal Chad Draxfield, who's part of a unit of the Royal Engineers based at Catterick Barracks in North Yorkshire. In this phone call, I was invited along with the senior officer in the case, Detective Inspector Russell Woods, to attend a meeting with a Mr Wilberforce at the MOD offices. I was given a code number to recite at the reception desk to facilitate our visit.

We arrived at the appointed time. After entering the eight-storey Ministry of Defence building, we showed our warrant cards and were searched before being invited to a large reception area. I approached the front desk and read out the code number I had been given in Friday's phone call.

Five minutes later, a girl whom I assumed came from the counter approached us and announced: 'If you'd like to take the lift to Minus Four, your host will be there to greet you.'

We travelled in the lift until we were four floors down. The door opened. There to meet us was a charming, elderly man, aged about seventy, in a grey suit and waistcoat. His hair was silvery grey. He had the chain from a pocket watch protruding from his waistcoat pocket. He had shiny black shoes and was holding a black walking stick with a carved handle. He declared: 'Gentlemen, I'm so glad you could come. My name's Wilberforce.'

He reached out to shake both our hands and we introduced ourselves.

'Pleased to meet you, gentlemen,' he said. 'If you follow me, we can go somewhere comfortable and have a quiet chat. My secretary's making tea and coffee. Which would you

prefer?' We both opted for coffee. Mr Wilberforce called out: 'Three coffees!' as he proceeded down the darkened corridor.

Finally, we came to a sumptuous meeting room on the left. The spacious room had high ceilings, false sash windows with long, beige curtains. It was lavishly furnished with a three-seater brown leather settee and two matching armchairs on a thick, light-green patterned carpet.

Mr Wilberforce put down his walking cane and took a seat behind a huge antique Victorian writing desk. A portrait of the Queen hung from the wall behind him alongside a colour photograph of Royal Marines raising the Union Jack at San Carlos in the Falklands on May, the twenty-first 1982.

As he invited us to sit on the settee, the inspector asked: 'May we ask who you are, sir?'

'My identity's immaterial,' he said rather sharply. 'Now gentlemen, I understand colleagues of yours have been making inquiries about a member of our special team, a certain lance corporal.'

The inspector said at once: 'Lance Corporal Chad Draxfield's wanted for the murder of a man in the Kent hamlet of Chivingden on November the fifth.'

There was a hint of indignation in his voice as he had had to make a journey to London and speak to a mysterious intermediary in order to progress his investigation.

'We don't call him by that name,' said our host. 'To us, he's known by the codename Rocksnake. Let me explain, gentlemen. I'm one of the founders of an intelligence branch of

the British Army that's known as the Joint Corps Research Branch. This is a covert military intelligence unit of the Army, part of the Intelligence Corps.

'It was established two years ago to collect intelligence regarding the jihadist groups ISIS and Al Qaeda. We recruit and run agents and informants. In addition, we operate within the realms of covert reconnaissance and counter-terrorism.'

The inspector was becoming agitated. He was perplexed as to why he was being given a lesson in modern military history when he simply wished to arrest a soldier and interview him about a murder.

'Excuse me,' the inspector said. 'I don't mean to be rude, but I've come here regarding a major murder inquiry. I need to talk to Mr Draxfield. Can you help us or not?'

I added: 'My colleague doesn't mean to be impolite, Mr Wilberforce. It's just we don't quite understand why you're telling us all this.' At that moment, a smartly-dressed young woman entered with a silver tray containing three cups of coffee and a silver sugar bowl.

Mr Wilberforce appeared to be a patient, sympathetic man. He handed round the elegant China cups and offered sugar to us.

'I quite understand your impatience, gentlemen,' he said. 'If you'll bear with me a moment longer, everything'll become clear. In the past few weeks, we've received disturbing information indicating the jihadist group ISIS, the so-called Islamic State, may be moving to the Tora Bora

mountains in eastern Afghanistan to establish a branch of their global terrorist network there.

'Until now, Taliban forces have been dominant in this region. But there are signs the leaders of ISIS are vying for control of this area, which includes vast cave complexes. They aim to set up a major new global terrorism centre in this inaccessible location. But what chills the bones, gentlemen, is they've been devising powerful new weapons that pose a threat to the West and they plan to store them there. It's vital for our defence we combat these efforts. Gentlemen, I know you've both signed the Official Secrets Act, so I trust I can speak to you in confidence about this?'

The pair of us nodded.

'Our way of life's taken centuries to create,' Mr Wilberforce continued. 'But evil forces are at work which could destroy it in a matter of a few years. We've established a special campaign, named Operation Benedict after the patron saint of cavers. It consists of an elite squad of British and American men and women with unique skills.

'Rocksnake as a person has a unique combination of talents. He's a survival expert and an explosives genius as well as being a proficient soldier. But it's his skills as a talented caver and experienced mountaineer that make him such a key member of this team. What's more, he knows this region like a mother knows her child. He played a key role in bombing the mountain hideout of one of Osama bin Laden's chiefs of staff when he was twenty-five.

'So you see, gentlemen, he's been seconded from the Royal Engineers to Operation Benedict. His presence is urgently

required to help flush the enemy out of the nooks and crannies of Tora Bora and eliminate them.'

The inspector interrupted to say: 'It all sounds like the SAS.'

Mr Wilberforce replied: 'We've some reciprocity with them. However, we tend to be involved in more long-term operations. The SAS are the celebrities. They're like the fire brigade of covert military operations. They get in and then get out. Our people tend to focus on special projects behind the scenes.'

He suddenly turned towards me.

'Chief Superintendent, I've noticed you've been writing away furiously.'

'Yes, sir,' I replied. 'I'm just taking a few notes to aid my memory for later.'

'OK. That's fine, provided, of course, it's solely for police purposes.'

'This isn't getting me any closer to interviewing my murder suspect,' the inspector complained. Then came a bombshell announcement from our host.

'Rocksnake is not in the country at the moment,' Mr Wilberforce revealed.

'What? He's left England already?'

'Yes, inspector. When your colleague Graham Kirwan called at the barracks in Catterick on Friday, he was already on his way to the airport. As we speak, he's in the Middle East.'

The inspector flew into a rage on hearing this. He took to his feet and began pacing up and down the carpet.

'My murder suspect was in Yorkshire on Friday,' he fumed. 'He should've been handed over to my man for questioning. Instead, the Army let him jump on a bloody plane!'

'Calm down, Russell!' I said loudly.

'With respect, sir, no, I won't calm down. The British Army are impeding an official police murder investigation!'

'I'm sorry you feel like that,' said Mr Wilberforce. 'I can sympathise. I really can. But Operation Benedict's essential for the survival of the Western world as we know it. Gentlemen, the future of our whole civilisation's at stake. You want me to put that at risk for the sake of a twopenny-halfpenny murder of which this man may or may not be guilty?'

The inspector, to my mind, became rather confrontational. He placed both his hands upon the desk and glared at Mr Wilberforce.

'I'm a police officer anxious to seek justice for the widow of this man who was maliciously killed. His widow's aged just thirty-two. She's been left with no income, no means of supporting herself. She's got two little boys - who are aged twelve and ten. What am I to tell her? "We've a good idea who slaughtered your husband, but the man's gone off caving in the Middle East and we're not allowed to chat to him about it?"'

Mr Wilberforce leaned back in his chair in a bid to avoid my colleague's angry stare.

'I can sympathise. I really can. The whole thing's really bad timing,' he said.

The inspector had not finished. He said: 'I'm fighting to see premeditated murder's adequately punished and the young widow, Gemma Sharp, and her two young children receive the justice they deserve - the British justice they've been led to expect. The British justice that's such a crucial part of the Western democracy and civilisation you're so eager to preserve.'

'Inspector Woods, there'll be no British justice without Operation Benedict. No British Parliament, no British monarchy, no British anything. This operation simply has to succeed. There's no question about it. We need Rocksnake to perform his tasks as only he knows how. Our freedom and our whole way of life won't survive unless his skills allow him and his colleagues to do their job unimpeded.

'After our operation is completed, however, the situation will be different. When he returns from this sensitive mission, you can slap him in your cell, interrogate him all you like and haul him up before a judge. If and when he returns to Britain, you of course will be free to question him. But I'm afraid not until then.'

'That's a helluva lot of good,' the inspector sneered. 'So justice must be put on hold - for weeks, for months! Who knows, for years! Don't the Sharp family have the right to some form of closure?'

I intervened at this point. 'Russell, you must calm down. Mr Wilberforce has tried to explain the situation as best he can. You must try and control your temper.'

'I should ask for one small favour,' said Mr Wilberforce, turning his attention to me. 'I understand you've got

some of Rocksnake's personal possessions. Of course, I realise some of them need to be retained by the police for evidential purposes. However, his Army letters and some ID were, it seems, removed from a house where he was staying. If we could have these returned to his barracks in Catterick, this would be much appreciated.'

The inspector had heard enough. He informed me afterwards, as far as he was concerned, our host's attitude smacked of audacity. Not only were the Army obstructing his investigation. They were seeking the return of the suspect's property.

'I think it's time to leave, John,' he said. 'I can't see we're going to achieve anything here.'

'I agree with you,' I said. 'We feel frustrated, but I think we've got to accept the suspect's abroad and cannot be contacted in any case. Thank you for your time, Mr Wilberforce.'

Our host accompanied us back to the lift, but the inspector refused to shake the old man's hand. 'This won't be the end of the matter,' my colleague declared.

'Everything I've discussed with you is, of course, confidential, gentlemen,' said Mr Wilberforce. 'I trust it'll remain that way.'

'You have my word,' I said as our meeting with Mr Wilberforce came to an end. I confirmed that the information would be restricted and released only on a need-to-know basis. J.D. Packha m, Chief Superintendent.

After we had both finished reading the report, I handed it back to the sergeant.

'So it looks as if you've got to play a waiting game,' I told him. 'Sadly, there's nothing you can do - short of sending a team of officers into that hostile region with a map, a compass and a pair of handcuffs.'

'And what would be the point of that?' the sergeant replied. 'It would be like digging for a lone turnip in a minefield. You're right. It's a waiting game. But make no mistake, he'll turn up one day and he'll be brought to justice.'

Anne intervened to say: 'I'm glad the police are thinking of letting Gemma Sharp see this report and know about the efforts that have been made to trace this man. She's finding it very hard to cope.'

The sergeant placed the report back inside his briefcase and stood up, as though he was preparing to leave.

'There's one more thing I need to tell you,' he said. 'When the two officers returned to police headquarters, the first thing the inspector did was to inform me that Draxfield was, regrettably, on a clandestine mission overseas. He said : "He's in a remote area and can't be reached." He was so angry that, at this moment, he didn't reveal any of the confidential information received from the mysterious Mr Wilberforce.

'But, as part of my inquiries, I had need to speak to Draxfield's parents. So later in the day I asked if the inspector could assist me in any way by obtaining information about them. The inspector duly called the Ministry of Defence.

'"Could I speak to your Mr Wilberforce, please?" he asked. The female operator replied: "I'm afraid I've no one of that name here. Would you like to go through to the Reaper Force?"

'The inspector told her: "No, it's definitely Wilberforce, Operation Benedict," and the girl goes: "No, sir, sorry. I've never heard of him or Operation Benedict. Would you like to go through to inquiries?" You can imagine how totally bewildered he must've felt. He could hardly speak. He just said: "No, it's OK" and put the phone down.

'And then last night he made another startling discovery. He was browsing the internet and spotted an online report about the Whitehall building in which he and the chief superintendent had travelled in the lift four floors down. It was stated, officially, the building had only three levels in the basement.'

EPILOGUE

Nine months have now passed since those memorable events in our lives. Much has happened over that time.

Yusuf, still gaunt and frail, was finally released from detention on condition he resided with Anne and me at the cottage. He has to report regularly to an immigration centre as his application to stay is still being considered by the Home Office. He is also having to wear an electronic tag. Anne was deliriously happy at this outcome, although we discovered he will be unable to work officially until his status is finally established.

I am not sure how Janice Carslake achieved this. She is the kind of lawyer who succeeds while most others fail. She had argued it would breach his human rights if he were to be sent back to Eritrea as his life would be at risk.

He is safe -- at least for the moment -- from Sam Tedros, who is currently serving a five-year prison sentence after being convicted of various crimes.

A huge party was held in Anne's classroom at the farm in August to mark Yusuf's twenty-fourth birthday. The event contrasted sharply with the simple celebration Anne and I had organised with cupcakes and beer for his previous birthday when he was new to us and insisted on no fuss. Kristina was among the party guests, although for the moment she has ended her relationship with him. Sue Wickens, Ted Moreton and dozens of Yusuf's fellow-workers were also present, along with Mrs Carslake, Anne and me.

Anne made a speech in which she thanked everyone who had supported the campaign to prove Yusuf's innocence. She invited all those assembled to join in a toast to his future. Secretly, she had told me, after her success in finding the killer of Lucas Sharp, her next quest would be to find Yusuf's mother and reunite the pair.

After the partygoers' clinked their glasses together, a Romanian band began to play traditional folk music in the yard outside - two fiddlers and an accordion player. They were ably supported by Kristina on tambourine.

I turned towards Anne, who looked alluring in a sleeveless light-blue summer dress. 'Shall we?' I said.

I took her hand. We danced. We swayed. We shook our hips in time to the music as other farmhands followed our lead and took to the tarmac dance floor.

'I really love you, Mrs Shaw,' I whispered. 'You've been so brilliant.'

'Have I?' she replied, kissing my right cheek. 'I don't suppose I'm too bad for an out-of-work librarian on the wrong side of thirty. You scrub up quite nicely yourself, Mr Shaw - in a good light.'

But, as the band launched into their second tune, I was shocked to see the guest of honour had slumped to the ground. Sue Wickens and I rushed to Yusuf's side. Sue, who had been trained in first aid, found Yusuf - who had only returned to live with us a short time earlier -- was conscious, but suffering from a shortness of breath. His skin was cold and he was complaining of chest pains.

Anne and I drove him to Ashford Hospital, where he was

admitted for blood tests. The following day doctors revealed he was suffering from anaemia - a deficiency in the amount of red blood cells in the body. The condition affects the way the blood carries oxygen.

We tried to explain the illness to the patient when we visited him on his ward the next day.

'You've got anaemia,' I said. 'It's usually caused by a lack of iron.'

'What's wrong with knee?' he asked.

'No, anaemia. It's a blood condition,' I persisted. 'The doctors say they'll probably let you go home in a day or two. You need iron supplements.'

'Can you bring Fiesta to me?' he pleaded.

'Don't be silly, Yusuf,' said Anne. 'You must know cats can't be taken into hospitals.'

'I leave! I leave!' he said.

'You'll stay right here,' Anne insisted. 'We want you to get better as quickly as possible.'

As we waited outside his ward during one of the doctors' rounds, I recalled some of the other dramatic events that had occurred.

Chad Draxfield never returned from Afghanistan. It was reported in the newspapers he was killed in action. A jihadist fighter struck as he explored the Tora Bora caves. There were more than fifty bullets found in his corpse, apparently. His body was brought back to England and he was buried somewhere in Oxfordshire.

Anne had discovered a close bond existed between him and Neil Bennett. On one occasion, while the pair were potholing in Somerset after some rain, Draxfield nearly drowned when a cascade of water suddenly flooded a narrow passage they were in. Somehow Bennett managed to save his life. After that the soldier became totally devoted to his friend.

Bennett had become clinically depressed when his marriage collapsed and Lucas Sharp came on the scene. Draxfield could not bear to see his friend so unhappy and vowed to solve what they together called 'the problem of Lucas Sharp.'

I had a drink with Graham Kirwan in the Merry Friar the other evening. He told me some time ago, on the advice of his lawyer, Bennett had changed his plea to Not Guilty and his trial is due to begin soon. The Crown Prosecution Service are proceeding with a charge of murder against Bennett. The prosecutors took the view that, while he may not have been present at the murder scene, he gave support to the main perpetrator and by doing so became liable for the same offence. They are still considering whether to charge Luke Bennett with any offence. Brandon Hill was handed a one hundred-hour community punishment order by a court and fined £1,000 for the illegal sale of fireworks. He has now moved in with Gemma Sharp.

Graham also mentioned Jane Taylor, who owned Lilac Cottage, had died in hospital after a long illness and an inquest is to be held in a few weeks. I heard rumours she might have been poisoned, but I think this was ill-informed tittle-tattle.

At the time of writing, Yusuf is still being treated in hospital. We expect him out any time now. He keeps talking about wanting to play with the cat. We are looking forward to having him back at the cottage. He is such a sweet, gentle guy.

Whenever I visit him in the ward, he immediately says: 'How's Fiesta?' After I have assured him the cat is as mischievous as ever, he asks: 'Are there still foxgloves growing in the lane?'

ACKNOWLEDGEMENTS

My warm thanks go to my friends Richard Brooks and Chris and Roseann Ellis for their review work and advice; to my understanding partner Lin for her help and encouragement; to Simon Dormer for assistance with my website; to Paul Hooper for bringing me up to date with Crown Court procedure; and to Joshua Lau for his immigration advice. A special thanks to my literary agent, James Essinger, for his hard work, patience and support. Lastly, my sincere gratitude to artist Ross Marklew from Pontypridd, South Wales for the illustration which appears on the front cover.